I0706438

Bright Futures

Samantha Benson

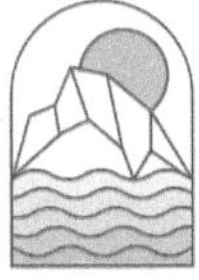

www.samanthabensonauthor.com

Copyright © 2024 by Samantha Benson. All rights reserved.

ISBN (paperback): 978-1-961611-03-0

No part of this book may be reproduced in any form or by any electronic or mechanical means, including information storage and retrieval systems, without express written permission of the author, except for the use of brief quotations in a book review.

This is a work of fiction. Names, characters, places, events, and incidents are either a product of the author's imagination or used fictitiously. Any resemblance to actual persons (living or dead), places, events, and incidents are entirely coincidental.

The author acknowledges the trademarked status and trademark owners of various products referenced in this work of fiction, which have been used without permission. The publication/use of these trademarks is not authorized, associated with, or sponsored by the trademark owners. Any trademarks, service marks, or product names are assumed to be the property of their respective owners, and are only used for reference. There is no implied endorsement of any of the terms used.

Editors: Brent Burchett; Lisa Hollett, Silently Correcting Your Grammar
Formatting: Stacey Blake, Champagne Book Designs
Cover: Sarah Hansen, Okay Creations

Honestly, I wrote this book for me. Good job, Me!
You're doing amazing, sweetie.

Bright Futures

Part I

Ovulation

Chapter One

Tatum

I T'S NOT EVERY DAY THAT I, A GROWN-UP, PROFESSIONAL, EDUCATED woman, am called the C-word in the course and scope of my job.

You know the one.

The ol' "C-U-Next-Tuesday."

Harsh language has never fazed me, but even I—a purveyor of f-bombs if ever there was one—believe the C-word is to be used sparingly and with discretion.

Like bronzer. A little bit gives you a nice glow. Too much and you're a bad 90's throwback.

Back to the C-word. I also recommend you never use it in the presence of a court reporter who is literally being paid to take down every spoken word.

Mark Jackson, the current spewer of the C-word, and whom I am currently questioning at a deposition, apparently has not received this memo.

"You fucking cunt!" he spits at me, eyes flashing with anger. His lawyer, Carson, sits next to him, unnecessarily restraining him with an arm across his midsection, the way a mother unnecessarily reaches her arm across the passenger seat when she brakes suddenly.

"Mark," Carson says through clenched teeth. "Calm down."

"That's on the record, right?" I ask Gabe, the court reporter seated at the head of the table. He nods, his eyes wide as his fingers fly across his machine.

"Off the record," Carson snaps. I smirk at him, and he glares.

"Bitch, you have no idea what you're talking about. *No idea.*" Mr. Jackson continues with his diatribe. Gabe has, unfortunately, ceased his typing by this point.

"*Mark*," Carson barks. "Outside." Carson all but carries his client out of the conference room.

"By all means, take five," I tell Carson innocently. He ignores me, following his client outside the conference room's glass doors.

"She can't just ask me stuff like that!" Mark tells his lawyer incredulously as he leaves the room. "Fat fucking bitch…" The words fade as Carson manhandles him across the lobby to the exit.

"Jesus," Gabe mutters to my left. "Short fuse on that one."

I hum but say nothing. Mark Jackson does, indeed, have a short fuse, which is one of many reasons why my client, a local hospital, fired him from his position as a nurse.

The "many reasons" include, but are not limited to, his constant barrage of sexual innuendo and inappropriate comments to his colleagues. Comments that are all documented neatly in his personnel file and about which I was questioning him in a painstaking fashion before he erupted.

Seemingly unable to come to terms with the fact that he's a total douche, Mark Jackson instead is suing the hospital for wrongful termination.

Some free legal advice—if you decide to sexually harass your colleagues over a period of years, including in text messages that your colleagues don't delete, you should know that information is going to come out if you later decide to claim your employer fired you unlawfully.

I have a motto when it comes to texts, emails, messages sent by carrier pigeon—write as if your words will be presented to you at a deposition one day.

Because everything comes out. It always does.

I stand up and stretch my body, rolling my shoulders out, before checking my phone. After a few minutes with no sign of Carson or his lovely client, I put it down and turn to Gabe.

"Big plans this weekend?"

"No way. Other than staying put. It's graduation weekend, you know." Gabe rolls his eyes.

"Dammit, seriously?" How could I have forgotten that?

"Yup. Our little town is about to double in size for a few days."

Our little town is St. Bishop's, a small city smack in the middle between Los Angeles—three and a half hours to the south, not counting traffic—and San Francisco—four hours to the north, not counting traffic. The graduation Gabe refers to is the college graduation, held each June and increasing St. Bishop's population of 40,000 by at least half. It is a weekend of debauchery and crowds. The hotels and restaurants love it, and rightfully so, given the amount of money it brings in.

The locals who live near the downtown corridor, however? Not so much.

"I have been so busy, I totally forgot," I respond. "I should have rented out my house." I'd done that for several years prior, making a quick buck in the process, and staying with either my brother or mom in Estero Bay, my hometown, about fifteen minutes north on Highway 1.

"You should have," Gabe agrees. "Anyway. Carlos and I are staying in and bingeing *Our Flag Means Death*. He's making pozole," Gabe adds.

My stomach grumbles in response. "That sounds really good. Well, I am staying in too." No way do I want to be out and about with a bunch of drunk co-eds.

"Ooh, Carson looks mad," Gabe pivots as Carson marches back through the doors, his client nowhere to be seen.

"Can we talk?" he asks me, skipping the formalities. "Off the record."

I sit back down in my chair across from him and spread my hands wide. "Anytime. Especially if your client is ready to dismiss his ridiculous lawsuit," I can't help but add.

Carson raises his eyebrow at me before making a show of inspecting his fancy cuff links. Carson is probably in his mid-thirties, Black, very handsome, and a successful plaintiff's-side employment lawyer I have come up against several times over the years. He's straight off the pages of *GQ* today in his bespoke navy suit. Dude is good-looking and charismatic, which serves him well in this profession and in the courtroom. He's tough and hardworking and, most importantly, not an asshole.

A rarity in this profession, I have found.

"What would your client say," Carson says smoothly, still not meeting my eyes, "if I could convince my client to dismiss his case, with each party bearing their own costs?"

Meaning that my clients wouldn't be able to recover anything for defending against this stupid lawsuit.

"I'll have to take it to my clients, of course," I respond sweetly. "Does that mean you want to suspend the deposition for the day?"

Carson grimaces briefly before recovering. He's usually the one representing victims of sexual harassment, rather than representing the harasser. I certainly don't know how Mark portrayed his firing to Carson, but I would place a healthy wager that Mark didn't mention anything about being fired for harassment. I assume Carson is no greater fan of his client than I am.

"My client wishes to proceed," he tells me, reluctance etched across his face.

"Can your client control himself? His language is pretty abhorrent," I remark.

Carson gives me a speaking glance. "Offending your delicate sensibilities, Tatum?" he asks dryly.

I smile slowly. "You know me better than that. But you should know there's more of Mark Jackson's greatest hits yet to come, so be prepared."

Carson sighs good-naturedly, apparently resigned to his client's antics. "Bring it."

I do what the man says and bring it.

Mark Jackson is *not* my friend by the end of the day.

But hey, I am not here to make friends with sleazy men who see a female-heavy workplace as their own harem.

"And am I reading this correctly?" I ask in a monotone voice, as if I could not care less about Mr. Jackson, his testimony, or the world at large.

"On April 11," I continue, "you texted Ms. Manriquez, your coworker, quote, 'I have something to show you in On-Call Room D.' End quote. Is that right?"

"Objection. The message speaks for itself," Carson mutters, writing something on his notepad. "You can answer," he adds to his client.

"That's what it says," Mark sneers.

"And Ms. Manriquez texted you back with a question mark, is that right?"

"That's what it says," Mark repeats.

"And then what did you respond with?"

"Objection. The message speaks for itself. Answer," Carson barks to Mark.

Mark mutters something in a low tone that no one can hear.

"I'm sorry. I didn't get that," Gabe pipes in from the end of the table, his hands paused over his machine.

"It says 'In On-Call Room Deez Nuts,'" Mark says loudly. I maintain a straight face, but my god, is it difficult. Mark's face is red, and Carson looks like he's ready for the floor to swallow him whole.

"Mark, what did you mean by the phrase, 'Deez Nuts'?"

"Objection. Calls for speculation," Carson interjects.

"Speculation? It's his text. He can tell me what he meant by the phrase 'Deez Nuts.'" I turn back to Mark. "What did you mean by that phrase?"

"It was just a joke!" Mark whines.

"Are you aware that 'Deez Nuts' is often used to refer to a man's testicles?" I continue.

"Objection. Calls for an expert opinion," Carson interjects.

I have to laugh. "Really? I'd like to meet such an expert. My questions aren't meant to elicit expert testimony, counselor. I merely want to know your client's personal knowledge of this phrase." Again, I turn to Mark. "I'll ask you again. Are you aware the phrase 'Deez Nuts' is sometimes used to refer to a man's testicles?"

"Yeah! No! I don't know!"

"And what did Ms. Manriquez do, if anything, to make you think that this kind of messaging would be appropriate?"

"She was always flirting with me!" Mark bellows, his face now the shade of a tomato. "Always following me around, asking if she could sit in on some of my cases."

"She was assigned to you as a new rotating nurse, wasn't she?" I ask calmly.

"Yeah. So what?" Mark eyes me suspiciously.

"Wouldn't that explain why she was, in your words *following you around*?"

Mark sets his lips in a firm line. "Nah. It was more than that."

"Well, what was it?" I press.

"I could just tell, okay? I can tell when a woman is interested!"

I'll just bet you can.

"Interested in, as you wrote in your text to your colleague Ms. Manriquez, 'deez nuts'?"

"Objection!" Carson's voice booms as he again puts his arm in front of his client's chest. "Calls for speculation."

"Did you think that because Ms. Manriquez was, as you put it, *following you around*, she was actually interested in *your* testicles?"

"*Objection!*" Carson's expression is between panic and disgust.

How fun.

"Did she ever say or do anything that caused you to believe she was interested in your testicles, specifically?"

"More interested than you are, you fat fucking bitch!" Mark shouts.

He can't even find something new to call me?

How disappointing.

"Objection," Carson inserts again, weakly.

I raise an eyebrow at Carson. "Your client already…answered the question. But what's your objection?"

"Badgering the witness," Carson tells me smoothly, but it's a stupid objection, and he knows it.

"All I am doing is asking your client his basis for sending this text to his colleague. If you think it's badgering, take it up with the judge."

"Maybe I will," Carson tells me, standing and buttoning his suit jacket. "We're done here."

"I'm not done with my questioning, and if you end this deposition unilaterally, I'll bring a motion to compel your client to answer further questions."

"Do it, then," Carson tells me carelessly. "Off the record."

He's posturing for his client, I know. He's hoping my client will agree to a walk-away deal before anything else happens and, more importantly, before I get to ask his client about any of the other, more colorful texts he sent to his colleagues.

"Yeah. Do it," Mark jeers at me, watching Carson and me volley comments back and forth. He stands to join his lawyer.

"Shut *up*, Mark," Carson instructs him.

Mark clamps his mouth shut but continues to gloat at me before walking out with Carson.

As if he's the winner here.

I heave out a sigh.

"We're off the record," I confirm to Gabe.

Chapter Two

Tatum

AFTER A DAY WITH CARSON AND HIS LOSER CLIENT, ALL I WANT is to curl up on my couch with a glass of wine.

Thankfully, the deposition today was near my downtown office. All I have to do is walk the seven short blocks to my house to make that dream a reality.

I feel icky after all that time with Mark the Douche. I realize that Carson has to drive to Los Angeles, on a Friday afternoon, on a weekend that's not only graduation in St. Bishop's, but likely a million other colleges up and down the coast, from Santa Barbara to Malibu. Meaning a four-hour trip could take upwards of eight.

That makes me feel a little better.

Gabe has already left, as have most of the other workers in the building. I check my phone briefly while packing up. I have a text from my mother and another from my best friend Lucy Yashimoto. A missed call from my other best friend, Summer Mahoney.

I head out, my bag hefted over my shoulder, shooting off a quick text to my client contact at the hospital to let her know that Mark's deposition is done for the day and I'll send her a formal update next week.

I mentally put away Tatum lady lawyer, slip my earbuds in, and select a Lizzo song. I scrounge in my bag for some saltwater taffies, my eternal weakness. I find one, unwrap it, and pop it into my mouth.

Cherry cola. Delicious.

It's a warm June evening, and as I suspected, all the restaurants and bars are packed with excited college students and their families. The streets of St. Bishop's are old and narrow, with large Ficus trees occasionally popping up from the concrete, cracking the pavement and providing a nice canopy over Main Street. I step carefully around the uneven sidewalk.

My nose fills with the smells of garlic and oregano from Giuseppe's, a popular Italian restaurant, which is so crowded that people are forming a line out the door and down the block. Farther on, I inhale the smoky, sweet scent of barbecue at Old Bishop's, which is just as crowded. Despite the crowds, I don't see many familiar faces, which isn't all that surprising, considering the town will be packed with out-of-town visitors this graduation weekend. The locals stay away on a weekend like this.

Toward the end of Main, I nearly crash into a group of co-eds, stumbling and laughing outside Frog and Peach, a local bar. "Sssoorry! Sorry, ma'am," one of the dudes calls out to me.

"No problem," I mutter, but they're all on their way and don't hear me.

Did I just get ma'am-d?

I'm thirty-one, not 100, for chrissakes.

But in this moment, I might as well be 300. I graduated college a decade ago and law school even more recently than that. Right now, though, I feel as far removed from the drunk shenanigans going on around me as ever.

I turn the corner and dart around an elderly couple with a small terrier. That reminds me of my own four-legged friend at home, and I hasten my step to get the hell out of the busy downtown corridor and onto my quiet street.

My home is a traditional Craftsman house, three bedrooms, one bathroom, with low ceilings and narrow doorways. It's small, but it's mine, and I've spent the past several years making necessary repairs with help from my brother, brother-in-law, and grandfather. My grandfather, to be honest, only comes because I feed him and give him a root beer. Which is totally fine, as I also get to enjoy the root beer and his company.

My street is several blocks off Main, and while there're more cars parked than usual, it's peaceful compared to the craziness of downtown. Unlocking my front door, I am instantly greeted by Janet, the love of my life.

"Hi, girl! Hiiiiiyeeee," I squeal as she practically stands on her hind legs to greet me. She's a golden retriever and absolutely insane at nearly two years old.

Janet barks and yips and licks anywhere she can get her mouth. "Gross. At least buy me a drink first," I mutter with a smile. Janet gives me the unconditional love that only a dog can.

And she won't call me "ma'am."

I awaken much later with a start to what sounds like…

…a growl?

I pause and catch my breath, sitting up in bed. After putting my phone on DND and enjoying a delightful dinner of potato chips and red wine, along with *Law & Order* reruns, I crashed hard.

Rubbing my eyes, I reach for my phone on the nightstand. Nearly five o'clock in the morning. This time of year, the sun rises early, and thin streaks of blue light peek through my curtains.

"*Grrr…*"

I hear the noise again and shiver. I know it's Janet, being her best badass self from somewhere in the house, but I'm discombobulated since she's usually so calm.

"Hey, girl," I coo to her from my room, making kissing noises. "C'mere."

She whines in response, which can only mean that I have to drag my ass out of bed and investigate.

Dammit.

Swinging my legs over the side, I grab my UCLA hoodie from the foot of the bed, drag it over my head, and pad into the hall.

"Where are you, sweet girl?"

More whining, from the front of the house.

I pass the kitchen on my left and continue toward the front door. Janet sits sentry at the front door, which is solid brown oak, with no windows. She whines softly as I approach.

"Hey, girl," I whisper, even though it's only just the two of us. "What are you looking at?"

She turns her head to me and thumps her tail, whining again.

"Okay, okay." I debate the possibilities. Is there a murdering, chainsaw-wielding psychopath quietly waiting on my front porch at five a.m.? That seems unlikely. Don't they go around in the dead of night to do their best chainsaw-wielding activities? Isn't five a.m. cutting it a little close, even though it's Saturday?

I snort a laugh at my logic. Janet whines again, unaware of the debate going on in my brain.

"Should I open the door?" I ask Janet.

She doesn't respond.

"I should open the door," I tell her affirmatively.

No response.

Decision made, I double back to my room, grab my phone, and call the one person I know is likely to be awake at five a.m. on a Saturday morning.

"Girl, you okay? It's five a.m.," Lucy says by way of answering the phone.

"I'm good, I'm good."

"Didn't hear from you yesterday, and I figured you were out partying with the young kids," Lucy says.

"Very funny. I was beat, man. I came home and crashed." Janet, tired of this interruption, whines again, and I rub her ears and shush her.

"Is that Ms. Jackson? What's going on?"

"It is, and we're good. Well, actually, she woke me up, growling at the door."

"No shit?" Lucy seems unfazed by this, although I can't blame her. We don't have a lot of serious crime in St. Bishop's.

"She won't come away, so I need you to stay on the line with me while I open the door and see what's up."

"Ah, and you knew the baker would be up. Check you out, Nancy Drew. I'd go back to bed, for sure." Lucy must put the phone down, because I hear her speaking in a muffled voice to whoever is with her at her bakery. "I'm all ears. If it's a psychopath with a chainsaw, I will promptly scream and then hang up and dial 9-1-1."

"That's what I said!" I exclaim loudly. "Well, thought, actually. But honestly, do you really think it is likely that someone with a chainsaw would be waiting quietly outside at this hour?"

"Jesus God, Tatum. Open the door. I've got shit to do."

"Okay, okay."

I undo the dead bolt and latch, grab the handle, and pull the door open a few inches. I've got my other hand on Janet's collar in case she decides to bolt.

Of course, if there is an axe-wielding psychopath out there, I'll let my dog do her thing.

Not sure when the marauder changed from wielding a chainsaw to an axe, but here we are.

Peeking out, I see…nothing. Nothing but my neighbor's Pride flag across the street, the rainbow bright in the early-morning light. Nothing but the streetlight flickering slightly before going out. And nothing but my white garden gate…

My *open* garden gate.

"What the hell?" I mutter.

"What's happening? Is it a chainsaw?"

"No chainsaw. No axe," I murmur. Janet whines again, pulling against my hold, and I let her go. She immediately darts out on the porch and to the left, as the porch stretches across the front of the house. And as my eyes follow her, I see what has her all worked up.

"Dude. It's a dude!"

"With an axe?"

"No, he's not moving. He's lying on the porch," I tell Lucy, exhaling.

I walk over to what appears to be a young man—younger than me, anyway.

It's hard to tell, because he has messages written in Sharpie all over his face. I laugh in spite of myself. "I think it's a dude who got super, super hammered last night and lost his way home." I move a little closer, but not too close, as I get a hit of stale liquor and cigarettes. "Yeah. I can smell it on him."

"Gross," Lucy chimes in. "But also, glad he is not there to murder you."

"Same. I'm going to call…someone. Who do I call to report a drunk dude?"

"The police, I guess?" Lucy surmises. "Although, he's just passed out, right? Not drunk."

"That's true," I tell her. "They'd probably just put him in the drunk tank until he wakes up."

"Don't let him barf on your pretty porch."

"No way. I'll get the hose out if that happens. Anyway, I'll figure it out. Thanks for having my back."

"Thanks for being safe. Text you when I'm done here."

I hang up with Lucy and regard the dude. He looks Asian and is wearing a black T-shirt and jeans. Miraculously, both of his Chuck Taylors are securely tied on his feet.

His chest moves up and down, his mouth gaping open as he breathes loudly.

"So, he's a mouth breather," I remark to Janet, who is currently licking a spot on his arm.

An arm that is also covered in Sharpie messages.

"Janet!" I hiss. "No. Come here." But the guy remains still. Janet backs away, finding this guy less than appealing.

I look at the spot where Janet was just licking him, the Sharpie printed in bold, capital letters.

"FOR A GOOD TIME CALL 805-555-2595"

Well, that's one option besides the police.

Chapter Three

Jake

"J AKE! JAAAAKE!"

I groan, rolling to the side of my too-small bed, in my too-small room, in my dumpster fire of a college rental home.

"Mphmblemn," I reply to whoever is banging on my door. Thank god for locks.

"*Jake!* I really need to talk to you," the female voice demands again.

"I seriously doubt that," I mutter, wiping my hands down my face and sighing.

"*What?*" the voice screeches through the other side of my bedroom door.

"Nothing! Nothing. Jesus, don't get your panties in a bunch!" I yell toward the door.

"Don't pull that sexist shit with me, Jake."

"Oh, Jesus Christ," I mutter, pulling my comforter back over my head and burrowing into my pillow. Surely if I ignore her, she'll go away?

And last night was crazy. Isn't she hungover? Why is she awake?

Why am *I* awake?

"*Jaaake!*"

Fuck it.

"I'm coming. Please don't speak any more. I am begging you." I move out of bed slowly. I didn't drink a ton last night, but I did imbibe.

I unlock the door to see the very awake, very pissed-off face of my roommate's on-and-off girlfriend.

"Jesus, Annette," I mumble. "It's like one in the morning."

It's not, but I don't care. I need my beauty rest.

Annette's breath hitches, and she eyes me up and down before her eyes flash and she goes back to being angry.

Well, she's the one who banged on *my* door and woke *me* up, so she can deal with *my* nudity.

Not all the way, mind you.

I have boxers on.

With SpongeBob print.

"Where is Brandon?" Annette snaps, referring to said roommate.

"He isn't in my room, that's for damn sure," I drawl, leaning against the doorframe. Annette looks like she's dressed for a picnic in the South, or what I imagine the girls wear at, like, Alabama, not at our school in sleepy Central California. Pearl earrings, flouncy skirt, blond hair styled just so.

Honestly, the fact that she's all done up at whatever ungodly hour this is after a night of graduation parties is impressive. At least, I would be impressed if I weren't so sleepy.

"He texted me last night a bunch of nonsense, and I—I was worried," Annette says, pushing her eyebrows together in what I think is meant to be a show of concern, but really makes her look constipated. "He's not in his bedroom."

"I don't know what to tell you, Annette," I respond, yawning and scratching my chest. "I saw him at a party, and he was still there when I came back and crashed."

"What party?" Annette snaps, her eyebrows arching.

"I don't know. Some house on Dexter." I start to close the door. "Anyway, if I see him, I'll tell him you were looking for him, okay? Okay. Bye now."

I move to shut the door before she can respond.

"I'm just worried!" she wails pathetically from outside.

I ignore her, knowing exactly what she's worried about…

…which is the idea of Brandon sticking his dick into someone who is not Annette. Brandon is great, but an absolutely shitshow when it comes to partying. Throw in graduation weekend and a so-called last chance to live it up with some people we may very well never see again, and…who knows where Brandon is, but I'm sure he's fine.

I'm also cynical enough to know that it's more than Annette's undying love for Brandon that has her concerned. It's his epic trust fund. Annette has had her hooks into my roommate from day one.

It's hard to trust people wanting to be your friend when there's a lot of money around.

I know a little bit about that.

For now…back to bed.

I've just nestled back under the covers, my shades pulled tight and my diffuser on—don't judge; I live with four other guys, and it smells like a tranquil spa in here—when I hear my phone buzz.

"Who the hell else is up at this hour… Oh shit."

It's a text from an unfamiliar number with a local area code, along with a picture.

Of my boy Brandon.

Unknown: Friend of yours?

I double tap on the picture to open it up and immediately burst out laughing.

"Oh my god, dude. What happened to you, buddy?"

It's Brandon, lying on his back on what looks like a front porch, still dressed in his shirt, jeans, and, unbelievably, both shoes. His mouth hangs open and his eyes are closed, but what cracks me up is the Sharpie marker everywhere. *Everywhere*—his face, his arms, his neck.

And apparently, there's a dog involved? At least, there's a super-cute golden pooch sitting next to Brandon and looking expectantly at whoever has the camera, as if to say *"What are we going to do with him?"*

I text back.

ME: OMG. That's Brandon.

Unknown: Okay…?

ME: He's my roommate. Is he all right?

Unknown: He's alive and appears to be unharmed.

ME: Okay, that's good. I can come get him.

Unknown: That would be lovely.

ME: How do you have this number, anyway? Did he tell you to call me?

Unknown responds with another picture. This one is of Brandon's arms, clearly inscribed with the words *"FOR A GOOD TIME CALL…"* right over my number.

"That's fucked up," I mumble.

Me: I am so sorry. I don't know who did that.

Unknown: Whatever. I really wasn't sure who to contact about a passed-out guy on my porch. This seemed like my best option.

I laugh at Unknown and shoot off another text.

ME: What's your address?

Unknown: Hold up. Who the hell are you? How do I know you're not some axe-wielding psychopath?

ME: I guess you don't…? Although getting my roommate drunk to the point of passing out and strategically leaving him on someone's porch with my number written on his arm is a weird way to find victims…

You're the axe murderer, not me.

I bark a laugh again. Unknown is pretty funny.

ME: Look. My name is Jake. I can send you a picture of my driver's license, and you can look in Brandon's pockets to see if his is in there.

Unknown: No way am I moving your friend or putting my hands on him. He smells like cheap vodka, a late night, and bad decisions. My dog doesn't even want to lick him, and that bitch licks everyone, Jake. IF THAT'S YOUR REAL NAME.

ME: It is. Here's my driver's license.

I shoot off a photo and pull a shirt over my head.

Unknown: All right, Jake Lundquist, I am trusting you.

Unknown sends their address.

ME: And your name is…?

Unknown: Don't push your luck.

I smile and get my ass moving. My friend needs me.

JAKE: I am so, so sorry.

JAKE: OMW.

JAKE: You there?

TATUM: Less texting, more friend-retrieving, please.

JAKE: Yes. Absolutely, OMW.

JAKE: Do you want a coffee?

TATUM: Are you fucking kidding me? I want you to come get your friend. Who still hasn't moved, btw.

TATUM: I did roll him over a little on his side in case he barfs.

JAKE: OMG. That's great. Awesome. OMW.

TATUM: You said that before, and yet here we are.

JAKE: Yeah, but I really mean it this time

TATUM: No more texting. Silence your notifications and come get your friend.

JAKE: Okay. I will.

JAKE: So sorry about all this

TATUM: JAKE

<h1 style="text-align:center">Chapter Four</h1>

Tatum

I POKE MY HEAD OUT THE DOOR FOR WHAT FEELS LIKE THE HUNDREDTH time, waiting for "Jake Lundquist" to come get "Brandon." Sipping my coffee, I sit back down with Janet at my feet, petting her behind the ears like she loves.

"These kids," I sigh dramatically. Because yes, they are kids, compared to me. According to Jake's ID, he'll be twenty-three in less than two months. At twenty-three, I was finishing my second year of law school.

I suppose eight years is not a huge difference, but it sure feels like one when one particular twenty-three-year-old drinks to the point of passing out on a stranger's front porch.

Janet's ears perk up at a car door slamming out front. I get up and open the door to greet Jake Lundquist.

"Good morning…" My voice trails off when I get a view of the man across the threshold, who is definitely *not* the scrawny, grim-faced kid in the driver's license photo he sent me. Jake must've taken that picture when he had his learner's permit, for chrissakes, because the guy in front of me is a man, not a teenager. I lift my chin and am captured by twinkling bright-blue eyes, like he's about to tell me a joke and can't wait for the punch line.

Jake looks like a typical surfer dude, with a lean swimmer's body and broad shoulders. He's white, his skin tanned, with sun-bleached dirty-blond hair poking out of the backward baseball cap on his head. He's wearing the unofficial collegiate uniform of Rainbow brand flip-flops, shorts, and a T-shirt molded nicely to his muscled upper body.

"Hi! I'm Jake," he says with a huge smile, his eyes widening briefly as he extends his hand to me formally, as if we are meeting for business rather than regarding his drunk-ass roommate.

"Tatum," I tell him, clearing my throat and offering him my hand in return. We grip each other firmly, his palm warm and rough. Jake keeps smiling, his eyes crinkling at the corners as he quickly moves his eyes down my body and back up again.

"Hi, Tatum," he tells me in a calm voice, a dimple popping in his cheek.

Jesus. This guy is too hot for this hour of the day and this moment in my life.

Belatedly, I remember that I'm wearing sleep shorts that don't do much to cover my ass, a ratty hoodie, and no bra. My hair is pulled up on top of my head in a mess of a bun.

But honestly, fuck it. I didn't know waking up this morning that I would have a passed-out dude on my porch, let alone a hot, young swimsuit model on my doorstep.

"Friend's over there," I tell him, removing my hand from his to indicate to the left side of the porch.

"Huh? Oh right! Oh shit—shoot," Jake stammers, darting over to Brandon. "I am so, so sorry about this."

"Not your fault," I reply, moving to join him on the porch. "I mean, I assume it's not your fault. You didn't strategically leave your drunk friend on my porch last night, did you?"

"What? Oh my god, no way!" Jake looks at me with wide eyes. "I mean, it's graduation weekend, you know, and we all went out, and things were a little—"

"Jake," I interrupt him. "It's okay."

"I don't even know who wrote my number on his arm, to be honest."

"Well, I am glad they did, because I wasn't really sure what to do about him."

Janet has decided she is tired of our conversation and leaves my side to accost Jake, rubbing her head against his legs and panting excitedly.

"Well, hello there, princess," he croons, bending down to pet her head. Janet doesn't waste a moment to lick his hand, although in this instance, I can't say I blame her. "I mean…or prince?" He looks to me in question.

"You had it right in one. That's Janet."

"Janet! I love her. What a pretty girl," Jake tells her, still in a smooth, calm voice. Janet throws herself on the floor and shows him her tummy, and he bends his big body down to give her a scratch.

"She'll love you forever now," I warn him.

"S'all good. There are worse things than unconditional love, isn't that right, pretty girl?" His voice goes from chatty back to crooning, sounding like a phone-sex operator as he scratches Janet.

He pats her belly one last time and then turns to Brandon, who still hasn't moved and is breathing like he's in a hot yoga class.

"Aw, you put a blanket on him!" Jake looks up at me with a grin. Is he constantly smiling? It's a little unnerving.

"Well." I shrug. "I didn't want him to be cold, I guess."

"Yeah, that marine layer can be brutal, huh?" Jake agrees. "I cannot believe this. Can't believe he chose to pass out here, of all places," Jake mumbles. "He's gonna die when he really wakes up."

Jake nudges his friend on the shoulder. "Brando. Big guy." Nothing from Brandon, though.

"Honestly, he might not even have been that drunk. Dude sleeps like the dead," Jake tells me, standing back up to his full height again, his hands on his hips. "I can get him out of here, but first…" He looks a little embarrassed. "Can I have a glass of water? And maybe a towel?"

"Sure, no problem," I tell him, leaving Janet on the porch while I grab the requested items.

"Are you going to—oh!" I gasp as Jake immediately throws the entire glass in his friend's face. Brandon snorts and sputters a bit, the first sign of life I've seen from him.

"Brandon. Buddy." Jake speaks loudly in his face. "We gotta go, man."

Brandon mumbles something unintelligible, wiping his face and taking the towel Jake hands him. "What the fuck, dude?"

"Bro. You passed out on a stranger's porch."

"No shit?" Brandon rubs his eyes some more sits up slowly. "Fuck. My head, man," he whines, dropping his head in his hands.

"Yeah, I guess you had a wild night, huh?" Jake crouches down next to his friend and places a hand on Brandon's shoulder.

"Fuck if I know," Brandon mutters, his speech slightly slurred. "I was at this party on Dexter, and…" His voice trails off as he shakes his head slightly before moaning again. "Kill me now."

"Maybe not right now, but let's get off this nice lady's porch."

I jerk at Jake's comment. Kill *me* now. I am a nice lady? Is this the equivalent of being "ma'am-d"?

Janet takes this opportunity to nudge Jake out of the way and do her best to crawl into Brandon's lap. Apparently, she is no longer turned off by the stale bar smell.

"Oh. What—hello?" Brandon asks. "Is—is this the nice lady?"

"That's Janet. I am the nice lady," I tell Brandon sharply. Brandon looks up, his eyes widening.

"Oh fuck," Brandon whispers.

"It's okay. She's nice," Jake whispers back, looking at me with a wink, that dimple popping again. Jesus Lord.

"I don't know if many people have referred to me as 'nice,' but there's a first time for everything. This morning, for example, was the first time I found a stranger passed out on my front porch," I say, gesturing to Brandon.

"Oh my god, oh my god. I am so, so—" Brandon moves to stand up suddenly, tripping over himself in the process.

"Hey, maybe no sudden movements," Jake tells him, reaching his hand out to steady his friend.

"Yeah, good idea," Brandon mumbles. "Seriously, kill me now."

"You mentioned that already. But let's go get in the car and head home, and we can talk about it there."

"Yeah. Lesdoit," Brandon slurs, clearly miserable. "I am so, so sorry." He directs this comment to me without making eye contact before shuffling down the steps and across the yard. "So sorry," he calls a little louder. He hops into the passenger side of the black Jeep, slamming the door before I can respond.

"He's usually not like this. Well, sometimes. He's a…complex guy," Jake offers wryly, putting his hands in his pockets. Janet rubs her head against his side, and he obliges, scratching behind her ear.

"I remember my college graduation," I tell him, cringing at how old that makes me sound. *Hello, youth. I, too, remember my younger days!* "I mean—it's all good. You are a good friend to come get him."

"He'd do the same for me," Jake responds, giving Janet a final pat on the head and meeting my gaze again. His blue eyes are questioning.

"Well, good luck with…that," I tell him, waving in the direction of his car.

"Yeah, thanks. And thanks for not, like, calling the police on him."

"I thought about it. But he seems harmless."

Jake smiles and stares at me some more.

"So…take it easy, Jake. Come on, Janet," I say, turning to head into the house.

"Wait! Um, wait a minute?" Jake asks me hastily.

I turn back to him, my eyebrows raised.

"So—" Jake sighs and looks to his car, before clearing his throat and looking back at me. "So. Um, what do you do?"

I stare at him blankly.

"Like—" a beat "—for a living?"

"Are you—" It's my turn to pause. "Are you…making small talk?"

"I mean," Jake says in a rush, "I was just wondering—"

"No." I interrupt him, holding up my hand to stop him. "No way. Jake, you seem very nice and, I am sure, a good friend, but I am fucking exhausted. I had a not-so-great day yesterday on top of a kind of shitty week on top of a super-shitty…recent history. I forgot it was graduation, which is my fault, but Jesus H., I do not have any bandwidth to make small talk with the super-hot college bro on my front porch at six o'clock in the morning on a Saturday." I snap my fingers, and Janet trots into the house. I follow her in before turning to Jake one last time.

"I hope your friend feels better, Jake."

I close the door on his wide-eyed expression.

Chapter Five

Jake

"**S**O, THAT'S EVERYTHING."

I help Brandon pull down the rear door of the moving truck we've spent the better portion of this drizzly morning loading up with…well, basically, his life. Clothes, assorted kitchen items, and truly disgusting college furniture that really needs to be burned rather than carefully packed in a moving van. But Brandon insisted.

"That's everything," my friend concurs, running a hand through his jet-black hair and sighing. He's fully recovered from his graduation debauchery a week ago. And like most college students in this town, he is moving out. Only this time, it's not just for the summer.

"The end of an era, man," I comment, gesturing toward the five-bedroom house near campus that we've rented for the past three years.

Brandon huffs a laugh. "No doubt. If these walls could talk…"

…They would probably wax poetic about a bunch of twentysomethings playing beer pong and eating too many breakfast burritos. Nothing too crazy.

But I nod. "It's been real. Can't believe it went by so fast."

"I know, man." Brandon jingles his keys. "I better get to it, though. I don't want to get stuck in Bay Area traffic."

"Right." I clear my throat. "Well, dude, it's been fun."

I move in for a backslapping bro-style half hug, which Brandon returns.

"You be careful up there in the big city," I tell my friend, who rolls his eyes.

"I am literally going to be doing nothing but logging hours when the job starts in a couple weeks, but thanks for your concern."

"Yeah, yeah." I watch as he gets into the truck, starts it up, and drives away with a wave.

And then it's just me.

Our other three roommates cleared out earlier this week, their families helping them move within a couple days after graduation. My own parents went back to my hometown of Santa Barbara immediately after the ceremony.

And as the rent is paid up through the end of the month, I am in no hurry to leave.

I walk back into the house, the smell of cheap beer and aftershave unmistakable, no matter how many times I clean this damn place. Brandon and my other roommates could live unconcerned in a house with plates stacked in the sink for months. But I like a clean house and always did my best to keep this place moderately clean.

That said, I refused to do the bathrooms, except for the one I use. I have my limits.

It's too quiet with my friends gone. Up and down our street, moving trucks and vans have been coming and going all week. This town loses half of its population in the summer after finals, and the silence is a little eerie.

I could be spending the time figuring out where I am going to live after the lease is up. As I have no desire to trudge back to Santa Barbara and crash with my parents, I hear the clock ticking.

I could be spending the time looking over the latest proposal my father sent me immediately after graduation—seriously, he must have had it drafted weeks in advance—inviting me to come work for the commercial development business he runs. It was actually less of an invitation and more of a command.

But my gut reaction to that offer is the same as it ever was.

I could call and check in with my mother. I do this at least once a week to catch up and let her know that her only child is doing just fine.

But conversations with her lately usually leave me feeling less zen than when I started.

There's only one other option.

Time to hit the beach.

Estero Bay is only a fifteen-minute drive north on Highway 1, but it feels like another universe.

The bay is small, quiet, and fairly untouched by development. The town has several small hotels and motels, but no big, branded resort chains. There's a Starbucks—where isn't there?—and a Fosters Freeze—give me a fried burrito and an M&M Twister and I can die a happy man—but the town is full of mostly locally owned restaurants and funky shops. Most important to me, however, is the six-mile strand of beach at the north edge of Estero Bay, which has some of the best surfing conditions around. One of my older fraternity brothers introduced me to the area when I first moved to St. Bishop's, and I've been coming back ever since.

I've been surfing as long as I can remember. Growing up in Santa Barbara, it's easy to pick up; the weather's nice pretty much year-round, and my mom put me in lessons at an early age. It's a solitary activity, but the people you meet and come to see on a regular basis all share the same affinity for the ocean. You can go as big or small as you want, with the ocean largely dictating how you spend your time while in her waters. Sometimes, I come out expecting to go hard and get thrashed, only to spend an hour paddling out, sitting on my board, and thinking.

And not for nothing, but the best way to cure a hangover is to get your ass in the Pacific.

St. Bishop's patchy fog gives way to a thicker cloud cover as I drive toward Estero Bay. I can barely make out the giant rock that is the town's landmark, the fog's thick fingers curling around the stone. I drive past the Rock, park, get my suit on, and head toward the water with my board.

A few hours later, I am salty and starving. I unzip the back of my suit half-way as I head back toward the parking lot.

The beach is sparsely populated this Friday morning, the cloudy weather likely keeping folks at home with fuzzy blankets and hot coffee. I notice a large group of school-age children, all barefoot and dressed in matching blue T-shirts, participating in some sort of camp on the sand. A tanned man in sunglasses and a big straw hat calls to them through a megaphone.

"Port!"

The kids all jump to the left.

"Starboard!"

The kids all jump to the right.

"Bow!"

The kids rush toward the man.

"Stern!"

The kids all hurry away from the man, who repeats the directives again and again and again. These kids have got to be exhausted—I am exhausted just watching them run on the sand—but they keep at it, despite a couple of them tripping and falling a few times.

"They have a lot of energy, don't they?"

Turning to my right, I see an older man in a navy-blue windbreaker and bright-white New Balance sneakers. He's on the shorter side, with a head full of salt-and-pepper hair and a gray mustache. He leans on a thick, knotty walking stick with a large handle.

He looks like someone's friendly grandfather. Or at least, what I imagine a friendly grandfather looks like.

"I'm tired just looking at them," I respond.

"A young man like yourself! If you have the energy to swim in these waters, you can surely hop around the parts of an imaginary boat."

I grin. "Maybe. That set kind of took it out on me, though," I tell him, gesturing toward the ocean.

"Mmm-hmm. You go the Brew, get yourself a nice hamburger or the solomo. It's pork," he explains at my probably blank expression.

"Okay?"

"The Brew. It's in Estero Bay, and my granddaughter and her husband own it," the man continues, his chest visibly puffing out with pride. "Solomo is an art, you see—you have to marinate the pork for many, many days before it is grilled. It is quite tasty. You will see."

"Okay…?" Honestly, this dude is making me even hungrier.

"Go! Go get yourself a sandwich," he tells me with a smile, gesturing toward the town. He ambles toward the children's group, where a dark-haired little girl rushes toward him, yelling something in another language. He speaks back to her in what sounds like the same dialect, stooping a little to give her a hug.

I smile at the two of them, before my stomach growls again and reminds me that I need to get a "nice hamburger" or whatever pork product this man was talking about.

Chapter Six

Tatum

"I think I'm having a midlife crisis," I tell my older sister Julia.

She raises her eyebrows and pauses in the act of squeezing a lemon wedge into my iced tea behind the bar at the Brew, the restaurant she runs with her husband, Lincoln. Her hair—dark and thick and a lot of it, just like mine—is done in two tight French braid pigtails. She has piercings up and down both ears and colorful tattoos up and down both arms.

"Considering you are thirty-one, I'm concerned about your life-span."

"Well, I don't think I'm living to be 120 years old, so it can't be a quarter-life crisis," I reply.

"True enough. What's the problem?" She hands me my tea, and I take a big sip. "Also, what do you want to eat?"

The Brew has traditional pub fare, but my favorites are the Basque dishes that Lincoln has perfected over the years. Both of my parents have Basque ancestry, and my great-grandfather was a first-generation Basque immigrant to this country. His son—my grandfather—is still alive, retired from a career as a fisherman. He's spent his entire life here in Estero Bay, where Julia and I grew up with our brother, Nick.

"Something meaty," I muse.

"That's what she said," Julia cracks.

"You're funny. I'm on my period, and I need iron," I tell her.

"We've got solomo," Julia offers, referring to a delicious marinated pork dish that Lincoln usually serves as a sandwich.

"Not today. I'm basic. May I have a burger, please? With extra pickles."

"You got it." Julia types quickly into her iPad before directing her attention back to me. "So, this crisis occurring between the first quarter and the first half of your life—what gives?"

Before I can answer her, Janet, who has been lying peacefully on the floor, jumps up so suddenly that my tall bar chair wobbles a bit. "Janet Jackson!" I admonish her, turning around to see where she's headed. She ignores me, trotting toward the front door and the man who's just entered.

"She's got good taste, I'll give her that," Julia offers.

"Oh Lord," I mutter, because of course it's none other than Jake Lundquist, rescuer to Brandon and apparently Janet's favorite human of the moment.

Jake's blond hair is in disarray, a shade darker, like he just took a shower. He's still in the same college uniform I saw him in last weekend—Rainbow flip-flops, shorts, and a hoodie. His eyes widen at the golden retriever bounding toward him, before he breaks into a smile that I am pretty sure causes me, Julia, and everyone else in the restaurant to swoon a little.

"Friend of yours?" Julia murmurs from behind the bar.

"No. I mean, we're not friends. We met once. It's a long story." I stammer an answer to Julia and mentally brace myself for Jake to be in my orbit once again.

"Uh-huh. I am going to go take this order, but don't worry. I'll be ba-ack," Julia tells me in a singsong voice.

The first time I met Jake, I was in my pajamas. This time, I am a sweaty mess, having just completed a quick three-mile hike at Cerro Cabrillo, a mountain trail just outside of Estero Bay. I'm bloated, my hair looks like something that can only be considered "Medusa-lite," and I am ready to stuff a giant hamburger in my face. Maybe two hamburgers.

Jake still looks like a swimsuit model.

Janet comes trotting back to me with a big smile.

Dogs smile; it's a known fact.

"Hi, Tatum," Jake says with a friendly grin.

"Hello, Jake. Janet," I snap, and she sits right next to my barstool. Jake helps himself to the seat next to her.

"How is your day going? No comatose people on your front porch this morning?" Jake turns his whole body toward me, leaning on the shiny wooden bar.

I smile despite myself. "Not today. It's always nice and quiet this time of year after graduation." I take a sip of my iced tea. "Seems like the college kids are moving out and moving on."

"Yeah, I just helped Brandon—porch guy—pack up this morning. Just me now," Jake replies, giving Janet a scratch on the head as she nuzzles into his side.

"What about you? I mean, you are probably moving soon too, right? Since you graduated?" He did graduate, didn't he? It occurs to me that I don't remember much about our early-morning convo last weekend.

"I did, but I am…not sure about my next move. Literally and figuratively." Some of the good-natured ease leaves Jake's face as he speaks, and hey, I can empathize with that.

Having entered my midlife-crisis phase after all.

Maybe Jake's in his quarter-life crisis.

He's definitely the right age to be in a quarter-life crisis.

My sister interrupts the rushing locomotive that is my thought process when she returns with a hamburger the size of my head. Not really, but it's close.

"Oh, you are a goddess among women. May you be blessed with many children," I gush, the smell of grilled onions and meat reaching my nose.

"I am very happy with the two I have, thank you very much," Julia tells me. "Hello," she adds, turning to Jake.

"Hi!" Jake's face brightens at Julia's greeting. He says nothing more, and Julia's eyes dart between Jake and me. I still haven't made contact with my burger—it's going to be a beast to eat, and yes, that's what she said—so I make a casual introduction.

"Julia, Jake. Jake, Julia. Julia is my older, but not wiser, sister. Jake is…a recent college graduate." I decide that is the safest introduction.

"It's nice to meet you," Jake tells Julia, offering his hand to her to shake.

"Likewise," Julia says, still glancing back and forth, probably wondering why I, a woman in the throes of a midlife crisis, is friends with someone in his quarter-life crisis.

Jake saves me from saying any more. "Hey, this might sound weird, but are you the owner of this restaurant?" He directs his question to Julia. "Because I was surfing" —*that explains the damp hair that is not at all sexy and definitely doesn't make me think of Jake in the shower*—"and after, there was this sweet old man who insisted that I come and try something…called the salami?"

Julia smiles ruefully and shakes her head. "The solomo. And that sweet old man is my—our—grandfather. Honestly, I need to start paying him for all the good PR he is doing for this restaurant."

"Your grandfather! And so…your grandfather, too?" he asks me.

"The one and only," I confirm. "What's he doing out on the beach to-day, though?" I ask Julia. "Usually, he's hanging out on the Embarcadero with his friends."

"I think he's there to see Violet. She's doing Little Guards. Lifeguard camp, and Violet's my daughter," she adds for Jake's benefit.

"Well, he definitely put in a good word for the solomo, and I'm starving."

"Coming right up," Julia says.

"You know," Jake says, turning back to me, "I am glad to see you again, and—" he frowns suddenly, taking his phone from his pocket and looking at the screen "—sorry. I'll call her back." He declines the call, puts his phone on the bar, and redirects his attention to me.

"Anyway. I wanted to apologize again for Brandon's…predicament."

"Jake," I tell him, "it's really not your fault. I mean, I was in college. I did stupid shit too."

"At St. Bishop's?" he asks me.

"No, I went to UCLA for undergrad."

"Undergrad? You're a…" Jake looks at me questioningly.

"A lawyer. I went to Pepperdine for law school."

"A lawyer?!" Jake's eyes get comically wide. "Wow," he breathes out. "That's pretty impressive."

"It's really not," I tell him bemusedly. "Trust me, a lot of idiots are lawyers."

"Yeah, but you're not an idiot," he tells me with certainty.

"True enough." I am interrupted when Jake's phone lights up again. He shakes his head and declines the call.

"You can take that. It's okay," I tell him.

"Nah, it's just my mom. I don't mean—like, *just* my mom. I just—I'll call her on the drive back."

I nod and make a production of cutting my giant hamburger in half. Maybe if I start eating, Jake will leave me alone.

"So, a lawyer," he adds. "Criminal?"

"No way. No criminal, no family law, no juvenile. Civil. The boring stuff."

Jake nods. "Like, car accidents and stuff?"

"Sometimes. I do a lot of probate, a lot of employment defense. Some landlord-tenant. It's a small town, you have to be willing to diversify your practice," I tell him.

"Probate. Like…trusts and stuff?"

"Yes," I tell him, surprised he's familiar with anything having to do with probate—which, for the record, is the process of transferring money and property after someone dies.

Exciting stuff.

"I do some trust formation, but mostly a lot of litigation, like families and heirs fighting over the estate. The dead person's stuff," I explain at his questioning look.

"Gotcha." He's quiet for a minute, and his phone lights up yet again. "I'm sorry," he says, picking up the phone. "I'll be right back."

All the more time with my hamburger, I think to myself as Jake walks toward the hallway where the restrooms are, his phone to his ear.

Chapter Seven

Jake

"**M**OM," I SAY A LITTLE IMPATIENTLY INTO THE PHONE. "WHAT'S up? I saw your calls. I was going to call you in a minute—"

I stop speaking when I hear sniffling, like she's crying.

"Mom, what's going on?" I ask her a little more sharply. "Are you all right?"

"It's your dad," she tells me, her voice small and defeated.

I deflate a little. To be clear, it's *always* my dad, so this is not news to me. But the fact that she's called this many times is unusual.

Lately, her calls have been of the "You need to figure out what you are doing with your life and join your dad in his commercial enterprise" variety, which is a conversation I am not eager to have again.

I'd personally like to see less building on the Central Coast, not more. But what do I know?

Hence, my declining her calls.

But her tone causes me to pause.

"Is he okay?"

She barks a laugh, dry and bitter. "As far as I know," she responds.

I pinch the bridge of my nose in frustration.

My parents have fought for as long as I can remember. Why they ever decided to get married is, frankly, beyond me, as I can't think of two people more unsuited for each other.

It's not that they don't have a lot in common. They both really like money. They both come from wealthy families; they both ran in the same circle of upper-crust Santa Barbara elite. One of my great-great-grandfathers on my dad's side purchased an original Mexican land grant in Santa Barbara

County in the 1800s. My dad's family has been here ever since, acquiring more land and real estate investments.

My mother was born in the Los Angeles area, but relocated to Santa Barbara with her family when she was a child. Her father was an engineer, worked for the Department of Defense, and moved his family north to help develop the military base about an hour north of Santa Barbara.

Other than enjoying money, making money, spending money, and talking about money, my parents never seemed particularly interested in each other.

My dad's constant travel has been a decades-long argument. He leaves, he's gone for too long, Mom gets mad, he returns, they fight about it.

I am not so naive as to assume these fights are due to my mother simply missing my father and desiring him to be home more. There's a little more to it than that. Because for as long as I can remember them fighting—and they were always fighting—my dad has had girlfriends. I know it, my mother knows it, and I am sure all their friends know it. I figure it was part of the bargain my parents made when they married, but honestly, I don't know for sure, and I don't want to know.

"If there is no emergency," I tell my mother slowly, "then what is the issue? Why all the calls?"

This sets Mom off into another series of sniffles. I've never seen my mom cry, not really, and if she did, I can't imagine it would be a screaming, snot-filled fiesta. She would cry delicately, serenely.

Which it sounds like she is doing now.

"Your father has shared some unfortunate news with me," she tells me through her sniffles.

I wait for her to continue.

"Jake." She takes a deep breath. "Did you know you have a younger sister?"

Tatum

I am halfway through my burger and debating whether to just devour the whole thing and take a nap when I get home—*do it, why do we always bother cutting the food in half? You're going to eat the whole thing anyway*—when I sense Janet moving beside me from her position on the floor.

I look up to see Jake walking back to his seat, at the same time as Julia is bringing out his solomo. Which, yes, smells delicious, sitting atop a piece of crusty bread and melted Manchego.

But I can't focus on the solomo, given the expression on Jake's face. He looks like his dog died or like he's seen a ghost. Or like he's seen the ghost of his dead dog.

"You okay?" Julia asks him, in full Mom Mode, clearly noticing the absence of the smiling, good-natured man of several minutes ago.

"I'm fine," he says in monotone. "Actually—" he looks at me, looking nothing short of devastated "—um, can I get it to go?"

"Of course." Julia grabs a box and places it in front of him. After a pause, during which it becomes clear Jake is in no condition to box up his food, Julia sets to work on delicately transferring the sandwich and fixings to the container.

"Are you sure you're okay? And I know that's such a silly, knee-jerk question. But…are you?" I search Jake's face, looking for a sign that will tell me what transpired on the relatively short phone call with his mother.

He heaves out a sigh, shuffling his body to the barstool gingerly. Janet cocks her head at him and thumps her tail.

"Just some unexpected news, is all," he says softly, looking down at Janet and petting her head. "No one, like, died or anything."

"You're allowed to feel shitty over things besides death," Julia says matter-of-factly.

The corners of Jake's mouth turn up a little at her comment, but it's not a true smile. He keeps petting Janet, which, honestly, I'm good with; he seems like he needs her right now.

Julia meets my gaze and widens her eyes a bit, jerking her head toward Jake. *Help a brother out,* her eyes implore.

I raise my eyebrows right back at her in a silent conversation only sisters understand.

What am I supposed to do? I don't even know this guy.

Julia rolls her eyes. *I'm disappointed in you,* she tells me.

I roll my eyes right back and turn to Jake. He's looking directly at me, his blue eyes sad and sweet at the same time. He looks older than he did a few moments ago.

"I'm sorry I didn't get to talk with you more," he tells me quietly.

"Likewise," I respond.

He looks at me a beat longer than necessary and huffs a sad laugh. "Of all the restaurants in the world…" he mumbles before turning to Julia and putting some cash on the bar.

"Thank you for the sandwich. It looks and smells delicious."

"You're welcome, kiddo," she tells him, and I roll my eyes again. Julia is thirty-six, not 106.

Jake either doesn't notice the endearment or doesn't care. He gives Janet one last pat on the head and turns his sad eyes to me one more time.

"Bye, Tatum."

Chapter Eight

Jake

A ROCK THE SIZE OF—WELL, ESTERO ROCK—SITS IN THE PIT OF my stomach as I drive down the cul-de-sac I grew up on.

The rock has been there since I left St. Bishop's an hour and a half ago, getting progressively bigger as I get closer to my destination.

After the phone call to end all phone calls with my mother yesterday, I was done. Spent. Unable to form a coherent sentence and nearly unable to eat my solomo.

I persevered on that end, though. And that sandwich was goddamn delicious.

Seeing Janet run up to me at the Brew yesterday was the most welcome thing I'd seen in a long time. Well, the second-most-welcome thing. The first clearly belongs to Tatum the lawyer, who was as stunning and sexy as ever, perched on her barstool.

She must have come from exercising or something, her hair up in a messy bun and her cheeks ruddy, her curves clad in skintight leggings and a loose T-shirt.

And what curves they are.

I wish I could tell you I didn't notice that she wasn't wearing a bra on our first meeting, but that would be a lie. Tatum is clearly blessed in the breast department, and after all, I'm just a man.

It also didn't escape me that, in her rushed monologue to tell me to get the hell off her porch, she admitted thinking I am hot.

Super-hot.

I can work with that.

I knew she was smart upon our first meeting, and she confirmed it at our second. Smart, sexy, and seemingly comfortable with exactly who she is.

I want more of her.

But now is not the time.

My shoulders lock up as I steer my car through the gate to the big circular driveway leading to my parents' home. It's what I think of as quintessential Coastal California, with Spanish-style roof tiles, white stucco, and turquoise-blue front doors. The landscaping is immaculate, and it looks peaceful. And rich.

Stepping inside, I will be greeted with floor-to-ceiling views of the backyard, the glittering Pacific in the distance.

It's lovely.

Still, I would rather be anywhere else but here today.

After the bombshell my mother dropped on me yesterday, I knew that I had to go directly to the source. The source being my father, Jonathan Lowell Lundquist.

I knock on the front door and wait for my mom to answer. She is as she ever was—very pretty, very slim, and very pale, with darker blond hair pulled off her face. She wears a cream-colored blouse and navy-blue pants, her painted toenails peeking out through some sort of strappy sandals. Why we are so dressed up to hang out around the house, I'll never know.

"Hi, Jake," she says, smiling a bit at me. Her eyes are rimmed red, and her cheeks are slightly blotchy.

"Hi, Mom," I respond, pulling her into a hug. Her perfume and small stature are familiar, and nostalgia washes over me. Whatever choices she made in marrying my father, I do feel badly for her.

Frankly, I wish she would have been over and done with him a decade ago. But it's their business, not mine.

"I want to talk to you," I tell her, pulling back. "But I want to talk to him first."

She nods knowingly. "I understand. He's in the study."

Yes, this house has a study.

There's a reason why I was familiar with Tatum's practice area when she mentioned trusts yesterday. I'm a trust-fund baby.

I don't have total control of the trust until I am thirty. I'm twenty-three now, and the safeguard was put in place to ensure that I am mature and won't spend it all on coke and whores, I guess. Even though I am not, and have never been, interested in either.

I knock on the door to the study before letting myself in. My dad is seated behind a massive desk, scrolling through his iPad.

"Hey, Dad."

"Jake." He looks up, removing his glasses. There's no escaping his paternity—my dad is me, and I am him. Same hair, same eyes, same build. Looking at him is looking into my future. And I suppose, for him, looking at me is looking into the past.

"How are you doing?" he asks as I take one of the seats in front of the desk.

"I'm okay, Dad." I don't really want to make small talk, and I give him a look that, hopefully, says as much.

"Good, good," he says to himself, leaning back. We regard each other for a moment.

"I talked to Mom, you know."

"Yeah, I know," he exhales, pinching the bridge of his nose.

He says nothing more and has stopped making eye contact with me, so I decide to steamroll ahead.

"You got another woman pregnant?"

"Jesus, Jake," Dad mutters, like I used profanity in front of the Pope. "Not exactly," he continues.

"Well, it's kind of an exact science, Dad. Either you got another woman pregnant, or you didn't."

"I did, okay? I did," he tells me loudly. "Almost seventeen years ago."

Seventeen years ago?

I stare at him dumbly. When my mom mentioned my having…a sister, I just assumed my father had taken part in this procreation recently.

But I guess that isn't the case at all.

"Several years ago, I was…unfaithful to your mother."

I know there's more than one indiscretion, but this really isn't the time or the place.

"Carly got pregnant. She had a baby, a little girl."

Not so little now, though, if my math is correct.

"A girl? And what—what happened to her?"

"She lives with her mother. In the Central Valley, near Fresno."

"So, she's—So, I have—" I can't form my sentences correctly. I take a deep breath and try to relax my shoulders.

"She's almost my age," I tell my father softly, as if he doesn't already know that.

"She's sixteen," my father confirms, his tone just as quiet.

"She can drive," I tell my father blankly.

He raises his eyebrows. "I suppose—I suppose she can. I don't know if she has her license."

I sit and stare at my father, who avoids my gaze and turns his chair toward the window. His study also has a stunning view of the Pacific, and there's not a cloud in the sky, not a whitecap visible on the water. It's hard to tell where the water stops and the sky begins.

"I wasn't honest with your mother." My dad interrupts my train of thought, and I am really, really not here for apologies or excuses.

"Kind of an understatement, Dad," I mutter.

"I hope," my father continues as if I haven't spoken, "you will forgive me in time."

This is *so* like my dad. Admitting to some mistake. Taking ownership, I suppose, in some way, albeit perfunctorily and with no real remorse. And then immediately turning the tables on the other person, transferring expectations so that instead of it being his problem to solve—*I have a secret daughter, and I need to make amends for the bad deeds I've done*—it is now *my* problem to solve—*why won't you forgive your father so everyone can move on?*

But honestly, the words are easy to say. This revelation confirms what I already knew about my father. He can't be faithful to my mother, he never has, and while she's apparently been able to live this way forever, I am done with it.

I wonder, yet again, why they ever married in the first place. Monogamy is not for everyone, and divorce exists for a reason.

"I am not sure it's up to me to forgive your…indiscretion," I tell my father slowly. "Honestly, Dad, that's between you and Mom. Not me."

My father raises his eyebrows, waiting for me to continue.

"But," I continue, "I am twenty-three years old, and you're telling me that I have a sister I never knew about. That…that really fucking sucks," I tell him, my tone cutting.

"She's well provided for," my dad interrupts me. "And your inheritance, your trust, is secure—"

Jesus Christ.

"It's not about the inheritance!" I tell him sharply. "It's about me having a sister that I never knew about. Don't you think, did you *ever* think, I might have wanted to get to know her? Did that ever occur to you?"

My dad doesn't respond, and he really doesn't have to, because the answer is clear.

"Of course you didn't," I mutter.

I stand to leave, but not before asking one more thing.

"I want her number," I tell my dad. "Text it to me."

Chapter Nine

Tatum

"WHAT'S COOKING, GOOD-LOOKING?" A VOICE RINGS out from behind me. My best friend Lucy breezes— as much as one can "breeze" in Doc Martens—in and takes the seat across from me at the high-top table. We are in Sidecar, a great local spot in St. Bishop's with strong drinks and good food.

"Not much. Another day, another dollar."

Lucy wears a black tank top, black denim cutoffs, her signature fishnet stockings, and her signature expression, which veers between "unimpressed" and "let's take this outside." Her shiny black hair is cut short in a super-cute, trendy, angled bob that would make me look like a poodle.

"Did you have a deposition?" she asks, eyeing my blazer and dress. I changed out of my heels as soon as my workday was done, opting for comfy sneakers that have seen better days.

"Settlement conference," I tell her, sipping my drink.

"And judging from the fact that you are drinking a…calimocho?—" she asks, nodding to my drink "—at five p.m. on a Thursday, I am guessing it did not go well." She helps herself to the wasabi French fries in the center of the table.

A calimocho is red wine and Coke and the most delicious thing in the world. No, it's not classy. But serve it over ice and put it in a big Cabernet glass, and I am fancy as fuck. In high school, my friends and I would empty half a liter of Coca-Cola and fill it with cheap red wine—god bless the makers of Franzia, keeping the underage drinkers of the world lubricated—and sneak it into football games and school dances.

Now, I drink it openly and sparingly. There is nothing quite like a hangover caused by equal parts sugar and alcohol. Calimocho is not for the faint of heart.

"It actually went really, really well," I tell her. "This is a celebratory drink, not a pity drink."

"Nice. Well, in that case, cheers, my friend. I hate to have you drink alone, but I can only stay for a bit."

"I can drink with you!" A bubbly voice erupts behind me, and our other friend, Summer, bends to kiss me on the cheek, the smell of her coconut shampoo reaching my nose.

"Hallelujah," I reply with a smile as Summer takes the third seat at the high-top.

Summer's coppery-red hair is in loose waves around her shoulders, her freckled skin clad in a maroon sundress. She wears no jewelry except for the blindingly bright engagement ring visible on her left hand.

Summer Mahoney is soon to be Summer Echeverria, as my older brother Nick grew some *cojones* and recently popped the question. And while I had some misgivings about Summer and Nick's relationship in the beginning—both of them coming off not just long-term relationships, but marriages that did *not* end well—anyone can see they are meant to be.

I am very happy for them, only slightly weirded out by the fact that my best friend thinks my older brother is even remotely attractive, and only slightly jealous of my friend's happiness.

"Is Nicky still out of town?" I ask Summer.

"He is. In Miami with Brock for some…football thing," Summer answers, partaking in the fries with Lucy. "He'll be back on Sunday." She eyes my drink. "A calimocho? Are we living dangerously?"

"If by 'dangerously,' you mean having no more than two of these, tops, and then going to a place where I can be braless and eat endless amounts of snack foods, then yes," I tell her, only half joking.

"I'm in."

After the server comes and takes our order—one calimocho for Summer, one water with lime for Lucy, and more fries and shrimp toast for all of us—Summer glances around the space. "I forget how quiet it gets here in the summertime without all the college students."

"It's soooo nice," I comment, taking another swig of my drink, feeling a little more tension evaporate from my shoulders, the sweet, low hum of inebriation taking hold. Other than the three of us, there are a few groups around the large restaurant. I recognize a small group from the DA's office at a booth and some older hippie-types at the bar.

I also recognize a lone figure at the corner of the bar, a plaid snap-shirt hugging his torso, cowboy boots propped up on the rung of his barstool, ball cap pulled low over his eyes. His arms are crossed and his gaze is downward, his entire posture screaming *go away*.

"J.B.'s over there at the bar. He'd never be out here while school is in session."

Lucy turns to look and smirks. "Totally. Can you imagine all the college girls trying to flirt with him? 'Take me for a ride, cowboy.' He'd scare them all off."

"J.B. Desiard? Didn't he go to our high school?" Summer asks, glancing over her shoulder at the man with the crouched posture before turning back.

"He did," I confirm. "He works out at the Hayes ranch now, near the state park. I've done some property stuff for him."

"His family's ranch? Isn't he the only one left?" Lucy asks.

"I think there's a sister. She was a few years younger than us. I don't really know, and he's not exactly talkative."

As if his ears are burning, J.B. raises his head slightly from the bar and catches my gaze. I lift my calimocho in salute. He makes no movement, but his dark eyes flash in recognition, his chin dipping slightly before he brings his gaze back down to the bar.

"Guess he doesn't want company," Lucy drawls, turning back to us.

"He's a nice enough guy. Let's just say he makes Nick look like a chatterbox," I reply, and Summer laughs.

My brother is not known for his loquacious ways.

"I guess this guy's lease still isn't up," Lucy says, her eyes focused on the entrance to the restaurant.

I glance to see where she is looking, and wouldn't you know it?

You already know it, don't you?

I get a jolt of déjà vu as Jake Lundquist enters the restaurant, literally in the same ensemble I saw him in at my sister's restaurant a week ago before he left quickly and without explanation.

Not that he owes me an explanation, of course.

"Oh, sweet Baby Jesus," I mutter to myself as Jake moves with purpose toward the bar, his eyes darting briefly around the space. He pauses and nearly trips over his feet as his eyes meet mine. Just like last time, they widen as he recognizes me and changes course, moving toward our table.

"You know this guy?" Lucy asks me.

"Nooooo," I tell her slowly. "Yes. Kind of. Remember the axe murderer during graduation weekend?"

"The…axe murderer?" Summer asks bewilderedly.

"This is the axe murderer?" Lucy asks.

"There is no axe murderer," I tell Summer. "And no, that's not him," I add to Lucy. "The axe murderer was his friend."

"But…you just said there *was* no axe murderer," Summer responds, a perplexed expression on her face.

"His friend? There were two axe murderers on your porch?" Lucy asks.

"And now there are two axe murderers?" Summer murmurs, more to herself than anyone else.

I am saved from any further explanation when Jake reaches our table, his expression bright. He looks to Lucy and Summer before meeting my gaze again.

"Hi, Tatum!" he chirps. *Chirps.* Like a happy baby bird.

"Hi." I take a sip of my drink.

Jake's eyes do a once-over of me, and his smile gets bigger. "You look nice today. Like a real lawyer. Not that I didn't think you were, like, a *real* lawyer, of course. But you know. You look like one today. At least, what I think one would look like." Jake's cheeks redden, and he self-consciously shifts from side to side.

A slow smile spreads across Summer's face, undoubtedly recognizing a fellow awkward conversationalist. "Hi! I'm Summer," she chirps—again with the chirping—and holds out her hand.

Jake shakes her hand. "I'm Jake. Jake Lundquist." He smiles back, his expression fading slightly as he looks at Lucy, who has her usual expression on her face. "Nice to meet you…"

Lucy stares a moment longer than necessary. "Lucy." She permits him to shake her hand.

"Jake." He puts his hands in his pockets and regards the table. "So, where's my favorite girl?"

I cough, taking another sip of my drink to avoid responding, both Lucy's and Summer's expressions registering surprise.

"Your…favorite girl?" Summer asks.

"You know! Janet. I think she likes me," Jake mentions conspiratorially to Summer, sensing that she is on his side.

Summer's eyes widen almost comically. "You…know Janet?" she asks.

"Sure! Love that dog," Jake responds easily.

"And how do you know Janet?" Lucy asks suspiciously, interrogating Jake in lieu of making conversation like a normal person.

I sigh. "So, here is the story. Jake's friend—" I look to Jake questioningly.

"Brandon," he supplies.

"—Brandon was the axe murderer. He was not really an axe murderer," I explain hurriedly to Summer's exasperated expression. "He is Jake's friend, and he got really, really drunk on graduation and ended up passing out on my front porch. Someone had the wherewithal to write Jake's number—in Sharpie—on Brandon's arm."

"Along with a bunch of other dirty messages," Jake interjects with a grin.

"Yes, your friend was definitely tatted-up," I agree, meeting Jake's eyes.

Still blue, still honest, still hopeful. His jawline is strong and sharp, and his lips look soft. I wonder if they'd feel soft against mine.

Jake stares back at me, his easy smile growing into a grin. My cheeks heat up at his blatant interest.

"So, Brandon…" Lucy butts in helpfully.

"Brandon! Right." I clear my throat and tear myself away from Jake's gaze. "Janet sniffed him out early in the morning, and I called Lucy to, you know, keep her on the phone in case there was an axe murderer on my front porch."

"Makes sense," Summer chimes in. "Why call the police when your baker friend who is fifteen minutes away can offer witty commentary?"

"*Anyway*," I continue. "The axe murderer turned out to be drunk Brandon, Jake turned out to be his bestie, and that is how Janet knows Jake."

"It was definitely love at first sight," Jake says with a smile at me, before realizing how that sounds. "With Janet, I mean," he adds quickly, before winking at me. I roll my eyes at his flirtation, but not before my cheeks heat again. This guy is good, I'll give him that.

"Uh-huh." Lucy leans back as much as she can on the barstool and crosses her arms over her chest, sizing Jake up. "And what are you doing *here*?"

"Having a drink?" Jake responds.

"Did you graduate?" Lucy continues.

"Yes," Jake answers slowly.

"What was your major?" Lucy doesn't skip a beat.

"Architecture."

"Fun," Lucy offers.

"It was a lot of math," Jake responds with a shrug.

"Oh, I do love math," Lucy says, her eyes brightening a little before she continues with her third degree. "You have a job?"

"No. Well, maybe. Kind of. I mean, I could. My dad wants me to come work at his company…" Jake's voice drifts off, and his eyes dart this way and that, clearly looking for an escape route.

"Sounds fascinating," Lucy deadpans.

"Give the poor kid a break, Lucy," Summer admonishes her, before apparently deciding to seize life by the balls. "Jake, would you like to join us for a drink?"

He looks gratefully to Summer and pauses, seemingly torn between wanting to join our group and fearful that Lucy will interrogate him about his health history. "I wouldn't want to impose," he says, glancing at me hopefully.

I sigh, taking a sip of my drink and realizing it is *not*, despite my best efforts, going to be a two-drink-maximum kind of night.

I gesture toward the lone stool left at our table.

"Have you ever had a calimocho?"

Chapter Ten

Jake

TATUM AND HER TWO FRIENDS CLEARLY HAVE A BOND THAT GOES back decades. They banter back and forth over their drinks and one order of shrimp toast that turns into three.

"That solomo thing from your sister's restaurant was amazing, by the way," I comment to Tatum.

"So good, huh?" she agrees, deeply engrossed in her own food.

"Wait, you also know Julia?" Summer asks, raising her eyebrows. I understand from their earlier conversation that Summer is engaged to Tatum's brother.

"I mean, I met her. Tatum happened to be at the restaurant when I was in there."

"She did?" Summer's eyebrows rise higher. "So, you and Tatum have spent a lot of time together," she says, looking slyly at her friend.

"Not really," Tatum quickly responds. "I mean, it's just circumstance. It's a small town. County. Whatever." She swipes another fry.

It's not "whatever" to me, but I let it slide. "So, what type of lawyer thing did you have today?" I ask Tatum.

She sips what I believe is now her third drink. That wine and Coke concoction is way too sweet for me. "I had a settlement conference. Basically, my client and I are in one room, the other party and her attorney are in the other room, and a judge runs back and forth between the two rooms, trying to make everyone happy."

"That sounds impossible. Making everyone happy, I mean," I comment.

Tatum shrugs. "Well, I don't know if we are all best friends, but there's an agreement to settle." She raises her glass in salute. "I'm going to run to the restroom."

"I'll come with," Lucy interjects quickly.

They leave Summer and me alone at the table, which is fine with me.

Lucy is a little…abrupt.

I wouldn't want to encounter her alone in a dark alley.

"So, Jake, you said you are from Santa Barbara?" Summer asks kindly, marking her as the "nice" one of the trio.

"Yep. My parents still live there."

"No siblings?"

It's a natural question for the conversation, but I pause. "Actually…it's complicated."

"You don't have to talk about it if you don't want to," Summer tells me.

"No, it's fine, it's just very new and…" I take a sip of my Dos Equis and stare into space for a moment. There's a baseball game on the television and a Jack Johnson song playing in the background. I turn back to Summer, who looks at me patiently.

"I have a little sister I just learned about. Like, literally just learned about a week ago."

Summer's face turns sympathetic. "Like…from a parent's second marriage?"

"Ha! And no," I tell her. "From an extramarital relationship my father had. And when I say 'little' sister, I mean younger than me. Not, like, someone in diapers. She's in high school," I add.

Summer's sympathetic look turns shocked. "That's a huge secret for your father to keep for so long," she says.

"No shit. I mean… Yeah. Sorry," I tell her, but she waves away my profanity.

"Have you met her?"

"My sister? Not yet. I mean, I want to. I told my dad to send me her info. That's where I came from today, actually." I laugh ruefully. "I drove straight back from Santa Barbara, intending to get really drunk."

"And you ended up with us, instead," Summer says quietly.

"I did. Which is great," I add hurriedly. "I mean, you are all really nice. Well, you are nice. Lucy seems…nice."

Summer gives me a side-eye. "She's a great friend. She won't be mad if you don't think she's nice. In fact, she would probably be offended if you *did* think she was nice."

I grin. "And Tatum's…" My voice drifts off, and I turn my attention back to a baseball game I don't care about.

"Tatum's great," Summer says confidently. "The best. The best of the best."

"I believe it," I reply, meeting Summer's eyes and hopefully letting her see that I do. She smiles back at me in seeming approval.

"Good," she says, bringing her glass to mine.

We cheers.

<h1 style="text-align:center">Chapter Eleven</h1>

Tatum

"**J**AKE'S CUTE." LUCY DOESN'T MAKE EYE CONTACT WITH ME AS SHE washes her hands in the sink.

"Mmm," is my noncommittal response as I give her a sidelong glance.

"You hitting that or what?"

Lucy always gets to the crux of the matter without a lot of song-and-dance. It's one of the many reasons we are friends—we never feel the need to beat around the bush.

Or the hot young college grad, as it were.

"No." I offer nothing further and grab a paper towel, then two more to wipe down the bathroom counter.

"Why not?"

"I'm just…not."

"You could."

"I could do lots of things. I could sail to the Channel Islands tomorrow and begin a new life. Get me away from your nosy ass," I add.

"You get seasick," Lucy reminds me.

"I'll take Dramamine," I mumble.

"Tatum Echeverria," Lucy says sharply, finally meeting my eyes. Hers are dark and lined perfectly, a wing drawn up from the outer corner of each eye.

"This dude is panting after you like a puppy dog. He thinks you're *swell*," she continues, "which, of course, you are. But I also happen to know that you haven't gotten laid in, like, a really long time."

She's not wrong. After my last relationship ended horribly, I've avoided even the suggestion of a hook-up, serious or otherwise.

"Takes one to know one," I mutter, knowing Lucy has also embarked on what she calls "born-again celibacy."

"True, but that's neither here nor there." Lucy pauses and cocks her head to the side. "I strangely remember having this same conversation with Summer in a bathroom at the Brew." She smiles deviously. "Only I was telling her to bang your brother."

"*Why*? Why are you so gross?" I moan. Seriously, I'm happy for Summer and Nick, but I am not here for the details of their boot-knockin'.

"It's summertime. This guy is here for a good time, not a long time, and you deserve some good dick. I bet he has stamina," Lucy adds for good measure.

"You don't know that. I bet he can't even find my clit."

"You'll never know until you try," Lucy responds. "And even if he doesn't find it on the first go-round, something tells me he'll be eager to please. Show him the way to good fortune. Light the path to your gilded—"

"Okay, okay, okay." I interrupt her soliloquy. I sigh and meet her eyes again.

"It *has* been a while since I—"

"—had someone raise a tent in your land of good and plenty," Lucy supplies.

I squint. "That doesn't even make sense!"

"It makes sense to me," Lucy responds innocently.

"*Anyway*." I pause. "Since Dr. Douche, I have been…reluctant to jump on the horse. So to speak."

Lucy's eyes flash at the reference to my ex. "Understandable. And Tatum, here's your opportunity. No strings attached. No pressure. I've been around him less than two hours, and I can already tell this guy would pay cash money to listen to you recite the penal code for an evening, or whatever it is you lawyers do," Lucy says.

"Not criminal law, but okay," I demur.

"Whatever. Go make a move. Release the hounds," she says, gesturing to my chest. "Get. Some."

I look at my reflection in the dirty, chipped bathroom mirror. "Get some," I repeat, more to myself than to Lucy.

She meets my eyes in the mirror. "You deserve it."

"I deserve it."

"Now go make like Mrs. Robinson and show that man a good time."

The bar bill is paid, I have pounded a glass of water, and I am about to make my case for a good, old-fashioned, one-night stand to Jake Lundquist.

"Jake, it was nice to meet you," Summer says cheerfully, standing up and stumbling a bit. "Whoa," she murmurs, leaning on Lucy. "Tatum, those calimochos are brutal."

"They are good for you!" I lie.

"Let's go, sister," Lucy tells Summer, linking their arms together. "Jake, it's been real. Can't wait to see you again. Or not. Whatever." Lucy waves her other hand and leads our friend out the door.

I turn to Jake, intent on convincing him that a little mattress dancing is in his best interest, only to see that he is already staring at me.

I open my mouth. Shut it. Sip some water. I feel relaxed and loose, but not so drunk that I will be sloppy, and definitely not so drunk that I'm incapable of making my own decisions.

"Hi," Jake says softly, his eyes darting around my face, a slight curve of a smile on his lips.

Is this man ever not smiling? It's a little unnerving for a cynic like me.

"Um, hi," I tell him, and his smile grows wider. I clear my throat to hide the fact that this guy really flusters me. Me! I used to eat men like him for breakfast. Other meals, too.

Jake places one hand on the table, palm up, his eyes holding fast to mine. In a trance, I take my hand and place it on his, palm down. His hand is warm and firm, and a trill of excitement rushes through me. I have to do it—I break our eye contact and look down at our hands instead. His skin is tanned, his forearm corded with muscle.

"I'm really glad I ran into you today," Jake murmurs, his hand closing around mine.

"Rough day?" I ask lightly, deliberately misunderstanding him. When he doesn't answer right away, I glance up and see that his face has shuttered.

"I'm sorry. What's wrong?" I ask him, trying to pull my hand out of his, but he locks his grip around me.

"It's nothing. Well," he huffs, "nothing that I want to share right now anyway. If that's okay with you," he adds thoughtfully. He strokes the top of my hand with his thumb, and it's the best thing I've ever felt.

"Of course." I am held by his eyes, unable to look away, unable to remove my hand, unable to feel anything else but this connection between us. Of course it's okay.

I don't know this man, not really.

He doesn't know me, not at all.

We don't owe each other anything.

I am about to tell him all these things—maybe not the best sell for a one-night stand, but I am nothing if not a realist—when he interrupts my train of thought.

"Can I walk you home?"

Chapter Twelve

Jake

TATUM AND I WALK THE ROUGHLY FIVE BLOCKS FROM DOWNTOWN to her house, hand in hand, in relative silence. The sun has set, purples and pinks and blues painting the sky. It's peaceful, the occasional sound of a dog barking or music from someone's home breaking the quiet.

I keep a firm grip on Tatum the entire way.

I don't know what persuaded me to take her hand in the first place.

I just knew I needed a connection.

I am unmoored, thrown off-balance by the time spent with my father, and equally off-balance—but in a good way—by the time I spent with Tatum.

And to be frank, it feels good to hold her hand.

It feels good to be around her, to breathe her scent, to see her dark hair—which was pulled away from her face the previous two times we met—falling around her shoulders and down her back. It feels good to see the different sides of her, however briefly. Lawyer Tatum in her nice clothes. Realist Tatum in her sneakers. Tatum the friend, laughing with her girlfriends. Tatum with her reddened cheeks when I stare at her a little too long, a little too intently.

All those things feel good in a way nothing else does.

And after all, I am just a man. A pretty girl way out of my league exhibiting a slight interest in me? I'm all in.

And I still haven't forgotten that she thinks I'm hot.

"Janet will need to go out for a bit," Tatum tells me as we make our way through the little white gate up the path to her porch. "A dog walker comes during the day, but she's probably been cooped up since after lunch."

"I can take her," I offer as Tatum unlocks the front door, and sure enough, I hear the enthusiastic barks coming from inside.

"Really?" Tatum asks. "I mean, that would be awesome. I need to get out of this dress."

I raise my eyebrows in mock surprise. "Really, Tatum? Buy me a drink first."

She smirks at me. "So confused as to what we just did at the bar…"

I smile and gesture toward her. "Do what you need to do. Just show me where the leash and doggie bags are, and we'll be on our way."

Tatum

I like to think of myself as a woman of action.

Having made the decision to "get some," as Lucy so aptly put it, and having the better part of twenty minutes to make myself passably fuckable, I decide once again not to beat around the bush and let Jake know how I envision this night going.

Men are visual learners. Show them some tits, and they fall right in line. A thong? They'll do whatever you want. Which is why when Jake returns with Janet, I have left no room for error. My robe is a silky navy blue that looks soft to the touch and feels even better, and I have a matching bra and panties set on underneath.

I hear Jake open the door, cooing sweet nothings to Janet, and damn if that doesn't get my blood pumping a little faster. I really don't know this guy. He's hot and nice, and I am pretty sure this connection I feel with him isn't totally one-sided. I have no lofty thoughts about our future together, but he seems like a sweetheart and likes my dog.

There are worse guys to give it up to, right?

Chapter Thirteen

Jake

JANET RUNS AHEAD OF ME AS SOON AS WE GET INTO THE HOUSE, WHICH I still haven't seen except for the living area in the front. A small kitchen sits off the living room, and I wash my hands.

I head back out into the living room, drawn toward the large fireplace in the center, framed by windows with forest-green curtains drawn closed on either side. There's a lot of plant life in this room, I realize, noting the potted fig leaf next to the gray couch and a couple of white pots hanging from hooks in the ceiling. Framed paintings hang on the walls. Some are abstract, just colors and shapes; some are portraits.

Another thing I notice, especially after living with dudes for the past five years?

This house is *clean.*

My girl is a clean freak.

The fireplace mantel holds several framed pictures, and I walk closer to take a look. There's a younger Tatum on the beach in Estero Bay, the Rock visible in the background, framed by Summer on one side and Lucy on the other. They are all laughing—yes, even Lucy—their mouths wide open and their arms wrapped around one another. There's Tatum in a graduation gown with a taller, lankier version of herself—her sister Julia, I realize, who is hugging another tattooed man. On Tatum's other side is a woman who can only be Tatum's mother, taller and thinner like Julia. And on *that* woman's other side…

"Huh," I say aloud.

"Huh, what?" Tatum's voice comes from behind me.

"Your last name is…" I continue without turning around, putting the picture back on the mantel.

"Echeverria," Tatum responds, and I move to examine another picture of Tatum, Julia, and two little dark-haired girls.

"And Nick Echeverria is…"

"He's my brother. He's getting married to Summer," Tatum answers as I turn around, and holy Mother of God, all thoughts of Tatum being related to a Super Bowl-winning quarterback vanish when I see what she's wearing.

Navy blue.

Silk.

Hair. So much hair, falling around her face, spilling down her back.

Small feet, bare. Toenails painted black. Toned legs leading up to thick thighs, covered by the smallest robe, knotted within an inch of its life.

And, if you'll forgive my crassness, huge tits. They are at war with the aforementioned robe, and I try hard not to stare at Tatum's chest like a cartoon character with bug eyes, but I can't help it.

After all, I'm just a man.

"Hi!" I blurt out, like an idiot. "I mean, you look nice. I mean, is Janet okay? Did you want to sit down? Have a drink?" I am nothing but word vomit, but I can't stop. I probably look like I am having a stroke with the way my eyes dart up and down, up and down, from Tatum's chest to her face and back again.

Tatum smiles, and it's a little evil.

"We already had a drink, remember?" She walks closer to me, determination in her eyes.

I hope her endgame is the same as mine.

"Right. Yes. We did." Tatum is now an arm's length away from me and stops. I lean forward unconsciously, willing her to be closer to me, smelling her perfume. She's so close that I can make out the tiny freckles on the bridge of her nose.

"And you only had a couple beers, so I assume that you are in full control of your faculties, right?" Tatum raises an eyebrow at me.

"Yep! Yes. I mean—" I heave out a breath and close my eyes for a moment, willing my mouth to stop blurting out words before I know what they are. "I am not drunk." I open my eyes and meet Tatum's hazel gaze. "I don't want to make any assumptions, but I am thinking—well, hoping really, that because you invited me into your house and let me walk your dog and are wearing…that…" I manage to choke out the rest of the words and lose the battle, my gaze moving back down to Tatum's breasts.

Tatum saves me, though, with five simple words.

"Jake, I want to fuck."

Chapter Fourteen

Jake

"I THINK I'M HAVING A HEART ATTACK," I MUMBLE, STUMBLING TO the couch and sitting down.

That's the only explanation for the rapid acceleration of my heartbeat and the adrenaline coursing through my veins.

Although, the beginning of an erection tells me I am fit as a fiddle.

"Really? You look fine to me," Tatum says innocently, moving closer to me, like she plans to trap me on her couch.

Not a bad idea at all.

"Do you need some water?" she asks, looking down at me.

"No. No, I'm fine," I tell her from my spot on the couch. I place my hands on either side of myself and clench them tight.

"You seem pretty wound up," Tatum continues, moving forward so that I have to manspread my legs to allow her to stand. I lean back and lick my lips as I take her in, all curves and hair and woman.

"Are you gonna—do you want me to—oh my god," I stammer as she pulls the tie on her robe, the knot losing its battle with her breasts, and I am blessed with the view of her breasts clad in a navy-blue bra. There's lace or something over the cups—I don't know, I admittedly don't pay a lot of attention to women's lingerie—but I see her dark nipples harden through the sheer fabric.

"Where you are is perfect, actually." Tatum responds to my stammering. She discards her robe on the couch and resumes her standing position and meets my eyes. "I haven't shaved in a while. I don't have the time, and I don't care."

I nod…and nod some more, doing my best impression of a bobblehead as I take in her ample thighs and pillowy stomach. Her sheer underwear matches her bra perfectly. *Fuck.* "No shaving. Got it. Okay." I rub my cock, now nearly fully erect in my shorts. I shift uncomfortably on the couch, trying to give the little guy some relief.

Tatum watches me, no hint of vulnerability, no sign of hesitation. From this angle, she looks down on me, the opposite of where we usually regard each other.

I fucking love it.

I'll worship at her altar any day of the week.

She gestures with her hands before putting them on her hips. "Take off your shorts, Jake," she tells me impatiently.

"Right! Right." I jump up and manage not to fall over as I undress. My socks are still on. Should I take them off? Is that lame if I am here just stark-ass naked—assuming Tatum and I are going to get completely naked, which, god yes, please, make this happen—but still wearing bright-white socks? Do they even match?

"*Jake.*"

"Huh?" I glance at Tatum, an amused look on her face.

"Sit down," she says gently.

I do as the good woman says.

Her smile grows.

"I should have known you'd have something like…that on your boxers," she says, gesturing her hand toward me.

Honestly, I never think about what print is on my boxers when I dress in the morning. I look down.

Lovely.

This particular pair has crosses and pictures of Cool Jesus, winking one eye, giving a thumbs-up with one hand and holding a joint in the other.

I shut my eyes briefly and open them to meet Tatum's gaze. "Um, yeah. My fraternity brothers…it was a Christmas gift. A joke."

"Your fraternity brothers," Tatum repeats.

"Yeah." My fraternity brothers had joked that, if I ever got far enough with a girl, then the good Lord Jesus would be there to remind me to hold off.

I don't tell Tatum that, though.

Tatum nods. "Well, as cute as those are, need them off."

"Right! Right," I tell her, eagerly hopping up again and pulling off my boxers. My cock immediately springs to attention, so hard that it rests along my abdomen as I sit back down. I sigh in relief as he's no longer constricted, glancing at Tatum…

…Who now looks at me with wide eyes and an open mouth. "Jesus Christ, Jake," she breathes, watching me stroke up my cock firmly, a bead of liquid seeping from the tip. "That thing's going to break me in half."

Another thing my fraternity brothers joked about?

The size of my dick.

My buddies mock-begged me not to hook up with any of the pretty girls.

"If one of them gets a look at that thing, all the others are going to know about it before sunrise the next day."

"Seriously, bro. Hold on to that V-card. Keep that shit locked down."

It's bigger than average, I guess. I mean, I usually don't get a good perusal of my friends' dicks.

I do, however, watch a lot of porn. I mean, a lot. And my dick seems pretty average compared to what I see in those films. And yes, they are films—they can be artistic, okay?

Well, sometimes.

Anyway. Tatum thinks I'm packing, and we've already established she thinks I'm hot, so this is all icing on the proverbial sex cake.

"No! No, it won't break you, I promise, I—we—we can go slow?" I ramble, squeezing my dick at the top and trying my best not to come before we get to the best part.

Or what I assume is the best part.

"Okaaaay," Tatum drawls, looking slightly nervous for the first time since we got into the house.

"It'll be like—like making out!" I tell her. She gives me a blank look, and I continue with my speech. I imagine I am on debate team giving the closing rebuttal. "You know—like, the best make-out sessions usually don't start with face-mauling. You need to ease into it, some nice, soft kisses, some nuzzles, kisses on the neck" —*girls love kisses on the neck, in my experience*—"and then you get to the tongue. But you just let your tongue touch hers a little, you know?" My voice gets quieter as I continue. "Just a little taste, just a little sample. And only then can you go for the deep, long kisses where your tongues get all tangled up and you're panting and, um. You know, rubbing on each other and breathing heavy and stuff."

Tatum's expression has gone from apprehensive to…I don't know what. Her mouth is slightly agape, and her cheeks are ruddy, her eyes a little glassy.

"I mean. In my experience."

Tatum clears her throat. "No, no, that's—" she coughs "—that's good. That sounds good. Slow. Yeah."

I give her a little smile. "You want to come sit on my lap?" I waggle my eyebrows, and she rolls her eyes.

"You want to take off your panties?" I add hopefully.

"I don't think so," Tatum tells me primly, coming to straddle me on the couch, and *ohmygod*, this is amazing. Her hair is everywhere, and I get the sudden urge to roll all that hair in my fist, angle her head toward me, and tongue her mouth deeply.

My cock agrees with this scenario, jumping a bit against my stomach.

"Goddamn, Jake," Tatum whispers. She wraps her arms around my neck and rolls her body, ever so slightly, against mine, letting me feel her warmth. I can smell her lotion or perfume or whatever—something sweet and warm, like toasted vanilla—but also something else.

"You getting wet, beautiful?" I ask her, my voice dropping an octave.

"You want to find out?" she asks me huskily.

"Fuck yes. Fuck yes," I tell her, wrapping my arms around her back to pull her close to me. We don't kiss, but we angle our heads alongside each other, breathing each other in as Tatum continues rolling her body, her movements getting longer and harder, rubbing herself on my cock.

"Mmm. Feels good," she whispers. "You think I'm ready for that big dick of yours?"

I almost choke at her words.

"See for yourself, Jake," she purrs, rubbing harder against my cock, jerking her body like a dancer. Or a stripper.

Yes, I have been to strip clubs.

I'm a virgin, not a monk.

I make eye contact with her as I run my hand down her back, trying my best to be slow and gentle.

Even though I want to throw her down on the floor and hump her like a dog in heat.

I reach her backside. I haven't even gotten a good look at that thing, and I make a mental note to do a thorough inspection later. I can't help but grab a healthy handful of her ass, squeezing firmly. "God, Tatum. I want you so much," I grit out.

She arches her back into my touch, her center getting that much closer to my cock as she does. Her movement puts me at eye level with her glorious breasts. She still wears her bra, and I make another mental note to lose the bra the next time we do this.

Please let there be a next time.

I shove my face unabashedly between her breasts, licking and kissing her smooth olive skin. Her tits are so big that I am in danger of being smothered alive. But honestly, if death-by-motorboating is in my epitaph, I will die a happy man.

Actually, scratch that. I won't die a happy man unless I can get inside this woman.

I lean back against the couch to get a full view of her. I look down to where she's undulating against me and see a large damp spot on her panties, right in the center.

"Looks like you might be ready," I huff out, bringing my hand around to her front. I slowly trail my fingers alongside the seam of her underwear, rubbing her through the fabric, not directly at her center but along the side. She whimpers and shimmies her body a bit.

"Fuck. *Fuck*," I mumble.

"Check. Me," Tatum pants out.

I obey her command and let my fingers slide under the fabric to run along her skin. I move my fingers past her crisp curls and feel the warm wetness of her core. She's nearly ready. But just to make sure…

"Beautiful. Let me have a taste of you," I breathe out, Tatum's eyes rolling back in her head as she gyrates. I move my fingers directly to her opening and dip one in, feeling her body coat me in her arousal.

"No. No time. I'm ready, Jake," she whispers in staccato. She gasps when I dip my fingers farther, feeling her smooth insides squeeze my finger so tight, sucking me in.

"Just a little taste," I tell her, pumping my finger gently in and out of her a few times. "Let me get some of you." Tatum moans loudly, and I lean my head forward again to be cradled by her breasts.

This.

This is already heaven—me fingering this goddess, her rubbing all over me, her smell in my nose and her taste in my mouth.

"Oh my god, I want to die here," I blurt out as I keep pumping my finger in and out of her. I think Tatum laughs—it's hard to be sure with the noises she's making—but I do hear her comment to "Hurry up and get in me before you die."

"I will—I will," I tell her. "I don't want to hurt you, beautiful. Let me get another finger in there, huh? Can you do that for me?"

Tatum's arms are wrapped around my shoulders, and she meets my eyes directly. "Do it," she whispers, spreading her legs wider.

We both look down to see my finger retreat, shiny with her wetness. We both suck in a breath as I add my middle finger to the mix, slowly penetrating her, her underwear pulled casually to the side.

"*Oh fuck*, Jake," Tatum cries, her head lolling on her shoulders. I pump shallowly a few times, and she shudders before bringing one hand to her center. "I want to come," she tells me, meeting my gaze again through heavy lids.

"*Fuck yes*, you do." I pump a little faster but not deeper, every inch of her sucking me in. I hold her gaze. "Do it," I repeat her words back to her.

She rubs herself just above where my hand is, her breath erratic, her movements jerky. "Jake. *Jake.*" My name on her lips is the best sound I've ever heard.

"Come, Tatum," I coax her. "Come all over my hand. *Please.*"

She opens her eyes again and looks at me, desperation on her face. "Kiss me?" she asks.

"*Yes,*" I tell her, and our mouths meet in a mash of lips, tongue, and heat. It occurs to me that this is our first kiss. Our first kiss is an explosion of taste, touch, and smell, all my senses heightened as Tatum clenches around my fingers, her hand moving quickly between us.

"Jake," she pants between kisses, our movements sloppy and neither of us giving a fuck. "I'm coming, *ohmygod*, I'm coming," she moans, and I swallow her words, her gasps, her cries with my mouth. I have no finesse and I have no playbook as she comes around my fingers, and it's the greatest experience of my life.

"So good, Tatum. You're so beautiful. Come, come," I whisper into her mouth, sucking on her bottom lip as she cries out. "Good girl. Come on me."

Tatum's whole body tightens up before she slowly releases, the waves subsiding and her muscles loosening. She keeps kissing me, slower and softly, and removes her hand from between us.

Leaning back, I take her in. Her hair is wild and tangled, her cheeks rosy, her lips puffy. She really is beautiful.

She looks at me with a serenity in her eyes that I haven't seen before. And I'm no dummy; I know an orgasm releases all sorts of endorphins and other good juju, and it's not that Tatum couldn't get herself off alone any day of the week.

But it's nice to see that look on her face, just for me.

"I think I'm ready for you now," she whispers with a glint in her eye.

Tatum

Jake looks equal parts excited and apprehensive.

"Are—are you sure? Because we don't have to do anything else. Honestly, that was amazing, and I—"

"I definitely want to. But only if *you* want to," I reply, a little touched by his words.

Obviously, I know I'm not obligated to give it up to Jake just because he gave me an orgasm. But it's nice to hear that he knows that too.

"You have a condom?" I ask him as I stand up to remove my underwear, which, yes, were pulled to the side the entire time he finger-fucked me.

It was hot as hell.

"I don't, actually," Jake replies, not meeting my gaze.

"Oh." I am surprised. Doesn't every guy carry one in his wallet? But no matter.

"Well, I have some. I'll be right back." I leave before Jake can judge me for having a ready supply of condoms in my house. Not that I think he would, but you never know.

I grab a few from the side table in my bedroom—fortune favors the optimistic—and smile at Janet, dead asleep in her dog bed on the floor.

I pad back out to the living room, grabbing a towel from the bathroom on the way—fortune favors the prepared—thankful all the curtains are closed as I am clad in only my bra. Jake is still sitting naked on the couch, his head resting back on the pillow, his hand firmly gripping his dick…

…Which is so erect, it looks painful. For him *and* for me.

"You okay?" I ask him, making my way back to the couch and setting the condoms to the side. Couch sex is highly underrated, if you ask me. The buoyancy of a well-made couch just can't be beat.

"I'm good," he responds, his eyes widening when I come to straddle him again. "Holdonholdonholdon—" He sucks in a breath and squints his eyes shut as I touch his dick, which jerks in my hand.

"*Tatum*," he moans. "Jesus."

"I'm sorry!" I exclaim. "Are you sure you want—"

"I do. I totally, one hundred percent do," he moans. "I am just barely hanging on here, and I don't want to come before we even get the condom on."

I smile.

I can work with this.

"Jake," I whisper, as I slowly lower myself onto him so that our chests are pressed together and his dick is standing straight up between us. "You can come any time you want to." I lean forward and speak softly directly into his ear before taking the lobe in my mouth and sucking gently. Jake shudders, his head lolling to the side.

I wrap one hand around his dick, much gentler this time, and squeeze a little as I move my hand to the top, where it meets his. "Any time you want. Because once you break me in, I want you to work me over, okay?"

I squeeze him harder as I stroke up to the top where our hands meet again. Jake roars as his hand joins mine, down his dick, back up again, and he erupts between us, his eyes squeezed shut and his head dropping back to the couch. "Oh my *god*," he moans as he comes, and while I'm no expert on the subject, it's a lot.

I am really glad I grabbed that towel.

Five minutes later, Jake is cleaned up, his breathing is more or less back to normal, and I think we can agree he is not going into cardiac arrest.

His erection, however?

Is just as hard, long, and strong as it was ten minutes ago. And it shows no sign of dissipating.

"So, it's just…like that? All the time? Even after an orgasm?" I gesture to Jake's cock, the third person in this ménage.

Jake huffs a laugh and rises from the couch, the towel in his hand. "I mean, I guess? I don't know? I've never paid too much attention…" He looks embarrassed.

Never having had a penis, I can't know for sure, but I imagine most guys packing what Jake's packing would definitely be paying attention. "I'm sorry. I don't mean to objectify you or anything."

"It's okay. Honestly, I am glad to be of service." Jake meets my eyes as he speaks, a devilish grin on his face. "Can I put this somewhere…?" He holds up the towel.

"Laundry's behind the kitchen. There are three baskets in a row to the right of the machines. The towel can go in the farthest basket." I don't miss a beat with my instructions.

Jake raises his eyebrows but gives me a salute before walking out of the room. He's naked except for his white socks, and sweet baby Jesus, that ass is something to write novels about. I bite my lip, acutely aware of my tender center.

Jake returns, his cock bobbing against his stomach, his easy smile turning hot as he sees me lying on the couch, my feet flat on the cushions and my knees propped up.

"Hey, beautiful," he says easily, as if we've known each other forever, as if we're together, as if everything is so simple.

"Hey, handsome," I reply, and his smile gets bigger.

"Something you're interested in?" He comes and sits next to my feet on the couch, his eyes a darker shade of blue as he glances down between my legs.

"You know there is," I tell him softly, letting my legs fall apart slightly. Jake sucks in a breath and moves suddenly, leaning toward me and placing his hands against my inner thighs, spreading me open. And I mean *open.*

"Jesus, Tatum," he growls. "I can't decide whether I want to eat you or fuck you."

"Maybe…maybe both?" I murmur as he holds my legs open, inspecting me. It's raunchy and dirty, and I *love* it.

"I know you need it, though—to be worked over, right?" he asks me softly, and before I can answer, he slides one long finger into me, so shallow, so teasingly, and I whimper in response. "Come sit on my lap again."

Yes, please.

I push myself up with Jake's help and straddle him again. He gets one of the condoms and hands it to me, grunting as I roll it on.

"There," I whisper. "All ready."

"I can't believe you still have this on," Jake tells me, looking at my bra. I have to laugh—Jake in his socks, me in my bra, not a stitch of other clothing between us.

"Take it off," I tell him with a shrug. He unlatches the hooks in the blink of an eye, and *oomph.* All the heavy-breasted people cheer with me at the euphoric feeling of a bra coming off.

"These are…my favorite things. In the world. Ever," Jake says, his eyes glued to my breasts. "So beautiful," he murmurs again, one hand firmly pressed to the small of my back, the other moving to caress the side of my breast.

Jake leans forward and kisses me gently, licking inside my mouth, while his hand continues its exploration. As his kiss grows hotter, he applies more pressure, plumping and squeezing my breast, but never going right where I want him most.

"Jake," I whisper pleadingly.

"Don't bother me," he tells me. "I'm busy." He moves his other hand to my other breast, back to stroking and light touches, and I need more. I shift around in his lap, trying to lodge my breasts—really, either of them will do—where I want them most.

In his mouth.

I turn away from his kisses and push his head down. He laughs, and I catch his eyes for a moment.

"Stop teasing me," I tell him with faux indignation.

"Sweet, impatient Tatum," he says. "Remember what I said?" he asks me, his bright-blue eyes boring into mine. "Fucking you is going to be like a kiss." And he leans close and kisses me softly, gently, with closed lips.

At the same time, he places his hands under my bottom and lifts me— no easy feat, I assure you—so that the tip of his dick is nudging right at my entrance. I lift up on my knees to assist him as he gently strokes my back.

"A little kiss, right?" he says softly, easing up on his hold, allowing gravity to drop me just a tiny bit on his cock. I hiss because, yes, this thing is a monster.

But I want more.

"A little kiss," I pant out in agreement.

"Maybe with some tongue," Jake replies, kissing me deeper, allowing our tongues to tangle, easing up more, as I drop farther down onto him.

"Oh my *god*," I mutter, stuck between wanting him to go for broke and drop me down in a rush and rethinking whether I want this monster cock in me at all.

"You're doing so good, beautiful," Jake murmurs to me between kisses, and if that doesn't have me lighting up like a firework and gushing like a geyser all at once.

"Ohhhh, more of that, please," I tell him, angling my head so he can kiss me on the neck. He promised that too, didn't he?

"Hmmm? You want me to tell you what a good girl you are, spreading wide and letting me get inside you, nice and slow?" Another inch down.

"You want me to tell you how good it feels to have that tight pussy suck me in, one inch at a time?" Another inch.

"Or you want me to stuff you so full I can't find my way back out? I'll just stay inside you, keeping it hard for you, letting you feel every inch of this fat dick?"

Another inch, or maybe several inches, who knows.

"Yes, yes, please, do it," I babble incoherently, turning my face back to Jake's, trying to find his lips with mine. But he's finally done what I wanted and moved his face back down to my breasts.

"So good, Tatum. You're doing so good. And I'll work you over like you wanted. You're going to get real acquainted with my cock while I get better acquainted with these tits."

And he drops me completely, bottoming out inside me, placing his mouth around one of my breasts and sucking, kissing, rubbing his mouth all over me. I can feel his cock in my goddamn chest, it's so big, and I am nothing but a sweaty, horny, desperate mess as I rub myself on him, grabbing the back of the couch and pressing, pressing, pressing as hard as I can against his body, feeling him everywhere and never wanting him to stop.

"Oh my god, Jake—please don't stop," I moan, riding him harder as he moves to my other breast.

"No way am I stopping. Not when I just got started," he mutters, keeping me steady with one hand on my back as I ride him hard. "Fuck yes, Tatum. You are fucking unreal, you know that?" He moves his head back down to my other breast, sucking hard, and I tighten around his cock in response.

"Feels so good, so good…" I can barely get the words out as Jake brings his lips to mine, kissing me wetly, before sliding his hand up my back to grab my hair in his fist and angling my head down, sucking on my neck as he does.

"This fucking hair. Unreal. All of it. Jesus Christ…" Jake is babbling now too, assorted phrases and words punctuating his kisses. He pulls down on my hair, hard, and I cry out with pleasure, the tightening feeling in my core growing stronger.

"Touch me, please—touch my clit," I beg, frantically hoping he can, indeed, find my clit. Jake brings my head back up so we are eye level, his eyes glassy with arousal and his jaw slack.

"Do it like you did me," he grits out before grabbing my hand. "Do it with me."

He moves my hand between us, his right on top of mine, and presses my fingers down firmly. I am a sopping mess down there as I move our fingers right where I need them most. Jake's forehead is plastered with sweat as he buries his face in the side of my neck and thrusts up into me, hitting a spot I never knew existed.

Everything coalesces into a train wreck of an orgasm, the kind that rushes through you at a million miles an hour. Everything is tight and sensitive and sharp, my pussy contracting around Jake so hard—honestly, it would be painful if it didn't feel so fucking good—and I shout my release into the room, clinging to his shoulders like I'll get swept away if I can't keep my grip on him.

I don't have the energy to alert Jake that I am, in fact, coming, and that it might, in fact, kill me, but he must feel me go off because he pumps up into me even harder. "That's a girl. That's my girl," he mutters, "coming so good. Fuck. *Fuck*. Tatum…" His voice trails off on a strangled sound as he thrusts up into me one more time, before moving both hands to my jaw, angling my head toward his for a kiss.

Jake keeps his mouth on mine, moaning into me, then sighing and relaxing as we both come down the other side of the wave. I release my death grip on him, letting my body drop lazily over his, nestling my head into the juncture between his neck and shoulder. He wraps his arms around my whole body, pulling me tighter to him, holding me securely and breathing into my hair. His cock softens inside me, but let me tell you, it's still a monster.

We stay like that for a minute…or maybe an hour. My legs start to twitch from being spread open for so long.

"You okay?" Jake asks my hair, his voice ragged.

"M'perfect," I mumble back. My leg twitches again. "But I may need to move shortly."

"Here." Jake reacts before I can protest, lifting me off him, his now-flaccid cock sliding out of me with a slick sound. He turns me around and cradles me in his lap like a baby.

A large, thirty-one-year-old baby.

My limbs are languid as my breathing slows, and I close my eyes. Jake speaks a few moments later, his tone low.

"I knew when I finally did it, it would be great, but I didn't know it would be *that* great," Jake mumbles into my hair.

My skin prickles.

"Did it…with me?" I ask casually, staring at the wall ahead of me instead of craning my neck up to look at his face. This means I am having a postcoital conversation with the Frida Kahlo print I have on that wall, a self-portrait with thorns around her neck.

I'm not going to lie—that was some epic sex. But something in Jake's voice gives me pause.

"Did it…with you." Jake waits. "And just did it…period."

I stare at Frida in disbelief.

She stares back.

I feel those thorns around *my* neck.

Because if I am hearing Jake correctly…

Chapter Fifteen

Jake

"You're a virgin?" Tatum screeches, jumping out of my lap and leaving me wet and cold.

"Not anymore, beautiful," I tell her with a dopey grin, running my hand through my hair. Also wet.

I don't care. I just had sex with Tatum Echeverria, the sexiest goddamn woman on the planet.

Said woman is currently stark-ass naked, waving her hands frantically as her eyes dart around, looking for something. Her robe, I realize, as she grabs the silky blue fabric and hurriedly wraps it around her body.

My body cries with disappointment at seeing hers covered up.

Not for long, I tell myself.

"You just—You're a—I'm not—" Tatum begins her sentences in fits and starts, not meeting my eyes, her face flushed and her hair an absolute fucking disaster as she runs her hands through it. She closes her eyes, exhales, and then looks directly at me, her hazel eyes bright. "I need to go check on Janet."

She turns and flies down the hallway, her ample ass cheeks bouncing underneath the fabric.

I am slightly concerned—but only slightly. I had a feeling that Tatum would balk at my revelation, and you don't corner a scared cat, or whatever animal metaphor it is. Is it a rat? Whatever, Tatum is definitely more feline than rodent.

I'd consciously avoided telling Tatum about my virginity before we fucked. Was it calculated? I don't like to think I am a calculating guy, at least not in an evil mastermind kind of way.

I am not particularly religious, and I wasn't really planning on waiting until marriage, if that day ever comes. All I knew was I was waiting for the right time.

And the right time never presented itself.

Until Tatum.

I sigh and lean my head back against the couch cushions, feeling depleted. But honestly...not that depleted, as I glance down to my crotch, raising my eyebrows.

Apparently once this thing gets started, it's ready to rock and roll all night, and maybe even party every day.

And by "thing," I mean my penis.

I still have the condom to deal with, and I make my way to the kitchen to dispose of it and wash up a bit.

I nearly jump out of my skin when something furry and fast brushes against my calves, yelping when I look down to see Janet, tongue wagging. She sits back on her heels and looks at me expectantly.

"Who's a pretty girl?" I croon.

She lets out a bark.

At least one female in this house still wants me around.

I sigh, reaching down to scratch behind her ears, doing my best to protect the family jewels as Janet nudges her head to be closer. "Hold on, hold on," I murmur. "Let me get a little bit dressed."

After finding my boxers—I swear Jesus gives me a "Way to go, brother!" grin—I turn to Janet. "Let's find your mom and see if we can salvage this evening, huh?"

Janet barks again in agreement.

Janet, my faithful accomplice, leads me down the hallway to where I hear water running. The door to the bathroom is open just a crack, steam billowing out into the hallway.

Janet sits on her heels again and looks at me as if to say "Here she is!"

Dogs always include exclamation marks at the end of their sentences. Don't ask me; I can't explain it.

"Go lie down, pretty girl," I tell her, gesturing toward another open door to what I assume is Tatum's bedroom.

Janet instead looks at me expectantly.

I move toward the door. "Tatum?"

"Yeah?"

Well, shit. Now what do I say?

Are you okay? Why wouldn't she be? We didn't do anything wrong.

Can we talk? That sounds too dramatic.

Do you agree that what we just did was the greatest experience in the history of the human race, and maybe other species too, and can we do it again?

"Fuck," I mumble, running my hands through my hair.

Still damp.

"You there?" Tatum asks when I don't respond.

"Can I come in?" I ask her.

"It's a free country," she calls back.

It's also her house, and she could obviously tell me to leave if she wants me to.

Which she doesn't.

I take that as a win.

I open the door and shut it on Janet. "It's okay. You stay right there," I tell her, which seems to appease her.

Tatum's bathroom is like the rest of the house, at least the parts I've seen.

Neat as a pin and filled with greenery.

She has a claw-footed bathtub with a shower curtain closed around it. The smell of vanilla permeates the steam from whatever shampoo or body wash she uses.

It makes my mouth water.

"I didn't mean to make you run off," I tell her, leaning against the light-pink countertop and facing the shower.

"What?" Tatum asks through the curtain.

"I said, I didn't mean to make you run off." I speak louder.

"It's no big. Totally fine. Don't worry about it." Tatum's words run together quickly.

Well, okay, then. Avoidance, thy name is Tatum.

"Hand me the white towel, please?" Tatum saves me from responding further when she turns off the water and opens the curtain. She is obviously naked, save for a clear shower cap thing covering her hair. Every inch of her skin is glistening, water droplets running down the sides of her body.

And like before, she gives no fucks. She does not try to hide any of those inches or cover herself up. Instead, she looks at me expectantly and holds out her hand.

My eyes, of course, go directly to her beautiful body, her breasts hanging unbound.

I meant what I told her. They are my favorite things, and I want to spend several years getting better acquainted with them.

Something catches my eye that I didn't see before. On each breast, I see a line of ruddy pink bisecting the bottom half, cutting through her skin. Like surgical scars.

"Did you have surgery?" I speak before I can think about it. It's none of my business after all.

"What? Tatum asks, her brow quizzical. She follows my gaze to her breasts. "Oh." She lifts them up high, allowing me to see the scars fully. "Yeah. I had breast reduction surgery when I turned eighteen."

My eyes widen, and I meet her gaze. And again, I speak before I think.

"They were *bigger*?" I ask her incredulously.

Tatum rolls her eyes, but her face relaxes and she looks at me with amusement. "They were bigger. Gave me all sorts of back problems, and putting on a bra was its own cardio workout. Now, Jake," she says, her voice softening, "please hand me my towel."

"Right," I mumble, grabbing the white towel and crying again internally as she covers up my favorite things with the fabric.

"I was just cleaning up," she says casually, as if we are work colleagues instead of…whatever it is we are. "I thought you would be gone when I got out."

I hear the record scratch in my head.

"What?!" I exclaim, pushing myself off the countertop.

"You know," Tatum continues in an unbothered tone, looking everywhere but at me. "We had sex. It was great."

"It was *fantastic*," I bark, and I can't help the increased volume in my voice.

"Says the virgin," Tatum says primly, stepping out of the tub onto the woven green bath mat beside it.

Oh, hell no.

"Tatum Echeverria," I tell her thunderously, daring to take another step closer. She keeps avoiding eye contact and makes a big production out of drying herself. What I would give to be that towel right now.

"I may be—*have* been—a virgin, but I'm not stupid."

I take another step closer, dipping my chin to meet her gaze. Her hazel eyes flash, and her cheeks are slightly pink.

No way she is as unaffected as she claims to be.

"That," I tell her as I take one more step closer, "was *fan-fucking-tastic.*" Another step.

"And I may not know what games people play when it comes to this sort of thing," I continue, taking one hand and tracing the top of her towel where it wraps around her torso, just above her breasts. "But I—" I let my fingers linger right above the knot on her towel, where it tucks in securely "—am not like them." I grab that knot firmly and pull her toward me.

Tatum looks up at me, her eyes wide and her lips parted. She still wears her shower cap. I want to rip it off, fist her hair and demand she kiss me like I want to kiss her. I want to fling open her towel, drop to my knees and feast on her until she tells me she is as affected by what we just did as I am.

But all I do is pull her firmly toward me, so she can feel my growing erection through the fabric separating us. She sucks in a breath, her gaze darting down and back up to mine.

"I am not like them," I tell her in a softer tone, leaning my head down farther to speak directly against her mouth.

"And all I'm thinking about is when I can fuck you again."

Chapter Sixteen

Tatum

IF YOU HAD TOLD ME THIS MORNING THAT BY THE END OF THE DAY, I would be a dirty, Mrs. Robinson-esque virgin conqueror, I would have laughed in your face and stolen your drink when you weren't looking.

And yet, here we are.

Never mind that Jake is packing heat that any straight woman would want. And probably gay men. I don't know, I'm not a gay man, and I've never taken it fully in my ass.

But I definitely wouldn't start with Jake's.

Surely he must have had opportunities. For fuck's sake, he's a hot, friendly, amiable guy in college at a renowned party school. He was in a fraternity, for crying out loud.

A thought occurs to me as I lie next to him in my bed, draped over his body like a blanket. Look, I was all ready to tell him to hit the road, which, frankly, I thought he would want to do after our living room sexcapades.

But after his little declaration in the bathroom—and his not-so-little erection nudging me in the stomach—I decided to live and let live.

In this case, "living" meant letting him tear away my towel and go at me like a man who hadn't eaten in a month. We ended up in my bed, he ended up pounding me from behind, everyone's happy.

Except maybe for Janet, who was relegated to the living room.

"Were you in a religious fraternity?" I ask suddenly.

Jake huffs. "Only if you worship at the altar of Jäger. No, it's a regular, old-fashioned party fraternity. Why?"

I think another moment.

"Are you…religious?"

"Not really." Jake shifts so that he's sitting up a little straighter, his back against the headboard. I move to roll over and face him, but he grabs me around the middle. "No way. Come here. I demand snuggles."

I hide a smile as he tucks me against his side, my head resting on his chest. He smells so good—crisp from whatever deodorant he uses, a little sweaty from the workout we just put in. He has sparse hair on his chest, and I rest my hand next to my head, feeling his heartbeat underneath. Strong and steady.

"I guess I am just trying to figure out why you are…were…a virgin for so long."

"First of all, virginity is a social construct." I snort, but he goes on. "There's nothing any different about me now that I have put my dick in the sweet recesses of your body."

I burst out laughing, hitting him on the chest and looking up. "That's gross!"

"On the contrary, I thought it was pretty amazing." Jake waggles his eyebrows, making me laugh again. I put my head back down on his chest, tracing nonsensical patterns on his skin. He begins to play with my hair, smoothing it back from my face and tucking it behind my ear, drawing lines on my scalp. It…isn't entirely unpleasant.

"But seriously. Maybe I am sensitive because people can be a little… obsessed with why I waited. And some people feel like it's their right to know why. Like, why is everyone so concerned about who I am or am not putting my dick in?"

"Some people are overly concerned with others' sexual choices anyway. Especially women's sexual choices," I offer.

"Yeah! Yeah, like, obviously, there have been opportunities."

I'll just bet there have.

"I just…" He heaves a sigh. "My parents…probably should not have been parents." I still my hand, waiting for him to continue. "That's unfair. My mom loves me, and she's a good mom." I notice he makes no comment about his dad. "They probably shouldn't have been parents *together*, if that makes sense."

"Trust me, there are a ton of ex-couples out there who you wouldn't believe decided it would be a good idea to procreate together," I tell him, thinking of all the successful family law attorneys I know. Divorce is a recession-proof business.

"And as good as I knew sex would feel…and as good as it *did* feel…I just didn't think anything would be worth the risk."

I turn my head again to face him. "The risk…?"

"Of pregnancy." Jake speaks plainly. "I don't want to get a girl pregnant. The easiest way to avoid it was to not have sex."

"I mean…we used condoms."

"For sure. But you know, those don't work 100% of the time. And birth control can fail, and—"

"'The only true form of birth control is abstinence,'" I finish. "Good Catholic girl here. That shit was drilled into our heads," I tell him dryly.

Jake smiles, twin dimples appearing on his cheeks. "Well, it's true. So, I didn't have sex."

"You make it sound so simple."

"Isn't it? I mean, once you make a decision, any decision, there's nothing more to do about it. You want to be a vegetarian, you don't eat meat. You don't have an existential crisis every time you go out to dinner." I feel him shrug. "So, I knew I wasn't going to have sex. The decision was already made."

"But you did other stuff," I supply.

"You make it sound so sexy," he tells me with a laugh. "I mean…yes, I have done other 'stuff,' as you put it. Um, I did have a girlfriend my sophomore year, and…well, I have, you know. Gone down on a girl." He pauses again. "And I've gotten a blow job. I mean, blow jobs. Plural." He clears his throat, as if he's embarrassed.

Given the size of his dick, I can imagine how that went.

I hope she used lots of spit and relaxed her throat muscles.

"Speaking of oral." Jake clears his throat.

I laugh again, giving him a shove in his side. "Were we? Speaking of oral, that is?"

"It came up kind of organically," Jake says. "But. You know. We haven't done that yet. Together."

I sit up to face him. "You want to go again?" I ask, raising one eyebrow. Dude has just had three orgasms in two hours.

"What can I say? You bring out the best in me," he tells me with a lopsided smile. *Jesus.* This guy is going to be the death of me.

And my pussy.

"I'm a little sensitive. You know. Down there," I tell him, gesturing toward my crotch.

"Poor Tatum," he says softly, sitting up and pushing me farther up on the bed so now I rest against the headboard. "I'll tell you what. You just relax and let me do the work."

I sense where he's going and have a brief moment of panic. I probably smell like condom and sweat. "Wait! Wait—you don't have to—"

"But I *want* to," Jake interrupts me, moving his lithe body down my bed, spreading my legs open abruptly. "I mean…" He looks up at me questioningly. "If you want me to."

Well, okay, then.

I'm not perfect. I know my faults, and I know my strengths.

And when an eager man wants to give you oral, you shut up and say thank you.

"Do your worst," I tell him breathily.

Jake

Tatum may be sensitive, but she is still eager.

And I love that about her.

I don't know for certain, but I have a feeling that she feels responsible for a whole lot. She gives off a take-no-prisoners vibe. I get the sense that it's hard for her to let go, that it's a challenge for her to relax, that it's nearly impossible for her to get out of her head.

If I can do that for her even a little bit, I'll consider it a success.

I make myself at home midway down her bed, lying flat on my stomach and propping up on my elbows.

"Open up for me," I murmur, spreading her thick thighs farther apart. Tatum sighs and complies, letting me move her around like a rag doll.

"I mean it," she continues. "I am a little sensitive down there..." Her voice trails off into a bigger sigh as I take my hands and frame her center, spreading her open like a flower.

"And I meant what I said too," I reply. "I'll take good care of you."

And with that, I dive in and stripe a big lick, from the top to the bottom. Not *all* the way to the bottom.

We'll work up to that.

But I go slow, not only because of Tatum's claims that she's sensitive, but because I want to savor this. Every sound, every smell, every taste—I don't know when I'll get it again, but I want it all.

"Remember, just like making out," I tell her, before proceeding to do just that with her pussy. I give her openmouthed kisses, allowing my tongue to dip inside her briefly. I nibble around her clit, placing soft kisses all over her pink, swollen skin.

"I love being inside here, Tatum," I whisper before gliding my tongue around her hole, picking up her wetness as I go. "I love being inside you."

She breathes a little faster, her stomach muscles tightening and releasing, her legs shaking slightly. I keep a firm grip on her thighs.

"And you took me so well," I continue between kissing her. "So well," I groan as a fresh slick hits my tongue.

"Tell me, beautiful. Is mine the biggest cock you've ever had inside this tight little box?"

Tatum's hips rise off the bed, and her sighs turn to moans. I lap at her clit in little flicks, inserting two fingers inside her slowly. "Oh my lord, *Jake*," Tatum moans, grinding down against my mouth.

Fuck yes. "Ride my mouth, Tatum." My chin is drenched, and I don't give a flying fuck. "Come on my mouth, beautiful."

I flick her clit one more time before taking it inside my mouth and sucking, pumping my fingers inside her at a leisurely pace. Tatum tenses up from head to toe, going taut around my fingers before they are soaked again. I hum in appreciation, not willing to separate my mouth from her until I know I've wrung every last drop from the best pussy I've ever tasted.

"Jake, Jake," Tatum chants, her voice softer in comparison to the shrieking orgasms she had earlier. She lolls her head from side to side, her hands on my head, thrusting up into my mouth. "Oh. *Oh.*" She chokes a sob and pushes down on my head, hard, and I get her message, sucking on her clit firmly.

When she relaxes her muscles and releases her grip on me, I lift my head from her center and wipe my mouth with the back of my hand. She casually runs her hands through my hair, and I am content to rest my head on her thigh.

We lie like that for a moment, not speaking, coming down from our highs and catching our breaths.

"Feel better, beautiful?" I ask into her skin. The silence responds.

I look up to her head to see Tatum's eyes closed, long lashes a shadow on her cheeks. Her lips are slightly parted, her breath heavy.

She is fast asleep.

Chapter Seventeen

Tatum

GROWING UP FEMALE IS FULL OF MIXED MESSAGES.

Anyone who has seen the Barbie movie knows what I am talking about.

Be sexy, but not too sexy. Be in control of your narrative, but not so controlling that you turn off other people, particularly straight men who might be interested in you!

Some of that messaging concerns sex. It's important to be in control of your own sex life, the messaging says. Have as many partners as you want. It's what an independent, girlboss, twenty-first-century woman would do! Be safe about it, but get that dick!

Sex and the City taught me that empowered women had sex and a lot of it, while also being very financially secure and going out to brunch constantly.

Also, Carrie Bradshaw is a horrible friend, and I will die on that hill.

But I digress.

Over time, however, I have realized one glaring problem with this philosophy.

Most—not all—of the time, the sex I've had?

It has not been memorable.

Some of it is great.

Some of it is fantastic.

Some of it is memorably *bad.*

But most of it?

Has been fine.

Like a nice pedicure.

Or a really good piece of cake.

There's a reason there are several "better than sex" recipes online. Because sometimes a nice Midwestern lady's riff on Duncan Hines *is* better than mediocre sex.

But now?

I had the absolute best sex of my life with a twenty-three-year-old college graduate who, from what I can tell, only wears Rainbow flip-flops.

The *best* sex of my life, by far. Perhaps the sex that will ruin me for all other men.

What the hell am I supposed to do with that information?

Part II

The First Trimester

Chapter Eighteen

Tatum

"A ND IS THAT THE ONLY TIME YOU COMPLAINED TO YOUR employer?"

Another day, another deposition. I am surrounded by the smell of weak coffee and warming sandwiches left over from lunch. Let me tell you something, shredded lettuce does not age well, especially this long into the afternoon.

Contrary to the Mark Jackson debacle a couple months ago—perhaps the least sympathetic plaintiff I have ever seen—this plaintiff, whom I am currently deposing, is respectful, quiet, and yes, sympathetic.

"I did," she says softly, her limp brown hair falling around her face. "I complained to Dr. Gonzalez again before the holidays."

"Ms. Hart, did you complain to Dr. Gonzalez verbally or in writing?"

I already know the answer to this question, but I have to ask it anyway.

"I complained in an email," the plaintiff, Melanie Hart, tells me.

I pull out three copies of a single sheet of paper and hand it to Melanie across the table. Her attorney, Lorena Galvan, snatches the sheet, gives it a once-over, and nods before placing it back before Melanie.

"Ms. Hart, is this an accurate copy of the email you sent to Dr. Gonzalez?"

"It appears to be."

"Can you read it for the record, please?"

Ordinarily, Lorena would object on the basis that the document "speaks for itself" or some other legal jargon nonsense. But this email is great for her client.

And really bad for mine.

"Dear Dr. Gonzalez, I am writing to tell you that I am uncomfortable with the dress code the office recently adopted. This is a chiropractic office, and we need to be able to move with ease and not be restricted by our clothing. Your request that we, the office staff—all female—wear white tank tops with a logo that says 'Gonzo's Girls' across the front and short skirts does not make sense. Frankly, the outfit makes me feel like I am working at Hooters. And if I wanted to wear a Hooters outfit, I would go apply at Hooters."

Not only is Ms. Hart sympathetic, but she, and the other plaintiffs who have joined her in suing my client, have a great case.

Dr. Henry Gonzalez—the "doctor" is specious—is a handsome, single, charming man in his midforties who operates a chiropractic clinic in St. Bishop's. For some reason, in his infinite wisdom, he decided it would be a great idea to (a) hire an all-female office staff between the ages of twenty and twenty-seven, mostly college students looking for part-time work; and (b) implement the aforementioned dress code.

It hasn't escaped me that every single one of his employees looks like she could model in her spare time.

Ms. Hart and her co-plaintiffs have now sued Dr. Gonzalez for sex discrimination, sexual harassment, and retaliation for complaining about the discrimination and harassment.

And having heard what they have to say and having met Dr. Gonzalez, I believe them.

"I previously told you in person that I was uncomfortable wearing this outfit. You told me that the outfit is part of your 'rebranding'"—Lorena inserts a well-placed huff at this comment, and honestly, cosign—"and if I didn't like it, I could find another job. I told you I need this job to support myself and my son while I attend community college."

Yes, Ms. Hart checks all the boxes: earnest without being *too* earnest, sympathetic, believable.

"I enjoy working here," Ms. Hart continues reading, her voice wobbling slightly. "I simply want a valid explanation as to why my coworkers and I should be expected to wear an outfit that doesn't seem to be necessary for the job we perform."

"Thank you," I tell Ms. Hart as she sets the document to the side. "Did Dr. Gonzalez respond to your email?"

"No."

"What happened next?" I ask Ms. Hart, again knowing the answer, my shoulders tightening in anticipation.

"He fired me."

Usually, after something at work leaves me feeling depressed, some family time makes me feel better.

This is because there is always good food involved.

I came to the Brew hoping for comfort in the form of traditional Basque soup, served with beans and a lot of very spicy salsa.

And bread. Got to have bread.

But right now, the smell of Lincoln's cabbage soup is making me feel worse, and the salsa is giving me wicked heartburn.

"Why are you looking at my food like it insulted your mother?" Julia asks me, leaning over the bar at the Brew.

"Our mother," I correct her. "I don't know, man. I feel off."

"Off?" My grandfather is next to me, happily slurping his soup. "Off, how?"

"Everything is making me feel ill," I tell them. "I had one of my favorite taffies, the POG kind?" I say, POG being shorthand for passion fruit, orange, and guava, a delicious Hawaiian concoction. "It just tasted like…blah."

"Blah," Julia repeats, her brow furrowed in concern.

"Blah," my grandfather echoes.

"Everything is blah," I tell them, trying not to sound like a Negative Nancy, but, well, if you can't complain to your family, who can you complain to? "My deposition left me feeling blah. My favorite taffy left me feeling blah. And now," I continue, my voice rising, "your delicious soup—" I gesture to Lincoln, who has joined us at the bar "—has left me feeling blah." I push it away and grab a piece of bread, biting ferociously.

"Blah," Lincoln muses, moving close to Julia and wrapping an arm around her shoulders. His black hair is long and pulled back into a man bun. Lately, he's been rocking a mustache that would make Tom Selleck jealous.

"You know, Julia couldn't stand the smell of cabbage when she—"

"Can I talk to you for a minute?" Julia interrupts him, turning out of his embrace. "About a shipment. Or something. Come on." She grabs his hand and pulls him to the other side of the bar, but not before she gives me a look that only an older sister can give.

A Look, with a capital "L."

"What's her damage?" I mutter.

"Hmm?" My grandfather is distracted, adding more salsa to his soup.

"Never mind." I reach to grab more bread before discovering I've eaten it all. "Sorry, Pops," I tell him. "I will get you some more bread."

"Don't worry about it," he says, slurping more soup. "I put some in my pockets when Julia is not looking." He gives me a wink.

I smile despite my bad mood. "You know she'd just bring you whatever you want, Pops," I tell him.

"I know. But I have to get my fun where I can."

My mood does not improve as the evening goes on.

I felt like I had twenty-pound shoes on during my walk with Janet. Nothing sounds good to eat—not even my taffy—so I am currently sprawled out on my couch, *Law & Order* reruns the perfect distraction from my funk. I try to relax and let the winning combination of Benjamin Bratt's dreaminess and Jerry Orbach's—*RIP*—witty remarks soothe my troubles away.

It's not working.

It also doesn't help that we are having a crazy heat wave. September into October is usually an endless-summer weather pattern on the Central Coast, with hot days and cool, pleasant nights. But the temperature today hit ninety in St. Bishop's, and it won't cool down much tonight. Tomorrow is supposed to be even hotter. I don't have air conditioning—most homes around here don't—so I have fans strategically placed all around the room, pointing right at me.

So I sit and I sweat and I force myself to drink ice water.

My phone lights up with a text from my sister.

JULIA: I am here. Let me in.

Sure enough, there's a knock a minute later, and Janet bounds up excitedly toward the door. "Here I come," I call and let her inside. She still has on the same outfit I saw her in earlier—her Brew shirt, cut-off denim shorts, and a fluorescent yellow handkerchief tied around her long hair.

"What's up? Is everything okay?" I ask as she enters and gives Janet some love.

"I'm good. Everyone is fine." She makes herself at home, going to the kitchen for a glass of ice water. "I just wanted to make sure you were feeling okay." She comes back into my living room and stands in front of one of the fans. "Ooh, that's nice," she says, lifting her shirt to give the girls some cool air. She's not as generously endowed as me, but anyone with breasts can appreciate a blast of cool air to the underboob.

"I'm fine. I must just have a bug."

"A bug?" Julia continues airing out the girls.

"You know, whatever bug is going around. You have kids, you can relate."

"True. When school starts, all bets are off." Julia shudders and drops her shirt back down before turning to me. "You know…I had a bug where I couldn't stomach cabbage soup. Or salsa. Or anything sweet."

I look at her wanly. "Okaaaay?"

"A nine-month bug." She looks at me expectantly.

"A nine-month bug. What kind of fuckery…" My voice trails off when I pick up what she's putting down.

I step back to sit on the couch. Only it's more of a collapse than popping a squat.

"Fuck."

I do the math so many women have done before me.

When was my last period?

When did I last have sex?

Could I be…

"Fuck!"

Julia's eyes widen. "No way. Really? Lincoln actually brought it up. I thought for sure, no way. Tatum's not…" She pauses and comes to sit by me, setting her hand on my thigh.

"Are you pregnant?" she asks incredulously.

Julia is five and a half years older than me. Our age difference means we had different friends and different lives.

Our paths continued to diverge as we grew up. Julia went to UCLA, met a guy two years ahead of her, fell in love, and married him in Vegas before she graduated. I went to UCLA, met a bunch of losers, had a lot of mediocre sex, got the hell out of there real quick to attend law school, and started working as a lawyer before I was twenty-five. Julia has a restaurant, tattoos, a nose piercing, and two children; I have a law practice, no tattoos or piercings, and no children. Julia is laid-back and breezy; I am self-aware enough to know that I am a little…tense.

Even when we stand next to each other, we don't go together. Julia is taller, skinny, and consistently dressed in a uniform of ripped jeans and concert T-shirts. I have built up my wardrobe of what I call "professional lady lawyer clothes," i.e., clothes nice enough to wear to a deposition, but comfortable enough that I don't feel like I'm wearing a straitjacket every time I get dressed for work. I gave up on button-down shirts years ago; they were not designed with big breasts in mind.

We have the same dark hair, though, and the Echeverria hazel eyes, which all three of us siblings acquired from our late father.

Julia is different from me in that she seems to have it all figured out. To put it simply—she seems so damn happy. She has her husband, her kids, her restaurant, her very chill, very relaxed outlook on life. No one's ever accused me of being chill or going with the flow.

So I can understand Julia's surprise when I confirm her suspicions.

"Bitch, I might be," I mumble, dropping my head in my hands.

Julia sucks in a breath of surprise, before scooting closer and wrapping an arm around my shoulders.

"No," I moan, pushing away. "Too hot."

"That's what they all say," she jokes. I raise my gaze to meet hers.

"Fuck," I whisper.

"Tatum," she whispers back. "This is not the end of the world. And whatever you want to do, I will support you. No matter what," she adds emphatically.

"Thank you. And I know," I tell her, leaning my head down to rest on her shoulder. Still too hot. I sit up and rub my hands over my face. "Jesus. No wonder I feel like shit. And my boobs are gigantic. More so than normal," I add at Julia's raised eyebrows.

"I didn't realize… I mean, I didn't know you and Dr. Douche…" Julia's voice trails off as she refers to my ex.

"Julia Echeverria Cruz! As if I would ever. He has his own family to worry about anyway." I huff and straighten my shoulders. "I haven't seen that crapbag in over a year."

Julia eyes me curiously. "Then who? I didn't even know you were seeing someone else. Not that you have to tell me everything," she adds, "or that you have to be, like, seriously seeing someone to get pregnant."

"Yeah, I definitely am not *seeing* anyone," I tell her. I try to laugh, but it comes out slightly maniacal. "This is the result of me throwing caution to the wind and stealing the virtue of a twenty-three-year-old college graduate with a super dick—and apparently super swimmers to go along with his super dick!" I cackle, truly on the edge between sanity and lunacy, laughing so hard I have the hiccups.

I might also be crying a little.

Not sure.

Julia opens her mouth in shock, her eyes comically wide. She pauses a moment and then joins me in cracking up.

"Like—" she tries to catch her breath "—a one-night stand? With who? A virgin—" She doubles over, but not before I hear her rasp out "Little Miss Perfect."

"Please. I am not perfect," I tell her between my hiccups, wiping my eyes. "I stole someone's virginity!"

This makes her laugh harder. "Virginity is a made-up thing anyway," she tells me, trying to pull herself together.

We make eye contact and lose it all over again.

"You don't have it all together after all, huh?" she asks me through her laughter.

"As if," I tell her. "You're the one with the perfect life."

"Me?!" She adjusts her bandana and wipes her eyes. "Dude, I love Lincoln, I love our life, but we have problems just like anyone else."

"Oh, really?" I ask her sarcastically.

"Yes, really. Do you know how high food costs are right now? It's fucking unreal. We have kids, we have stresses. I just try to…go with the flow. So does he."

I give a faux shudder. "I don't think I can do that."

"You don't have to, Tater Tot." She gives me a lopsided grin. "You just have to be you."

I hum noncommittally.

"Thank god it's not Dr. Douche's," Julia adds.

"Amen to that," I agree.

"So…what's his name?"

I sigh and rip off the Band-Aid. "Do you remember that blond guy in your restaurant earlier this summer? The one who got the solomo?"

"*Oh my god,*" Julia gasps, and this sets her off all over again.

"Stop laughing!" I demand. "This is serious! I am pregnant by a guy I don't even know!"

"You won't be the first," she tells me. Now she has the hiccups too. Serves her right.

"What's his name?" Julia asks.

"His name is Jake."

We both pause, eyeing each other to make sure no one will erupt again.

"You don't know his last name, do you?" Julia asks. I throw a pillow at her, and she laughs before chucking it back at me.

"I do too, you heathen," I muster. "It's Bloomquist or Elmquist or something vaguely Scandinavian."

Julia nods. "All right. And do you still talk to Jake from Scandinavia?"

"Not since…you know." I pause. "I mean, we texted a couple times. I don't even know if he's still in the county. He graduated, he's from Santa Barbara…" I can count the things I know about Jake on one hand. "I'm sure he has big plans, none of which involve knocking up a lady eight years older than him."

"Well." Julia side-eyes me. "He surprised you with his giant schlong. Maybe he'll surprise you again."

I throw the pillow again, hitting her squarely in her big mouth.

Chapter Nineteen

MY FIRST THOUGHT ON DRIVING FROM ST. BISHOP'S TO California's Central Valley?

It's hot, and there's a lot of brown.

The outside temperature is 106 degrees, according to my car thermometer. And while I am obviously aware that California has been in a drought for, well, practically my whole life, it's a little jarring to see all that brown.

I follow the directions the GPS reads out to me and pull off Interstate 5 toward the town of Murdock, smack in the middle between Fresno and Bakersfield.

I am here to meet Shelby.

My little sister.

I am already kind of a hyper dude, and right now, my nerves are working overtime. I feel like I am both interviewing for an important job and meeting a girlfriend's parents all in one day.

I continue obeying the monotone GPS instructions and pull into a Starbucks parking lot. *I'll be having decaf.*

I park, take a moment, and sigh.

I am nervous, but I want this.

I want to know this person, and in our abbreviated, awkward texts, it seems like she wants to know me.

"Let's do this."

My first thought on seeing the tall, young lady in the Starbucks?

She looks just like me.

I suppose it's more accurate to say that we both favor our father.

But it's an eerie kind of recognition, to see someone you are clearly related to.

Shelby, as mentioned, is tall and thin—built like me—with dirty-blond hair—also like me—that comes down to her waist.

That last part is not like me.

She has on denim shorts and a blue tank top that, upon moving closer, I see favors her blue eyes.

Eyes like mine.

She is sitting next to an older woman in a dark-pink dress patterned with orange and yellow flowers. It's a loud dress on a tiny woman. She has short gray hair curled tightly to her scalp, and from the way she and Shelby were chatting before I walked up, they clearly know each other.

Shelby jumps up quickly from her seat when she sees me, her eyes widening and her lips parting slightly. "Hi! Hi. Oh my gosh. Hello." She is flustered.

Also like me.

"Hello," I tell her, my voice surprisingly calm. "I'm Jake."

"Oh my gosh, of course you are. I'm Shelby. Shelby Jones." She smacks her hand to her cheek. "I am so dumb. You don't care about my last name. Sheesh."

"Simmer down, Shelby," the older woman next to her says. She looks at me and smiles, her face creased with age. "Hello, Jake. I am Chernell Jones, Shelby's grandmother."

"I hope you don't mind that Gram is here," Shelby continues, still talking a mile a minute. "I just got my learner's permit, and I need to have someone older in the car with me. And plus, I don't like to leave her at home alone—"

I smile at Shelby, hoping to calm her nerves. "It's totally fine. Hello, Ms. Jones," I add to Shelby's grandmother.

"You may call me Chernell," she says. "Or Gram."

I nod with a smile. Chernell will do for now.

"It's nice to meet you," I add to Shelby. "Do you mind if I…?" I gesture toward the seat across from her.

"Of course! Of course," Shelby says hastily. "Sit down. Please."

I do as she says.

Shelby and I regard each other, both clearly unsure what to say next.

"I am going over there to read my book," Chernell tells us, gesturing toward a couch. "Leave you two to get better acquainted."

"Okay, Gram," Shelby says softly, squeezing her grandmother's hand before she hobbles away, a little black leather purse slung over her wrist.

And Shelby and I are back to staring.

"This is weird, right?" I ask her, deciding not to beat around the bush.

Shelby smiles a little. "So weird." She bites her bottom lip. "I never thought…" She blushes a little. "I always wanted a sibling, you know? I'm my mom's only child. And even though I knew I had an older half brother—"

"Wait, what?" I interrupt her sharply, and she jumps a little in response. "I'm sorry. I didn't mean to startle you. I just…" I can feel my jaw clenching, and I do my best to calm down. "You knew about me?"

Shelby nods slowly. "I did."

"What—what were you told?"

Shelby sighs. "So, a little background?" she asks. I nod.

"My mother is a flight attendant. She works primarily with private carriers, VIPs, stuff like that. She's traveling, obviously, all the time, so it's always been just me and Gram." Shelby pauses before continuing. "From what I understand, her job is how, um, they met…" Shelby's face turns red.

I've forgotten how hard it is to talk about certain subjects when you're a teenager. "How my—*our*—father met your mother," I fill in for her.

"Right," she says, looking at me gratefully. "Anyway. Um, I grew up around here, with my mom and Gram, but I saw my father sometimes. On occasion. He came to a couple birthdays. And when I got older, my mother explained that, you know, my…*our* father had his own wife and his own family, but he would 'do right' by us." She clears her throat and looks down at the table. "I, um, just always assumed you knew about me too. But, like, didn't want to *know* me, you know?"

The muscle in my jaw ticks. I am going to kill my dad.

"Shelby," I say quietly. She looks up with apprehension in her eyes.

"Until a couple months ago? I didn't know you existed."

Shelby's eyes widen. "Really?"

"Really." I clear my throat. "I, um, always wanted a sibling too. My parents obviously didn't have any more kids" —*thank goodness for that*—"but if I had known I had a sister, I would have reached out a long time ago."

"Really?" Shelby repeats.

"Really," I tell her seriously.

Whatever issues I have with this whole shitshow, they are with my dad. Not an innocent kid.

I leave Starbucks with a weight off my shoulders, half a loaf of banana bread courtesy of Chernell, and plans for Shelby and her gram to come to visit me in St. Bishop's.

After we got over the initial awkward encounter, we played a little bit of Twenty Questions. We discovered we both like swimming, but Shelby has never surfed before. I promised to teach her when she comes to visit, and honestly?

I can't wait.

I had my phone on DND during my visit, and I check my texts before I begin the two-hour drive back to St. Bishop's.

To my surprise, I have a text from Tatum.

TATUM: Hi. Long time no see.

Kind of an understatement, but okay.

ME: Hi, yourself. How are you doing?

TATUM: I'm good. You busy?

Is this like a "you up?" text? It's a Sunday afternoon; I suppose it's an unusual time for a booty call, but you never know.

Of course, there's also the fact that I haven't heard a peep from Tatum in nearly two months.

>ME: I am actually on my way back into town. Should be there in a couple hours.

Tatum doesn't respond to that, and I decide to take life by the balls.

>ME: Dinner?

>TATUM: Sure. I have lots of food from my sister at my house if you want to come over.

Ah, we are forgoing the restaurant and getting right to the good stuff. Maybe.
I don't know.

>ME: Sounds good. I'll text when I'm close.

Chapter Twenty

Tatum

WHAT'S THE BEST WAY TO TELL YOUR ONE-NIGHT STAND THAT you are knocked up with his offspring?

Asking for a friend.

There's only one way to rip this Band-Aid off, and that's quick, which is my go-to plan for most things in life.

It was my plan for this event too, right up until Jake showed up at my front door, looking again like a goddamn swimsuit model, smiling at me easily, his blue eyes bright in his tanned face.

"Hi." I motion for him to come inside. Janet greets him, excited as ever.

"Hi! How are you? And how are you, my favorite girl ever?" he asks Janet, who thumps her tail on the floor.

"I'm good. She's good. Everyone's good." I take him in for a moment, noting that he is—again—wearing Rainbow flip-flops.

"Do you have other shoes?" I blurt out.

Jake looks up at me, still smiling, a quizzical expression on his face. "What?"

"Besides Rainbows. Do you have any other types of footwear?"

Jake looks at me like I have lost it, and you know what, maybe I have. "Ye-es," he says slowly, standing from Janet and approaching me with caution. "Yes, I am fortunate enough to have many other pairs of shoes that are not Rainbows. But it's hot as fuck here, and even hotter in the valley, so Rainbows are kind of my uniform for now." He pauses. "Is this why you asked me here? For a shoe interrogation?"

I deflate a little, knowing everything is out of left field. Me texting him after ghosting him for the past several weeks, my questions about his shoes.

I am a mess.

And now I am going to be someone's mother.

The thought pierces me right through the heart—*I am going to be someone's mother*—and I just feel so nauseous and tired and hungry but not for any food that any human has ever eaten on this planet, and I just can't help it.

I start to cry.

Jake's eyes grow large, and he rushes over to me, grabbing one of my hands in both of his. "Tatum! Tatum, oh my god. I am sorry. I didn't mean to make fun of you, and—are you okay? Are you sick? Is there something I can get you? Do you hate Rainbows that much—"

"I am pregnant," I wail, sniffling like a child and feeling the telltale lump in my throat that I am nearing a full-on bawl-fest.

Jake's hands tighten around mine, the only sign of movement as he otherwise turns to stone.

"And it's yours," I blubber.

Jake is nearly cutting off my circulation, distracting me from feeling otherwise shitty all around. He continues to regard me blankly.

"Jake?"

Nothing.

"Come on," I tell him, gingerly leading him to the couch. Janet follows us and takes a minute to inspect us both, before laying her head down in Jake's lap.

I guess between the two of us, she sensed that he needed a dog more.

Janet nudges her head under Jake's hand, which brings him out of his stupor. He scratches her chin. "Hey, pretty girl," he whispers, not meeting my eyes.

I am quiet, just watching them for a couple moments.

"So," Jake says finally, his throat scratchy.

"So."

"Are you—are you feeling okay?" he asks, looking me in the face, his eyes darting everywhere.

"I feel fine. A little tired. A little nauseous. Nothing sounds good when it comes to eating, which is new and definitely not my favorite. But all good, otherwise."

He nods again, a little distracted. "That's good," he says, turning back to Janet.

I feel like an asshole.

"Jake," I begin. Nothing to it but to do it. "I am so, so sorry. We were careful, but even before that, *you* were so careful, and then the first woman you have sex with, she ends up pregnant." I am on the verge of tears again, so I take a deep breath.

Jake's head snaps to mine, his blue eyes flashing. "No way, Tatum. This is not your fault. Fuck, I don't even like using that word, 'fault.' It's no one's fault. Yes, I had my reasons," he says with a wry look, "but I wanted to have sex with you. I made that choice, knowing the risk. It's nothing to be sorry about."

I smile bleakly.

"We're two consenting adults, Tatum," Jake tells me quietly.

I nod, but I still feel like an asshole.

Jake

If Tatum is expecting anger from me, she's going to be sorely disappointed.

She has thrown me for a loop, for sure, but this isn't the first unplanned pregnancy in the world, and it won't be the last.

Something occurs to me as I think—

"Do you… Um, are you keeping it?" I ask her. I keep petting Janet with one hand, and I take Tatum's hand in my other one. Her face is splotchy from crying, and she looks frail.

Very unlike the Tatum I've seen before.

"I think so," she says slowly, her brow furrowed. "I've been talking about it like, well, like I'm having a baby." She closes her eyes. "Fuck, that is weird to think about."

I smile, hoping it doesn't look like a grimace, my insides still a roller coaster of thoughts.

The irony, as Tatum already mentioned, is not lost on me. I resolved at an early age never to take the risk of an unplanned pregnancy, even before I knew what my father had done, even before I knew about Shelby.

I smooth Tatum's dark hair off her face and behind her ear. She leans into my touch like a cat seeking a scratch.

My eyes catch on all the photographs on her mantel. Her family, her friends.

"Family's important to you," I say, more of a confirmation than a question.

Tatum follows my gaze, sees the pictures, and nods. "Well, I happen to have a great family. They *are* important to me. But not just because they are my family—because of who they are."

I consider that a moment, but Tatum seems to have more she wants to say.

"Jake," she says, looking down at our hands, "I am not expecting a thing from you. You can be as involved or uninvolved as you want. And if you want nothing to do with me, or with the baby—"

Blood rushes through my ears, and I rear back as if I've been pushed. "How can you say that?" I ask her quietly.

Tatum's eyes snap to mine, registering surprise at whatever she sees on my face.

"It seems like a logical thing to say," she says, her voice tense. "You are young, you have your whole adult life ahead of you—"

"And you don't?" I interrupt her.

"Yes, but I'm older, and I—"

"You're what, thirty?" I don't give her a chance to answer before continuing. "Why the fuck do you think I waited to have sex for so long?" My voice is rising, and I'm acting like a dick, but I can't stop.

"I assume to avoid a situation just like this one," Tatum responds hotly.

"Yeah, but Tatum, I knew that when I decided to have sex, I had to be 100% willing to accept the consequences. I *knew* that going into this, and

I know it now." My jaw clenches, and I try to unlock my muscles. "I would never, ever abandon you. Or the baby."

Tatum looks at me with wide eyes.

"Okay, then," she says, dropping her gaze.

I know it's a little unfair to her—I still haven't told her about my father, not really, not his recent revelation and not about meeting Shelby.

But it occurs to me as we sit on the couch in a companionable silence, we have all the time in the world.

At least the next eighteen years.

"I'm sorry," I tell her quietly, holding her hand securely in both of mine.

"*You're* sorry?" she asks, her voice small. "What for?"

"Well…not that I don't have my charms, but I imagine an unplanned pregnancy with a dude you barely know wasn't on your bingo card."

Tatum huffs and wipes her eyes before heaving a sigh. "Kind of an understatement." She curls up her legs underneath her on the couch before leaning into my side and resting her head on my shoulder.

"I had a plan, you know? Keep moving forward. Graduate. Go to law school. Graduate. Get a job, open a firm, make money. Keep moving forward, on to the next, on to the next."

I wrap an arm around her shoulders, smelling her hair—is that strange?—before relaxing back into the couch.

The couch where we may have made a baby, I realize.

How fucking weird is that?

"I mean, sure, I have thought about becoming a mother in the abstract. Like…the way you think about what to do in the event of an earthquake," Tatum continues, unaware of my inner monologue.

I burst out laughing at her comment. "An earthquake, huh? I don't know for sure, but I bet there are some parents out there who can tell us having a baby makes an earthquake seem easy."

Tatum mumbles an agreement. "No doubt. My older sister, Juli? She and her husband have two little girls. Their first daughter, Sarah, was a moody little thing. She never slept, she never ate because everything upset her stomach, she never smiled. But Julia still couldn't wait to get pregnant with her second. She said it's a biological thing. The pain of childbirth, the long nights, the lack of sleep—it's all outweighed by the…by the love you have for your child."

Tatum's voice gets quieter as she talks, and maybe it's because she's thinking the same thing I am.

Her sister is married, and I assume planned her pregnancies with a guy she loves and is into.

Us?

Not so much.

I have no wise words and, let's be honest, no real-world experience when it comes to a baby.

But I sense that Tatum, for all her independence, needs something to hold on to right now.

I can try to give her that.

"We'll figure it out, Tatum."

We've got all the time in the world.

Chapter Twenty-One

Tatum

WHEN IN DOUBT, HIKE IT OUT.

This has been one of my life's mottos for several reasons. First, you don't need any fancy equipment or clothes to do it. A sturdy pair of hiking shoes does the trick, and I replace mine once a year.

Second, it's a good way to break a sweat with no bouncing. You laugh, but tell me how it feels to jump, jog, or do any other activity that requires a similar motion with F-cup breasts. It's not pleasant, and I have nearly given myself a bloody nose with the girls over the years. It's much better since my breast reduction surgery, but still.

Jogging is not for me.

Third—and this is probably unique to where I live—there are hikes literally in my backyard. Well, maybe not my backyard. The closest hike is a ten-minute walk. But an hour later, Janet and I can be at the top of St. Bishop's Peak, a 1,292-foot mountain overlooking the 101 freeway, feeling like we are on top of the world. The best hike is when we start in the fog and make our way to the top where the sun is shining, a thick gray blanket below us, covering the town. It's quiet and special and my favorite thing.

I had great plans to explain all of this to Jake—or at least show it to him—this morning. I figure, I am having a kid with this person, and what better way to get to know someone than during a picturesque hike?

One thing I did not account for, though, is my absolutely insane morning sickness.

Why is it "morning" sickness? Because let me tell you, I feel like shit morning, noon, and night. No amount of Saltine crackers and ginger ale will turn this ship around.

"Hold on, girl," I mutter to Janet as she pulls sharply on her leash, no doubt wondering why the hell we aren't making like mountain goats up the hill. I wheeze and try to catch my breath.

"You okay?" Jake asks from behind me, looking like a snack in a black T-shirt with the sleeves cut off, his sun-kissed torso visible every time he moves. His baseball cap is on backward, and I didn't know that was a kink for me, but you learn something new every day.

Even better? He has on athletic shoes.

Not Rainbow flip-flops.

"I'm fine," I tell him. "I don't know what's wrong, I just feel…not as peppy as usual, I guess."

"Nothing's *wrong*, Tatum," Jake tells me easily, reaching for Janet's leash. I comply and step back, my hands on my hips. "You are literally growing a human inside you. You'll probably feel weak and nauseous throughout your first trimester."

I squint at him through my sunglasses. "Okaaaay?"

"I can read, you know," he says with a wry grin. "I did some investigation into, you know, what to expect when *you're* expecting," he adds, gesturing to my still-flat stomach.

Well. It's never been flat, exactly. But not visibly pregnant.

"Oh." I am surprised. "Well, I definitely feel nauseous. All the time." I gesture toward the trail, and we start moving uphill again. Jake is now in front of me, giving me a great view of his ass.

I didn't get enough time with that ass.

"And tired," I continue, pushing thoughts of Jake and his ass out of my mind. "And not hungry, which has happened in my life absolutely never. And" —*this is where, once again, I have to pause to catch my breath*—"a hike that usually takes less than an hour and a half up and down is now going to take…a lot longer than that." I huff and puff as we climb a particularly steep pass, taking caution around the jagged rocks that poke up from the hillside.

"I'm in no hurry. Can't speak for Janet, though," Jake says. He steps to the side and positions his feet firmly on the slope, reaching for my hand. "Here. There are a lot of sharp rocks," he tells me, gripping me firmly and leading me up the slope to the flat surface at the top of the pass.

"Thanks," I mumble, embarrassed by how winded I am. We're about halfway to the top, and the trail at this spot is wide, with big boulders to sit on and take in the view.

I let go of his hand and do just that, stretching my arms and catching my breath. The hillsides this time of year are yellow and brown, overgrown with wild flowers and weeds. The sun is high in the sky, and looking toward the beach—toward Estero Bay, my hometown—I see a thick layer of fog ready to slink into town after sunset.

"Sit with me," Jake says softly, and I turn to see him staring at me with—what else?—a smile on his face. "We don't need to go all the way to the top today."

I'm too tired to argue.

He helps me up onto one of the boulders, the flat top big enough for both of us to sit comfortably. Well, as comfortable as one can be on a rock.

"Here," Jake says suddenly, reaching into his pocket. I hold out my hand, and he drops a couple taffies in my palm.

Not taffies.

"They're ginger lozenges. Supposedly they help with the nausea."

I look at my palm and then look up at Jake.

"Thank you," I tell him quietly.

He smiles. "You're welcome, Tatum." He stares at me a bit longer than necessary, his blue eyes bright and knowing.

"So. Did you have a nice week at work?"

I cock my head to the side at Jake's question and look at him curiously. "What?"

"I assume you brought me out here so we can get to know each other. Seeing as how you are currently pregnant with my child," Jake tells me, his eyes darting down to my stomach and back up again, his voice dropping an octave at the end of his sentence.

And *whoosh*! My libido apparently didn't get the email that we're expecting, because hearing Jake affirm that, yes, I am knocked up with *his* child makes my breasts tingle a little.

To be fair, they are incredibly sensitive and incredibly tingly all the fucking time now.

"You aren't wrong," I concede. "We're in this together, right?" At Jake's nod, I continue. "So let's do Twenty Questions on this rock. Because whatever you read is right. I am flipping exhausted."

Jake

"Are your parents still together?" I ask. I remember seeing pictures of Tatum's mother on her mantel, but no picture of anyone who could be her father.

"Unfortunately, no. My dad died when I was four. I don't really remember him."

Well, now I feel like a jerk. "I'm so sorry," I tell Tatum, reaching for her hand.

This is the third or fourth or hundredth time I've reached for her during this walk, and yes, I am slightly concerned about her footing while she's feeling so crappy. But also?

I like touching her.

"Thank you. It was a long time ago. And Mom never remarried." Tatum clears her throat. "And just for the record, I haven't told her yet about…this," she adds, gesturing between the two of us. "I will, and I am sure she'll be fine, but I just needed a little space."

"Who have you told?" I ask her, genuinely curious.

"Honestly, no one. I told you that my sister, Julia, figured it out?" I nod, recalling what she told me at her house a week ago. "So, I assume her husband, Lincoln, knows because they share everything. But I haven't told my mom or Lucy or Summer or my brother or my grandfather…" Tatum's voice trails off, and she looks out over the town several hundred feet below us. Her thick hair is braided down her back, a thin black headband holding the stray hairs off her face.

St. Bishop's is nestled between mountains and hills just like the one we are on right now. The sun is bright in the early autumn sky, a few sparse white clouds dotting the landscape. The clock tower from the Catholic church is visible, peeking out from the trees.

"I will, of course. I…I actually don't know why I haven't told them yet. My family is great, I told you that. I just…" Tatum sighs. "This wasn't part of my plan," she says, "and I anticipate they will be surprised to hear that I've diverged from my usual path."

"On to the next," I murmur, recalling what she said earlier.

"That's right," she says, raising her eyebrows. "Not that I ever knew what 'the next' would be, you know? Just that there was always something else to get to."

"Maybe this is your something else," I tell her, my heart pounding in my chest.

"Maybe," she answers, but I can tell she isn't persuaded.

That's okay for now.

"Anyway. Your turn. Are *your* parents still together? I remember you saying their relationship was…less than ideal."

See! She likes you; she remembers stuff you talked about. "They are still together. Long story short, my dad works all the time, travels constantly, and has been cheating on my mom for as long as I can remember." Discomfort creeps up my spine, like I need to brush a bug off my skin, the same way I always feel when I think about my father and his infidelities. "I, um, recently found out that I have a little sister I never knew."

Tatum's lips part, and she squeezes my hand a little tighter. "Holy shit! Are you serious? How old is she? Like, a baby sister? You're going to have a baby and also you have a baby sister?" Tatum's mind jumps from one thought to the next, and I smile.

"Definitely not a baby. Her name is Shelby, she is sixteen, and I actually met her last week. That was where I was coming from before you invited me over." It feels like a million years ago now.

"Shelby lives with her mother and grandmother in Murdock. It's between Bakersfield and Fresno," I add at Tatum's blank expression.

"Holy shit," Tatum repeats, whispering. "That's a lot to take in." She pauses. "God, no wonder you were freaked out when I told you about, you know," she adds, again gesturing between the two of us.

I've noticed Tatum is not eager to say the words "I'm pregnant" or "expecting" or "having a baby." There's been a lot of this gesturing during our conversation, like she can think about it but can't quite verbalize it.

"It was unexpected, for sure," I concede. "And Tatum, I could have handled that better."

She scoffs. "You handled it just fine." She angles her head toward me, her mirrored sunglasses hiding her eyes.

"Agree to disagree," I tell her with a wry smile. "Anyway. Shelby seems really sweet. She's going to come to St. Bishop's in a few weeks. I am going to take her surfing," I prattle on, excited at the thought.

Tatum smiles, open and honest. A real smile. "That's awesome, Jake."

"Yeah, I know," I tell her, feeling my cheeks heat. "I always wanted a sibling. Now I have one, albeit in an unconventional way."

Tatum nods in agreement.

"You're close with yours, right?" I add, volleying our game back to Tatum.

"For sure. We've always been close. Julia, Nick, then me," Tatum answers, referencing the older sister whom I've met and the famous retired NFL quarterback whom I have *not* met. "My mom busted her ass while we were growing up. She had to—it was three kids, plus my grandfather, who is really like another kid," Tatum adds knowingly.

"I can't imagine," I murmur.

"Have *you* told your parents about…you know?" Tatum asks suddenly.

And again with the gesture to her stomach.

"Not yet," I reply. "My dad… I am not really worried about his thoughts on anything, frankly, right now. But I do want to tell my mom."

"How do you think she will react?" Tatum asks slowly.

"Honestly? I don't know. I am her only child, and I am not sure becoming a grandmother was something she was expecting in the near future. But she'll deal." I dip my chin to look at Tatum, concern visible on her face.

"Was she expecting you to, like, move back home after graduation, and PS, where are you living right now anyway?" Tatum asks both questions in a run-on sentence.

"It's your turn to answer questions," I tell her, "but I'll let this slide." I give her a wink.

"As to your first question, I definitely wasn't planning on moving back to my parents' house after graduation." I shudder, thinking of the long windows and even longer silences. "I had the same house I rented with my friends for a bit, and when the lease was up, I moved to an apartment."

I don't bother mentioning that it's a really nice new condo in a building developed by my father's company, or that I am staying there rent-free with the assumption that I, too, will dedicate my life to residential and commercial development.

I guess I can share some part about this, though.

"My father has actually been after me to join the family business."

"Like the mafia?" Tatum asks with a smile.

"Ha! And no. He would never do something so lower-class. No, he's in commercial and residential development. Used to be solely commercial, but that took a hit post-pandemic, but it's pretty successful, I guess." I sell it short on purpose, but I am not really interested in finding out how Tatum is going to react to my family's money.

Not that I think she will be weird about it. By all accounts, she has her own life and has made her own success.

But some people are strange with money.

"Ew," Tatum responds to my revelation, wrinkling her nose.

Not the reaction I was expecting.

"And you are interested in that? In development, I mean?" Tatum asks, her hackles rising.

"Noooooot particularly," I tell her slowly.

"Because I have to be honest with you." Tatum removes my hand from hers and leans her body toward mine, as if ready to pounce. "There's a lot of back-and-forth in this area about growth and whether we need it, and if we do need it, how it's going to be sustainable." Tatum ticks off each item on her fingers as she talks about something she is clearly passionate about. "I'm an avid proponent of preserving our open space here, and I've done some pro bono work for the Land Conservancy. So, if you are telling me that I am going to be having a baby with someone who thinks that we need to build, baby, build—"

"Whoa, whoa, killer," I interrupt her.

First of all, did Tatum just finally say that she's having a baby?

With me?

With no weird hand gestures or innuendo?!

Because that's fucking *fantastic.*

Second—

"I don't have particularly strong feelings one way or the other. But, frankly," I add, "I don't want to join his business. For a lot of reasons, one of them being that I don't want to be tethered to him for the rest of my life."

Blunt, but needs to be said.

Tatum raises her eyebrows and nods. "Fair point."

Something occurs to me.

"Does that make me an asshole? I mean, you lost your dad at an early age. I want nothing to do with mine. And I know the situations are different, but am I just—"

Tatum waves her hand dismissively. "You just said it. Our situations are different. And just because you're family doesn't mean you're obligated or that you owe him anything." She pauses, inspecting her hands. "There are lots of people out there with shitty family members. Remember, I just happen to have a great family. But," she adds, nodding to me, "not everyone does."

"Okay. I know," I say, more to myself than anyone else.

"Your dad, for what it's worth, kind of sounds like a dick," Tatum adds casually.

I laugh, because it's true.

It's *so* true.

"And you deserve better," she says quietly.

I smile bigger, trying to catch her eyes through those big-ass sunglasses.

"Thank you," I tell her, holding out my hand to her, palm up.

"You're welcome," she responds, placing her hand in mine, color rising in her cheeks.

Chapter Twenty-Two

Jake

I'M DOING THE SAME DRIVE I DID A FEW MONTHS AGO, THE SAME feeling of dread circling me the entire way.

It's time to tell my mom about Tatum. And more specifically, about the Little Jake or Little Tatum who will be joining this crazy planet in less than nine months.

I can spend hours thinking about what the baby will look like. Blue eyes and dark hair? Hazel eyes and blond hair? I get giddy just imagining the possibilities.

It's been roughly a month since Tatum dropped a baby bomb on me, and she's still feeling pretty crappy most of the time. The ginger drops seem to help, or maybe she's trying to make me feel better. But her loss of appetite is pretty visible in that she's not as curvy as she was before.

Except for her breasts. Those things are as magnificent as they ever were. Even more so.

Is it inappropriate to secretly check out the mother of your unborn child with whom you had a one-night stand?

Asking for a friend.

After all, I'm just a man.

A man who is pretty fucking sexually frustrated.

I went years not knowing what I was missing, only to have it for one night, only to realize that it was the absolute best thing in the entire world.

And now, I just stare at Tatum and hold her hand like she's my junior high crush.

I've made it clear to her that I am here to support her and Jake Junior—I'm testing it out—and give her whatever she needs. *Whatever* she needs.

And I hoped that she might need me.

And my dick.

But so far, Tatum hasn't shown any indication that she is interested in a redux of our night together. And that's fine; it doesn't change my intentions toward her or Tiny Tatum—another work in progress.

I sigh, pulling up the circular driveway.

I want to have this conversation with my mom about as much as I want a hole in my head. Not because I am afraid of disappointing my mother, but because I have a feeling she is going to be disappointed, if that makes sense.

I made my choices, and I stand by them.

But I am not sure Mom will see it that way.

"Have you talked to your father recently?" Mom asks, drinking tea slowly from a delicate china teacup.

We are in Santa Barbara, not Victorian England, but Mom likes to cosplay British aristocracy.

"No." I don't really want to say more on that subject.

"He only wants the best for you, you know," Mom continues, setting down her teacup on the matching saucer, her giant diamond ring winking at me. Diamond tennis bracelet, diamond earrings, and her usual uniform of cream-colored blouse and dark pants. A display of scarlet roses is arranged in a gold vase on the table before us in the living room.

"I know, Mom. I am just not ready to talk to him. About anything," I add emphatically.

"Everyone makes mistakes, Jake." My mom looks at me directly, and I hear what she isn't saying.

This is the only time I will ever acknowledge your sister.

"I don't disagree. But…that's a long time to lie to someone."

"He didn't lie," Mom interjects sharply.

I raise my eyebrows at her. "Seriously?"

"He didn't lie," Mom repeats, jutting her chin out.

"Are you really going to say that an omission, a pretty big fucking omission, I might add" —my mother's jaw clenches visibly at my profanity; how crass—"is not a lie? Or that because he didn't outright lie, it's somehow less of a mistake?"

"I am not saying that. I just think that in the scheme of things, this happened a long time ago. It's water under the bridge."

I lean my head back on the white couch—bold move, Mom—and rub my temples. I could tell her that all that lost time is time I can't get back with my sister. I could tell her that an omission is still a lie.

I could tell her a lot of things, but I think the best way to steer this conversation to another location is to just be blunt.

"Mom, I am going to have a baby."

Mom looks at me quizzically, as if I've spoken another language. "What are you talking about?" She sips her tea.

"Just what I said. There's a girl" —and I can't help my crooked smile when I speak of Tatum—"there's a girl. And she and I are going to have a baby."

Now is the time when some of Tatum's casual gesturing in lieu of describing what we did might come in handy.

Mom sips her tea and frowns at the same time. Or at least, she attempts to frown. There're no visible lines on her face, but it's in her eyes.

She's frowning.

The teacup hits the saucer with a slight *clink*. "Jake. I don't know what kind of joke you're trying to pull, but this is really not well-taken."

I stare at her, my smile fading. "Her name is Tatum. And we are having a baby."

Mom's expression goes from attempting-to-frown to attempting-to-look-shocked. "You—you don't even have a girlfriend! And now you're going to come in here and tell me that you've gotten a girl pregnant? Of all the ignorant, immature things—"

"I came here to tell you because…because I love you, Mom," I interrupt her loudly. "Even though things are a little…strained right now. *I* won't lie to you," I can't help but add pointedly.

Mom sets her jaw. "You are twenty-three years old, Jake," she seethes. "And I assume that…this girl is someone you met at school?"

Try as I might, I can't help another smug smile. "Actually, no. Tatum is older. She's a lawyer."

That's right, Mom.

I knocked up a lady, not a girl—a lady who is a hell of a lot smarter than me.

Mom pales a little bit. "A…lawyer? How much older?"

"She's thirty-one. She has her own law practice."

"In St. Bishop's? What does she spend her time doing, disputes over cattle?"

I roll my eyes. A lot of people around here have Mom's attitude—anything north of the university in Santa Barbara is like *Deliverance*. But will the rich folks put on a shiny pair of cowboy boots to go drink wine at someone's mansion in the hills north of Santa Barbara?

You bet your ass they will.

They like to cosplay cowboys too, I guess.

"Jake, you know that this woman is only after you for your money," Mom says, worry starting to replace her shock.

I huff a laugh. "She doesn't know I'm rich, Mom. And even if she did, she doesn't need my money."

Sometimes I think Tatum doesn't need anything from me at all.

But that's not anything I want to discuss with my mother.

Chapter Twenty-Three

Tatum

THIS PREGNANCY STUFF IS, SO FAR, FOR THE BIRDS.

I still feel like shit. And while I haven't thrown up once, I would honestly welcome a change from just feeling like I *might* throw up all the time.

"I know that you don't want it right now," my mom calls from the kitchen, "but you might want the cabbage soup when you are feeling better. At least, your sister did."

"Am I turning green? I must be green, right?" I ask my brother, Nick, who is wrestling with Janet and his black Lab, Layne Staley, in the living room.

He came over with Mom and offered to take Janet for a walk, as ours have been shorter and fewer than normal. Mom's excuse was that she just happened to have made extra food, and wouldn't I like to stockpile my freezer with meals like I am preparing for a winter in Russia?

I wasn't lying when I told Jake that I have the best family.

"You don't look green to me," Nick tells me without looking up.

"You didn't even look," I point out.

He pets Janet on the belly, Layne Staley flopping down next to him, and glances up at me. He opens his mouth and raises his eyebrows in mock concern.

"You *are* green, Tater Tot," he tells me. "What if the baby is green too?"

I roll my eyes. "Was that an honest-to-God joke? You are too happy. I don't like it."

He smiles, the corners of his eyes crinkling, not disputing my assessment of his mood. Ever since he and Summer got together, he's basically a new person. A much happier person.

"You know she's just excited," he tells me, referring to our mother. "She'd have a million little grandbabies if it were up to her."

"A million?" my mother exclaims, entering the living room and taking a spot next to me on the couch. "Let's not get ahead of ourselves. I do love being a grandma, but there's only one of me to go around." Layne Staley comes over, seeking attention, and she pets him on the head.

"Thanks, Mom. I don't mean to sound ungrateful. I'll just be glad when food sounds good again."

"I know you will, honey," she responds, patting my hand. "I was the same way with all three of you. Never threw up once, but just felt like absolute shit the entire first trimester."

Mom is a lot like Julia in that they are both fairly relaxed about life and whatever it throws at them. When I told Mom I was pregnant, she was visibly surprised—as I knew she would be; it's not like I have a boyfriend or husband—but immediately held open her arms. "Do you want a hug?" she asked me.

And yes, I did want a hug from my mother.

"You'll get there," she tells me now, tugging on the rope that Layne Staley has brought for her to play with. "And then you will get to experience the joy that is Second Breakfast."

"Second Breakfast?"

"You're eating for two, you know. So, you have your first breakfast, your eggs or cereal or bacon or all three. But then a couple hours later, it's not time for lunch, but you're hungry. Second Breakfast. I usually had more eggs. I think I could eat a dozen a day."

"Like Gaston," Nick offers.

"He ate five dozen a day," I correct him.

I know my Disney.

"Must be how we all came out so big. The eggs," Nick muses, because did I mention that all three of us Echeverrias each weighed more than nine-and-a-half pounds?

I would be concerned about that, but I'm too nauseous.

"Maybe," Mom says. "Anyway. Tatum, I love you, and I'm proud of you—" she leans in to kiss me on the cheek "—and I'll try not to come check on you every day."

"Maybe once a week," I joke weakly.

"Maybe every other day," Nick says wryly.

"Stop with the jokes," I warn him.

"Never," he tells me, before leaning over to ruffle my hair. "Later, skater."

I lift my hand in good-bye and nestle back down in the couch, knowing my family can let themselves out.

"Oh."

I hear Nick's voice a moment later.

"Hello!"

And my mom's voice.

I turn around and lift the curtain from the window to see that my mother and brother have run into none other than Jake, who must have been walking up my front path.

Janet trots to the door, hearing the people outside.

"All right, all right."

No time like the present, in my unwashed, smelly, and slightly barfy state, to introduce the father of my unborn child to my family.

I should have planned this better.

I haven't shown up unannounced at Tatum's before, and I wasn't thinking clearly.

All I knew after leaving my parents' house was that I wanted to see her.

It never even occurred to me that she would have guests over.

And now that I'm thinking about it…does she have other guests over?

Like, of the male variety?

We haven't had a single discussion about *us*, assuming there is an "us" at all. And I'm not stupid—Tatum's a fucking catch. Why wouldn't other guys be interested in her?

I don't have time to think about that now, when I am faced with a woman who is clearly Tatum's mother and her brother, the former football player Nick Echeverria.

"Hi! Hi. Um, hi, I'm Jake Lundquist." I offer my hand to the woman, deciding it best to go with a friendly introduction to Tatum's mother.

Who will be the grandmother of our child.

Holy shit.

"Hi, Jake. I'm Elaine," she tells me. She looks like Tatum in the face and hair, although hers is shot with silver throughout. Tatum—and her brother, who is eyeing me like he's not sure whether to shake my hand or punch me in the face—must have gotten her hazel eyes from her father. Elaine is also taller than Tatum and much leaner, like Tatum's sister Julia.

"It's nice to meet you," I tell her honestly, doing my best to avoid the determined sniffs from a black Lab who is very interested in my crotch.

"Layne Staley, knock that off," Nick Echeverria says.

I am sure he goes by just "Nick," but until he tells me otherwise, he's Nick Echeverria to me.

"Alice in Chains? Nice," I comment, holding out my hand for Layne Staley to sniff.

"Little before your time, though?" Nick Echeverria asks me, cocking his head to the side and eyeing me carefully.

"Sure. A lot of the good stuff is," I respond easily.

I'm no dummy.

If Nick Echeverria wants to kick my ass for knocking up his little sister, I will take it like a man.

"But *Jar of Flies* is great, man," I continue, referring to the best Alice in Chains album.

Yes, I am hoping to score brownie points with Tatum's brother.

"Hmm," is his noncommittal response. He looks at me a beat longer and holds out his hand. "I'm Nick."

I know who you are! I watched you play growing up!

…is *not* how I respond.

"I'm Jake."

We shake hands.

Nick's grip is firm.

"We were just leaving. Tatum's inside," Elaine offers, nudging her son in the shoulder.

"Here I am." Tatum's voice rings out from the porch. She comes down the stairs gingerly, her hair absolutely everywhere. I think it has its own postal code at this point. A UCLA blanket is wrapped around her; the fog has started to roll in, and there's a chill in the air. Her bare legs peek out from underneath the blanket, her toes painted black, just like last time.

Last time.

I haven't seen her bare legs in…maybe since that night.

The night we made a baby.

I want to get under the blanket and touch every inch of her skin.

And now I try not to get a boner in front of Nick Echeverria.

"Hi!" I greet Tatum, as excited to see her as Layne Staley is about my crotch. "I hope it's okay that I came by," I add, *like an idiot without texting first.*

"It's totally fine. They were just leaving. Bye, Mom. Love you. Bye, Nick. Tell Summer to come over this week."

Nick raises his hand in salute before eyeing me one more time on his way out. He might be trying to communicate something to me telepathically, but I'm not sure.

"Jake." Elaine distracts me from Nick's steely gaze when she takes my hand again. "So nice to meet you. And I hope we get to see more of you soon, okay?"

"I would like that," I tell her.

Elaine smiles, squeezes my hand, and follows her son to the truck parked out front. I watch them leave and feel another furry friend at my leg.

"Hey, pretty girl," I croon to Janet.

"Oh my *god*," Tatum mumbles from the porch. I look up and see her covering her eyes and trying to pat down her hair.

"What's up? What's wrong? Is it really okay that I came by? Did… did you have other plans? Other, I don't know, other people coming over? Because I can go if you did—"

"*Jake*," Tatum barks at me from the porch. She's removed her hands from her face, and her skin is splotchy.

"Does it look like I have company coming over?" she asks me, gesturing to her blanket-wrapped form.

I mean, I wouldn't turn down an invitation to join blanket-wrapped Tatum, but I think it best to slow my roll here.

"I mean…not really? I still think you look great," I add. "Beautiful, even."

Tatum opens her mouth, closes it. Gives me a look that says *Are you bullshitting me?*, and then turns to go inside. "Janet, come," she calls.

Janet bounds up the path and into the house. Tatum turns around and looks at me questioningly.

"You coming?"

"Yes! I mean, yes."

Hopefully.

⌃

Tatum

Pregnancy hormones are wild, I tell you.

I am still a little barfy. Still a little tired.

But something about hearing Jake tell my dog that she's pretty also has me feeling a little horny.

This can't be normal, right? Why do I want to eat everything and *not* eat anything, sleep for a week, throw up, cry about everything, and get absolutely railed at the same time?

"I'm sorry I didn't text or anything before I came over." Jake continues babbling as he enters the house, closing the door behind him. He runs his hands through his hair, not meeting my eyes, his gaze apparently focused on…my legs?

My unshaved legs.

I am nothing if not consistent.

"It's okay," I tell him, but he keeps talking before I can say more.

"There's just some stuff—"

Jake pauses, huffing out a sigh, his hands on his hips as he looks at the floor.

"I just needed to—"

Another pause.

"*Jake.*"

He looks up when I bark his name, his eyes cloudy with emotion.

"It's okay," I repeat, more gently this time. I give him a wry smile. "Although I must tell you, I am not very good company these days."

"I think you're great company," he replies in a low tone. He assesses me, like he's weighing his word choice. "I just had a not-so-great day. And...I really wanted to see you."

I am equally alarmed and excited by his statement.

Alarmed because...this isn't anything, right? We had a one-night stand, I got pregnant, but that's show biz, baby.

Excited because...I am not sure why.

"That's sweet, Jake, but I am not up for much of anything, given that..." I gesture toward my middle. Of course I am not showing yet, but he gets my drift, his eyes going to my midsection and...smoldering?

"I just feel icky." *And a little horny.* "Nothing fits me and I don't want any food and my boobs are absolutely *killing* me, so like I said, not very good company, but—"

Jake dashes toward me, preventing me from saying anything further by pressing his tall, firm body right up against mine. His eyes are definitely smoldering, his blue gaze piercing in its intensity. Every inch of him is hard against my soft, the blanket around me dropping to the floor as he cradles my head in his hands. His touch is light as he holds me delicately, his eyes darting around my face, as if looking for something.

And I realize that truly *every* inch of him is hard as I feel the unmistakable pressure from Little Jake. Not that it's little, and I know firsthand. But that's definitely a healthy erection pressing up against my stomach.

My eyes widen, and my lips part on a gasp. Jake gives me a smirk.

"Don't sell yourself short, Tatum," he says, his voice like gravel. "I happen to think you are *great* company." He punctuates this statement with the slightest thrust of his hips, so I have no doubt as to his meaning.

"Okay—um, okay," I reply, my voice breathy.

"I want to tell you some stuff." Another thrust of his hips. "I want to tell you that you were the first person I thought of talking to after my bad day." Another thrust, and as he talks, his hands travel away from my face, over my jawline, into my hair. My rat's nest hair, but it feels so damn good to have his strong hands comb through the strands as he removes my hair tie, I nearly moan out loud, my eyelids fluttering.

"I want to tell you that I want to kiss you," Jake tells me, his expression serious, his jaw clenched as he thrusts again and massages his fingertips over my scalp.

This time, I can't help the moan that escapes my lips.

"I want to tell you some other things about myself. Because I want to know you, and I want you to know me." *Thrust.* My head lolls to one side, leaning into his touch.

"I want to do more of what we did last time, Tatum. I want to do it all—" *thrust* "—over—" *thrust* "—again."

"Oh my *god*," is all I can moan as his touch grows stronger. I remember those long fingers inside me, pumping me, taking me exactly where I needed to go, and all I can think is, *I want that too.*

"So, stop telling me about how you're bad company, because you're the only company I want."

And then his lips are on mine, warm and soft. This is no taking; this is seeking. He wants me, if the rod in his shorts is anything to go by, but his kiss is a question, a chance for me to tell him to go to hell.

But right now, the only place I want to go is my bedroom. And I want Jake there with me.

I press my lips back against his, flattening my body up against his chest.

He's hot and hard and smells so good, like mint and the ocean. My tongue darts out, and his lips open on a groan, his tongue tangling with mine, his hands leaving my hair so his arms can wrap around my body and pull me closer.

"I want you so bad, Tatum," Jake grits out.

"You can have me," I tell him between kisses. "You can have me," I repeat, almost to myself.

We stand like that in my living room, kissing, feeling each other, pressing our bodies together. It's straight-up Heavy Petting 101, and I am into it. Until—

"Shit—ow! Shit," I curse when Jake's hands make their way to my breasts.

He immediately raises his hands in retreat, his head lifting from mine, his eyes concerned. "Sorry! Sorry—are you okay? What is it?"

"My tits hurt," I grumble, gently running my fingers over the top of my chest. "They are bigger than normal and, like, crazy sensitive. I had to wear two bras to go hiking the other day."

Jake's eyes widen and immediately move to—you know where—my breasts.

"I'm so sorry," he whispers, his face ruddy, his lips swollen from our kissing.

"It's okay," I tell him, mimicking his earlier move by reaching up to cradle his face in my hands. "Jake," I add, seeing how upset he is at the thought of hurting me, "it's really okay. You can touch them, just…be careful."

I lean in to kiss him again, softly, gently. "I want you to touch them," I add quietly. "I want to do it all over again, too."

Jake moves his hands around my body, then lower to my ass, and he grabs himself a good handful. "I'll be careful," he murmurs. "So careful, Tatum." His words are belied by the firm grip he has on my sizable bottom, and he groans again into our kiss. "Jesus. I did *not* get enough time with this ass the last time we did this."

I smile against his mouth. "Come with me to the bedroom, and you can have all the time you want."

Chapter Twenty-Four

Jake

I OBVIOUSLY DON'T HAVE MUCH TO COMPARE IT TO.

Actually, nothing to compare it to.

But my first time having sex with Tatum was a rush. Everything was heightened—every sound, every touch, every smell. Every moan from her body, every kiss from her lips.

This time, I want to go slow. Not only because I still don't know if I'll continue to have the privilege of seeing her body, of being with her like this. But also because if she is sensitive or experiencing discomfort, I want to lessen that for her.

We don't speak as we enter her room. We say nothing as Tatum takes off her T-shirt and bra, although she sighs in relief as soon as her breasts are unbound. She climbs into her bed after removing her shorts, rolling on her side to look at me.

"Now you," she says softly, gesturing to my clothes, and I do what the good woman says and undress, leaving my boxers on.

"No Jesus this time," she quips, eyeing the blue plaid pattern on my underwear.

"Nah, he's sitting this one out," I tell her with a grin. My smile grows bigger as I see her lips part when she views my crotch.

I may not know for sure where Tatum and I stand with each other—I don't think either of us does—but one thing I do know for sure.

My girl is a size queen.

I can work with that.

"I meant what I said," I tell her as I crawl into bed with her. "I want to tell you some stuff."

"Uh-huh," Tatum says distractedly, moving closer to me, pressing her body against mine.

"I mean, since we are having a baby," I tell her pointedly, doing my damnedest to ignore how good her soft, warm body feels against mine, "there's probably more you should know about me."

"Okay," she breathes out, pressing the palm of her hand against my cock. I shudder in response and grab her wrist.

"Tatum," I tell her firmly, and she looks at me, her hazel eyes glazed over. "I'm rich."

"What—what?" She peers at me in confusion.

"I'm rich," I repeat. "As in, my family is rich. I have a lot of money. Most of it's in a trust from my grandfather, but it's going to be mine one day—"

"Jake." Tatum narrows her eyes at me, propping herself up on one elbow. "I appreciate that we do need to do more Twenty Questions." I smile, remembering our first round on the rock. "But right now, I don't give a dusty fuck about the size of your trust. What I am interested in right *now*—" she jerks her hand out of my grip and goes back to my cock—"is the size of your dick."

"Ohhhh," I moan incoherently as she grabs me firmly.

"You good with that?"

"Yeeeaaah. Yeah. I am good with that," I wheeze out through clenched teeth.

"Good." Tatum gives me an evil smile, and I'm immediately transported back to our weekend together.

"Now. Like I said, I am a little off, a little groggy, a little like how you are feeling like you *might* be coming down with the flu, but never actually do?"

I nod because she phrases the last part like a question, but she might as well be speaking another language.

Because as she speaks, she lays herself back down on her back, takes my hand, and places it directly over her center. She feels warm and inviting through the thin material of her underwear, and I groan again at the sensation against my hand. I cup her mound gently, and Tatum sighs and closes her eyes.

"But," she continues, her voice strained, "I really, really want to have an orgasm. And I really, really liked it when you fingered me last time, Jake."

I hum in response, letting my hand press more firmly against her through her underwear. "Did you now?" I ask, my voice low.

"Yes," she says softly. She rolls her head over toward me and opens her eyes, meeting my gaze head on, letting me see the want in them. "Yes," she murmurs again.

"I don't want to hurt you," I tell her honestly. "So tell me if something doesn't feel good or is uncomfortable or whatever." I massage the palm of my hand in slow circles all around her mound as I talk, essentially giving her a massage through her underwear. Tatum gasps, her eyes fluttering closed.

I take that as permission to continue and keep my hand flat against her, covering every inch of her center. Before long, there's the telltale sign of her arousal, damp against my hand.

Jesus. My cock is absolutely rock hard now, standing straight up in my boxers and all but demanding to get into that sweet, wet place. I close my eyes and exhale, doing my best not to repeat my premature finish like the last time.

After all, I'm just a man.

"You're making a wet spot on these panties, Tatum," I grit out. "I like that. I like that your body knows to get nice and wet for me."

"Feels so, so good," she slurs, her body lax, her hands clenching occasionally on the sheets.

"You remember we had to go slow last time so I could fit in this tight spot, right?" I ask her, feeling her dampness grow.

"Yeah," she mumbles around a moan.

"We're going to do the same thing this time, okay, beautiful? Get you nice and slick, so I can slide this fat dick right in."

"Oh *fuck*," Tatum cries. I give one final, firm press with the heel of my hand against her clit and then move my hand to lift the side of her underwear. She's already drenched and glistening, and I gingerly slide a finger inside, not moving farther than my first knuckle.

"That's a good girl," I mutter, my jaw tight as I finger her with slow, shallow thrusts. "Get me nice and soaked, Tatum."

"Jake," she moans, and it's the best fucking thing I've ever heard, my name on her lips as she writhes on the bed, her head lolling from side to side.

"That's it," I continue, letting my finger get deeper on each thrust. "Get ready, Tatum. I want that body ready for me to fuck."

I play with her like this for a few minutes more, adding another finger to join the first, turning them to curl against the front of her body, but never touching her clit. I tell her how good she is, how wet she is, how I can't wait to be deep inside her. I can't take my eyes off where I enter her, my fingers disappearing into her tight flesh, feeling her clench around me. It's the hottest thing I've ever seen.

Tatum responds with a refrain of blasphemy and calls to the man upstairs, and it's a miracle I don't come in my shorts. But I manage.

"I wanna come, Jake," Tatum says suddenly, and I shift my gaze from her center to her face to see her eyes blinking at me, determination visible in her face, a thin sheen of perspiration on her hairline. "Please. I have to come."

"Are you sure? You sure you're ready to take me inside you?" I press my fingers inside again, turning my wrist so that I rub on the fleshy part of her core.

"Fuck. *Fuck.* Yes, I'm sure, I'm sure—"

I maneuver my body so that I am sitting up next to where she's lying, keeping my fingers inside and taking my other hand so I can apply direct pressure right where she wants it most.

"I don't know, Tatum. I could honestly keep fingering you all fucking night," I tell her wryly, and I mean it. This is like the most erotic massage in the history of everything, and I am here for giving this woman pleasure.

"Just fucking touch me. Don't stop, don't stop," she babbles.

And I do. I keep fingering her, using the heel of my other hand to press against her clit in circles. I'm again riveted by the sight before me, almost as if I'm watching someone else do it.

"Jake, I'm gonna come," she sobs, grabbing my wrist suddenly, just like the first time we did this on her couch over two months ago.

"I'm gonna come," she repeats, her eyes widening, her legs spreading farther than I thought possible, as if she can't get enough of what I am giving her.

"Do it, beautiful. Come on my hand and get ready. Get ready," I repeat myself as well, my words almost nonsensical. I am the one who needs to get ready, to prepare myself for this woman and what she's going to do to me, what she already *has* done to me.

Tatum tenses up, her back bowing toward the ceiling, her body clenching unbelievably tight around my hand, before she goes off. She just…lets go, her body melting into the bed, her arms dropping at her sides, her eyes shut as she moans my name through her climax, drenching my hand.

The tightness around my hand is nothing, however, compared to the squeezing pressure in my chest.

"Fuuuuuuck," I mutter, trying to wring every drop of pleasure from Tatum that I can. "Good girl, beautiful. *Fuck*. Give it to me."

Get ready, indeed.

Chapter Twenty-Five

Tatum

I've had a lot of sex over the years.

I'm not ashamed of it, and I don't apologize for it.

Therefore, I have a healthy amount of experience to compare to my first—and now, second—time having sex with Jake.

I expected the second time would be as pleasurable as the first. Jake is eager to please, considerate, and—let's be honest—packing heat.

I did not, however, anticipate the rush of emotions I would feel during this second time with him.

I blame the pregnancy hormones.

I am wrecked from the shuddering orgasm he gave me with his fingers. I was content to do nothing more than disintegrate into the bedsheets as he used those magical hands on me, my core throbbing, the sound of my blood rushing through my ears as I closed my eyes and focused on what he was doing to me.

Watching him watch me? Having him devote one hundred percent of his efforts to making me come? The way he sat up alongside me, almost in a detached manner, to use both hands to work me over until I couldn't take it anymore?

I came so hard, I think I nearly passed out.

Now, Jake says nothing, removing his hands from my center, his chest heaving as if he just ran a marathon. He looks at me, his blue eyes darkened like a stormy ocean. He doesn't look away as he brings his fingers—fingers that were just inside me—to my mouth.

He says nothing as he presses his fingers against my bottom lip, silently entreating me to open my mouth.

I say nothing as I part my lips, granting him access, tasting the salty flavor on my tongue. My core clenches as he dips his fingers into my mouth. I don't look away from him as I let my tongue dart out, teasing his fingers the way I would his dick if I had the opportunity.

Jake says nothing, his face a mask of want and frustration, as he dips his fingers in and out of my mouth.

He groans when I keep my tongue out, letting him play with my mouth.

Just like he did with my pussy a few moments ago.

He lets out a curse and suddenly he's directly over me, his mouth mashed against mine and his tongue touching mine, but he keeps his fingers right where they are. It's a fucking obscene trio consisting of his mouth, my mouth, and his fingers, as we both vie to taste me on his fingers.

Jake says nothing as he removes his fingers, balancing himself on his elbows, keeping his mouth on mine as he lowers his body on top of me.

He says nothing as he grips his dick, running it through my center once, twice, a third time, before positioning it right at my opening, and giving a big thrust.

I yelp in surprise, but not pain, as my body welcomes him home.

And then he starts to fuck me.

And I mean *fuck* me. He traps me under him, kissing me, panting, cursing every so often, but remaining uncharacteristically quiet as he drills into me, letting me feel every inch.

Just like before, I am content to melt into the sheets as he works me over.

Again.

Our gasps, moans, and grunts fill the room. Before long, Jake lifts his head from mine, still balancing on his forearms, and grips my jaw in one of his hands. Not hard enough to hurt, but firm enough so that I am immobile. His pupils are dilated, his lips parted as he breathes heavily with each thrust, sawing me with his heavy dick.

"Gonna come inside you, Tatum," he tells me, his voice wrecked.

I realize then we haven't used a condom. I always use condoms, but it's not like I can get any *more* pregnant, right?

I obviously haven't been with anyone else since Jake—can he say the same?

He must see the internal monologue running through my head, because he grips my jaw just a little firmer. "Haven't been with anyone else. Only you. I'm gonna come inside you," he tells me, making it sound like a threat.

I spread my legs open more. "Do it," I breathe out. "Come inside me, Jake."

He mutters an expletive, leaning down to kiss me again, keeping my body anchored and pumping his hips faster, faster, faster, until he lets out a long groan and presses his hips firmly to mine.

"Only you, Tatum," he breathes out, his shoulders hunched up around his ears as he unloads.

I wrap my arms around his back, feeling his muscles tense and release as he reaches his peak. He lets go of my jaw and cradles my head in his hand, kissing me again, letting me feel the full weight of his powerful body before he shifts to the side.

"Only you," he mumbles.

Part III

The Second Trimester

It's not every day that I, an expectant mother, am called the C-word in a court of law. The hallowed halls of justice, if you will.

But, unbelievably, that is what just happened.

I am in the St. Bishop's courthouse, an old, tired government building well past its prime. Courtrooms are stuffy, windowless places where time drags on forever or completely stands still.

I'm here for pretrial motions in another employment case, which is set to begin trial in two weeks. Because we are still in the pretrial phase, no jury has been selected. It's just me, opposing counsel, the judge, her clerk, and Gabe, the court reporter.

Unfortunately, opposing counsel in this case is not as practical or amiable as Carson or Lorena. This opposing counsel is James Hutchinson, and he is a total dick.

He's a good attorney, no doubt, but makes every interaction so incredibly unpleasant that I end up dreading each and every phone call, deposition, and court appearance with him. I am convinced it's part of his strategy; if opposing counsel comes to dread you, surely that will bode well for settlement negotiations.

I've just prevailed on a motion in limine, a fancy term for a pretrial motion made to ensure certain evidence isn't introduced to the jury.

In this case, my client's three DUI arrests and two convictions.

A good look?

No, never. In the age of Uber and Lyft, why anyone is still getting a DUI is beyond me.

But are the DUIs relevant to this case, which involves claims of unpaid wages against my client, the manager of a local strawberry producer?

No, they are not relevant, as I argued to the court.

Judge Marla Herrera agrees with me, and the evidence of my client's DUIs is out.

Mr. Hutchinson vociferously argued the DUIs should be considered by the jury, and he is now fuming in his tailored black suit and gray tie. Very monochrome, maybe to match his salt-and-pepper hair and mustache.

"Any more issues to address before we adjourn?" Judge Herrera asks. I like her—she's smart and no-nonsense. She's a former criminal prosecutor, as are a lot of judges, but has demonstrated a knack for the issues in this civil lawsuit.

"Not from the plaintiff, Your Honor," Mr. Hutchinson replies.

"And none from defense, Your Honor," I echo.

"Very good. Then we will adjourn, and I wish you both a good weekend."

"Thank you, Your Honor. If I may, for a moment, extend my thanks to the court and opposing counsel for their professionalism and courtesy during what has been a very hard-fought case."

I try not to roll my eyes and wait for Mr. Hutchinson to continue. I want to go home. I want to eat some saltwater taffy—my nausea has left me, thank goodness—and approximately ten bacon-wrapped dates that I plan on picking up on my way home.

"And with that, I will wish Mr. Velasco" —*that's court reporter Gabe*—"and the court a nice Friday evening. Counsel" —*that's me*—"I'll see you next Tuesday."

Mr. Hutchinson leans into the microphone, totally unnecessary as no one is appearing telephonically or via videoconference, and says louder, "See you next Tuesday, Ms. Echeverria."

My lips part in surprise, my eyebrows rise.

Did he just…call me a cunt?

I look at him blankly, and he gives me a slimy smile.

"How nice," Judge Herrera says offhandedly, clearly not picking up on anything untoward.

My eyes dart to Gabe, my trusted court reporter, and he is giving me a look that says *Girl.*

"Um, have a nice weekend," I stammer.

"See you next Tuesday," Mr. Hutchinson says again, offering his hand to mine for a handshake, his eyes shrewd, as if asking me *are you picking up what I'm putting down?*

I reluctantly shake it, remember who I am, and try my best to squeeze the life-force out of his fingers.

"You sure will, counsel."

I really thought this profession would involve less instances of people calling me a cunt.

After the initial shock of Mr. Hutchinson's comment wore off, I entered the next phase of my response, which is straight-up angry pregnant woman.

I am in the middle of my second trimester. I am visibly pregnant, I am hungry constantly, and I am horny, also constantly.

I am also still tired and more emotional than I've ever been.

Which is only making me angrier.

However, I need to check myself, because today Jake and I are driving to Santa Barbara to meet his mother.

I sigh, finishing applying my mascara, and head to my bedroom to check out my outfit in the full-length mirror.

After looking like I'd just eaten a Thanksgiving dinner for the past few months, I now have a visible baby bump. My boobs don't hurt as much, and they've gone back to their regular size. Which is to say, they are still huge.

But I've never been able to do anything about that, and I don't intend to start now.

I have on an outfit that I would have selected for a deposition instead of a Saturday—a stretchy, forest-green dress with short sleeves and a full skirt. Put a blazer over it, and *bam*! Professional lady lawyer. I instead have on a cozy camel-colored coat. It's mid-October, and the weather on the Central Coast ranges from blazing hot in the daytime to the low 50s at night. And as always, when the fog rolls in, I get cold.

I put on my boots—also camel-colored—and smooth my hair in the mirror.

I don't know what it is about pregnancy, but I have more hair everywhere than I ever did before.

And I had a lot of hair before.

Again, nothing I can do about that now.

A knock on the door signals Jake's arrival, and Janet leaps up from her dog bed to go greet our visitor.

"Hi," I say as I let him in the house.

"Hi!" Jake offers me a big grin, per usual. What is unusual is his choice of wardrobe. No Rainbows, no shorts. He looks like he's dressed for church in a pair of dark pants and a blue button-up shirt the exact shade of his eyes. Those eyes sparkle at me in appreciation as he eyes me up and down.

"You look beautiful, beautiful," he tells me with a crooked grin.

"We look like we are going to high tea," I respond, self-consciously smoothing my hands down my dress.

His smile gets bigger. "Well, I have always thought my mother fancied herself a member of the aristocracy, so that checks out."

Jake's told me more of his mother and father and their bizarro relationship over the past couple months. It doesn't escape me, of course, that we are going to meet his mother, only, and not his father.

So far as I know, Jake has had minimal contact with his father ever since the truth came out about his sister. When I bring it up, Jake is not inclined to talk about it, which is fine with me.

I figure he will talk about it when he's ready.

Jake told me he came from wealth a few months ago. I shouldn't be sur-prised when we pull up to a gated neighborhood in the hills above Santa Barbara an hour and a half later.

And I'm not surprised.

But I am…nervous?

I twist my hands together in my lap. Jake finishes punching the ac-cess code to open the gate and reaches his hand over to my lap, palm up.

I smile at his frequent overture and take his hand in mine.

"You ready?" he asks as the gate in front of us opens slowly.

I shrug. "Ready as I'll ever be."

He smiles. "You have nothing to worry about."

"I know that. I am just wondering what your mother is going to think about this older woman who got knocked up by her baby boy."

"First of all, that's gross," he says matter-of-factly. "I'm not a baby. Second, she will think that I am fucking lucky a woman of your stature even gave me the time of day, let alone let me impregnate her."

I burst out laughing. "So sexy when you put it like that."

"Well, I'm trying not to get turned on right now with you in that tight fucking dress."

I raise my eyebrows. "Seriously?"

"Tatum," Jake tells me with a sideways glance, "you know I am always hard for you."

I roll my eyes and feel myself blush.

Yes, I do know this.

Yes, Jake and I have been fucking pretty much nonstop lately.

I went from being both nauseous and horny to just horny.

And hungry.

Turns out sex with a dude who is eager, curious, and knows what he's doing, combined with the complete lack of concern about getting preg-nant—been there, done that—is pretty damn delightful.

"You flatter me," I tell him.

"No way." He brings our linked hands to his mouth, placing a soft kiss on the back of mine.

"*You* flatter me."

Kimberly Lundquist is exactly what I expected.

She is thin, blond, and beautiful. She reminds me of Princess Grace—or, at least, what my idea of Princess Grace is. She has the biggest diamond earrings in her lobes and is dressed in a perfectly tailored cream silk blouse and camel-colored pants.

"We match!" I tell her, pointing to my boots.

No, I do not say that.

"It's lovely to meet you, Mrs. Lundquist," I say instead, shaking her delicate hand.

"Please, call me Kimberly," she responds, her face unsmiling but kind. She softens a bit when she turns to Jake. "How are you?" she asks as he leans in to place a kiss on her cheek.

"I'm good, Mom," he tells her. "How are *you*?" he asks pointedly.

I know the source of his focus. Jake is still mad at his father for keeping a secret for so long; he is still frustrated that his mother won't leave his father; he is still unwilling to have a real conversation with his father about much of anything.

But one thing has become apparent in the past few months that Jake and I have spent together. It's evident he loves his mom and is very protective of her.

"I'm well," Kimberly demurs. "Come into the sitting room," she adds.

I manage not to choke out an expletive as we enter the cleanest, brightest room I have ever seen. The clean freak in me rejoices, but the room isn't bright due to the color palette. Rather, it's decorated entirely in whites and creams, ample sunlight streaming in from the floor-to-ceiling windows along the far side, million-dollar views of the Pacific in the distance.

The only color is in the clear vases of burgundy roses placed throughout the room.

"You have a lovely home," I immediately say as we enter.

"Thank you," Kimberly replies automatically, gesturing toward the white couches.

How does she keep these clean?

I realize it's only her and her husband—when he's around—in this house, so it must be easier than I think.

I sit with Jake on the couch. He immediately takes my hand in both of his, cradling it in his lap.

"Well," Kimberly says, her eyes darting to my stomach ever so briefly. I notice the slight wince before she trains her eyes on her son.

And we begin our visit.

Chapter Twenty-Seven

I KNOW TATUM WAS NERVOUS ABOUT THE VISIT WITH MY MOTHER, BUT honestly, I don't know why.

Tatum is fucking awesome. She's smart, she's successful, and she's sexy as hell.

That last part probably goes unnoticed by my mother.

But I think it's a productive, if not a bit stilted, conversation. My mother asks all the right questions about Tatum's background, appropriately sympathetic when Tatum mentions her father dying when she was young, and appropriately interested when Tatum talks about attending law school and opening her own law practice.

"Will you be able to take time away from work when…?" My mom's voice drifts off as she gestures to Tatum's general vicinity or, more accurately, to her stomach.

What is with these women and their inability to talk about babies being born?

We really are in some bizarre aristocracy cosplay.

"I will. I'll probably set some office hours, or something similar, for clients to call me if something comes up. But I have a good associate working with me who can handle most of the day-to-day activities, and all my trials will either be over before the baby comes or won't take place until at least six months after."

"Jake, what about you?" My mother directs her attention to me, sipping from a glass of ice water with a wedge of lemon.

"Me?" I respond distractedly, removing my gaze from Tatum and meeting my mother's eyes.

"You've been working at that architectural firm in St. Bishop's," my mom replies. "Do you intend to stay there, or are you going to take your father up on his offer to explore development in the area?"

Ugh. The never-ending question of "When are you going to start working with your father?" is definitely not my favorite. It's true, I've been working for a local firm specializing in sustainable architecture, where the focus is not on the quantity, but on how projects can have a low negative impact on the environment and use sustainable and recycled materials in construction.

And…I actually really like it. It's nice to be part of a team that builds thoughtfully.

"I haven't given it much consideration," I tell Mom smoothly.

"He's expecting you, you know. To join him. Especially in light of…"

Again, with the fucking gesture toward Tatum.

"In light of what, Mom?" I ask slowly.

"Well, in light of the…the baby," my mother manages to reply. "Surely you will want a more…stable income at that time," she adds.

It's also true that I am not making nearly as much money as I would if I joined my dad's business and received an equity stake.

However, that is none of my mother's business, not that she is aware of how much money I'm making anyway.

"I'll be fine, Mom," I tell her firmly.

"I'm sure you will. I just think that you should talk to your father—"

"Mom, can we please not have this conversation again?" I hate to interrupt her or create drama, but I am not here for this.

"He misses you. He asks about—"

"No," I tell her more forcefully. "Mom, I'm sorry, but no. I'm not ready to talk to him."

I'm not ready to forgive him, is what I really mean.

Tatum, who has silently been watching this awkward-as-hell conversation, sets her glass down on a coaster—of course she does—and then shifts the angle of her body toward mine, so that our knees are touching. We are no longer holding hands, and I unconsciously place mine on her knee, palm up.

She takes my hand, linking our fingers.

I look down at our hands, hers smaller. Her skin is soft and warm.

I raise my eyes back up to my mother, who is looking at me both expectantly and a little sadly.

"I'll talk to him when I'm ready." I clear my throat, because I still don't want to talk about this, not even a little bit.

"I'm not ready now. Okay?"

Mom darts her gaze to Tatum briefly, before meeting my eyes again. "Okay."

Tatum and I sit in companionable silence as we drive north from Santa Barbara.

The drive from Santa Barbara to St. Bishop's is stunning. If there was ever a place to be silent and soak in the scenery, this is it. I opt to take a shortcut instead of the 101 the whole way through, choosing a state highway that climbs up into Los Padres National Forest. The road will eventually lead us through a few small towns—including Solvang, a Danish-style village with windmills and bakeries on every block—before dumping us back out onto the 101.

But after we make the initial climb up the San Marcos Pass, I have another idea.

"Are you hungry?"

"Starving," Tatum responds immediately. "Always starving."

I smile and continue driving a few more miles before taking a left into the mountains. "I've got just the place."

Cold Spring Tavern is part biker bar, part Wild West saloon, and part outdoor music venue. It used to be a stagecoach stop way back when, and yes, I took a field trip there to learn all about it in elementary school. This time of year, after the summer heat has dissipated and the shadows grow longer, it's stunning. The leaves brown and gold, birds chirping in the trees, the smell of meat cooking, and a three-piece band—stand-up bass, banjo, and violin—greeting us with a Coldplay cover as we walk toward the restaurant.

"Tri-tip!" Tatum exclaims excitedly as she walks alongside me toward the saloon.

"You know it."

"I mean, I've always been a big meat eater—"

"That's what she said," I can't help but interject.

"—but something about this baby makes me want red meat," Tatum continues, unfazed by my remark, "like, the unhealthy kind. No chicken. No salmon."

"No sushi," I add.

"Ugh, yeah, that does suck. But give me a hamburger or a steak or tri-tip, and I think I can live with it."

"Maybe your body needs the extra iron," I offer.

"Maybe."

"And Tatum, I've got an unhealthy amount of meat any time you want."

Tatum side-eyes me, her boots crunching on the gravel as we walk. "Couldn't resist, could you?"

I take her hand in mine and smile. "No way."

We find a place to sit outside and place our orders—tri-tip sandwiches and iced teas for both of us. After the waitress leaves, we relax back in our chairs. Tatum unwraps her silverware from the napkin on the red-checkered tablecloth and places the fabric on her lap just so, before looking at me expectantly.

We're less than twenty-five minutes from Santa Barbara, but it feels like a million miles away. In a very, very good way. I inhale and exhale, make an effort to relax my shoulders, and run my hands through my hair.

"You're a good son, Jake."

I jerk my chin up to meet Tatum's eyes, her comment unexpected.

"Your mom loves you. Who wouldn't?" she adds, and I raise my eyebrows. *You wouldn't…would you?*

Tatum doesn't pick up on my thoughts, instead continuing, "She cares about you, about your future. And I'm sure this" *—if one more person gestures to Tatum's stomach in lieu of using words, I am going to lose my shit—*"isn't what she had in mind for your future."

"I know." Leaning my head back, I watch the leaves blowing in the wind above me, the sun breaking through cracks to shine down on us.

"You know you're under no obligation to talk to your father, though, right?"

I meet her eyes again, sympathy evident across her face. "I do know that. I mean, I can appreciate that Mom wants us all to forget what happened and be a happy family, but…" I sigh. "I just can't. At least, not yet."

"Good," Tatum said. She leans back as our waitress approaches with our sandwiches. "I hope you don't mind, but I am now going to eat this whole sandwich in, like, less than five minutes."

I grin at her. "Same, beautiful."

Tatum falls asleep almost the instant we begin our drive back to St. Bishop's. Her mouth is open, her breath heavy as the sun gradually sets behind the mountains.

She's beautiful, the mother of my child.

I grip the steering wheel tighter, sneaking a glance at her stomach, something inside me stirring when I see the little baby bump.

I still have no regrets about what we did or the consequences. I still get just as excited to see Tatum as I did when I first met her. I meant what I said on the way to my parents' house; I still think she's the smartest, sexiest woman I've ever known.

And she's mine.

I release my grip on the steering wheel.

She's not mine, not really, her growing bump notwithstanding. We have tacitly avoided any conversations about "us" or our future, other than to generally discuss the baby. What sort of birth she wants, her maternity leave, that kind of thing. Nothing about where Tatum and I stand, separate and apart from our roles as parents-to-be.

But that's okay.

I can be patient.

Chapter Twenty-Eight

Tatum

"TRY THIS ONE. THE PINEAPPLE. A CLASSIC, BUT REALLY GOOD." I add three more pieces of taffy to Jake's basket.

"Black licorice." He reads from a sign and shudders. "Nothing good ever came from black licorice."

"Not your favorite?" I ask him.

"Reminds me of Jäger." He makes a face, but he's still cute.

"Ah yes, the drink of frat boys everywhere."

"Hey, I've grown up now." Jake reads from some of the other cards attached to dozens—hundreds?—of baskets displayed around Carousel Taffy, my favorite taffy shop in Estero Bay.

"Banana split. Yes, please. Root beer. Oh, hell yes. Eggnog. I'll pass."

"Make sure you get POG. It's my favorite. Oh, and butter popcorn."

"Yes, ma'am." Jake takes our taffy to the checkout counter, pays for our sugar, and meets me at the door.

"This going to tide you over?"

"I am sure Lucy is bringing food. And if she doesn't…" I point to the backpack I am wearing. "I may have brought snacks in here, too."

Jake grins, leans in, and gives me a kiss.

Right on the mouth, right there on the Embarcadero in my hometown, right in front of everyone.

Actually, it's early November and there aren't many people around, but still.

Someone could have seen it.

And I don't care one bit.

Jake pulls away from me, giving me a crooked grin, and puts on his sunglasses. "Let's go, beautiful."

My insides do *not* turn to mush every time he uses that endearment. It's definitely indigestion on account of the tiny human I am growing inside.

We walk to Jake's Jeep, where Janet is happily waiting with the window rolled down, and drive a quick five minutes to the strand, the long, narrow beach at the north end of the Rock. It's pleasant weather—not too cool and certainly not hot and, given that it's a few weeks before the holidays begin in earnest, not crowded. I see the fog patiently waiting a few miles off the shore, and I figure we have a couple hours before it returns to town for the evening.

"There's Lucy." Jake gestures to a tiny, dark-haired figure getting out of her car in the lot.

"Do you see your sister?"

"Mm, not yet," Jake hums, glancing around the parking lot.

Shelby, Jake's sister, is coming to the beach for the weekend. Jake is going to teach her to surf, and honestly, I've never seen him so excited.

Well, his resting heart rate is "excited," but he's more excited than normal.

"Go set up with Lucy. I'll wait for Shelby in the parking lot." And Jake leans in to kiss me again across the car's center console.

Just like that. In front of everyone.

There's still no one around, but...

Someone could have seen it.

He's been doing this a lot lately—touching me constantly, kissing me even more. Almost like he's staking his claim.

And I'm not mad about it.

"What's good, baby mama?" Lucy greets me as I reach her, umbrella open and blanket laid out. She wears black leggings, a ratty black T-shirt, and a black fedora. For Lucy, this is her beach outfit.

"Does that phrase work if I'm not *your* baby mama?" I ask her.

"Not sure. Can you imagine the child we would make together?"

"They would definitely be...acerbic."

"Oooh, good word. Anyway. You are having enough baby for the both of us," she says, gesturing toward my stomach. I'm not huge—yet. Which is surprising because…

"Did you bring any food?"

Always hungry.

"Does the pope wear a funny hat?" she responds, indicating the cooler beside her. "How are you feeling? How's boy wonder?" she adds.

"I'm good. He's good," I say, feeling the corners of my mouth turn up when she asks about Jake.

"Still having all that amazing unprotected sex we mere mortals only dream about?"

I snort. "Totally none of your business, but yes, we are, and yes, it is amazing."

Lucy sighs dramatically. "Oh, to get that eggplant of a dick whenever I wanted," she says wistfully.

"Aren't you celibate?" I ask her, knowing she's teasing me.

"True. But, you know, a girl can dream. And if my vibrator inventory is any indication, I am still getting it. Just, you know, not *it*." Lucy decided to swear off men, and women, after a bad breakup. It's been a long dry spell for her.

By choice, of course.

"Oh my god, it's Ken and Barbie. And…Sophia Petrillo?" Lucy asks, referencing the character played by the late, great Estelle Getty on the *Golden Girls*.

"Who?" I turn to look in the direction of the parking lot, and sure enough, Jake—aka Ken—is walking with a tall girl with long, blond hair—Barbie. And next to Barbie is a short older woman in what I can only describe as a belted old-lady dress. The woman is tiny, shorter than Lucy, who stands about five feet tall, and small-framed. Her dress buttons up the entire front, has a belt around her little waist, and is patterned with orange, yellow, and brown flowers.

"Very autumnal," Lucy comments.

Jake's grin is wide as he makes his way toward us.

"Hi, Lucy!" He greets her the way he always does—with enthusiasm.

"Boy wonder," she murmurs, which only makes his smile grow. Jake's uncertainty about whether Lucy likes him—"not, like, in a sex-me-up way, but, like, in an 'I am okay with you knocking up my best friend' way," he explained to me—has worn off. Especially once I told him that Lucy treats most everyone the same.

Acerbically.

"This is Shelby. My sister," he adds with equal amounts pride and hesitation. "This is Tatum and Lucy."

Shelby is tall to the older woman's short, and she really does look like a swimsuit model.

Just like Jake.

Jake's dad—their dad—must have some strong lifeguard genes.

Shelby has long hair and is lean like Jake. She wears a Fresno State sweatshirt over a black wet suit. "It's so nice to meet you," she tells us softly and a little shyly.

"Hi. I'm Tatum," I tell her, offering her my hand.

"I've heard so much about you," she tells me. "Congratulations, by the way," she adds, her eyes darting briefly to my stomach.

"Thank you," I tell her, turning toward the older woman. I notice Jake has set up a beach chair for her under the umbrella and is leading her to sit down.

"I'm Chernell Jones," the woman declares. "Shelby's grandmother."

"Um, I have my learner's permit, but I can't drive without someone older than twenty-five in the car with me," Shelby explains. "I told Jake I was bringing my grandmother."

"The more, the merrier," Lucy tells Shelby.

The thing about Lucy?

She is prickly, to be sure, but she has a huge soft spot for older people. The way some people feel about babies, she feels about the elderly. She is a member of the Estero Bay Yacht Club, where the average age has got to be eighty. Never mind the fact that Lucy owns neither a yacht nor a boat nor watercraft of any kind. She is also very close with her own grandmother, Glo, who lives in a retirement home just outside Estero Bay.

"Don't mind me. I will just be reading my book while you young people go swim."

"Oh, Ms. Jones, we're not swimming," Lucy tells Shelby's grandmother. "We're going to sit on the beach and talk about other people."

"And eat," I add.

"Please, call me Chernell," Shelby's grandmother responds, visibly perking up at the thought of snacks and gossip. "And you know what I always say—if you don't have anything nice to say, come sit by me."

Lucy snickers. Shelby rolls her eyes.

"You are *literally* the nicest person I know, Gram," Shelby says, putting her hands on her hips.

"Go surf. Swim. Bond with your brother." Chernell makes a shooing motion with her hands.

"You ready?" Jake asks her. "I brought a foam surfboard for you. They're pretty forgiving for newbies."

"Let's do it," Shelby says, removing her sweatshirt.

Jake removes his own shirt, and *hoo boy*, it's one thing to see him naked during our sexcapades, but it's an entirely different thing to see him the way God intended—on a beach, his golden skin on display, his smile bright on his face, his blue eyes piercing me right through the heart as he leans over my chair and gives me another kiss.

So many kisses.

I'm unprepared.

His mouth is moving as he pulls away.

"What—what's that?" I ask him, a little breathless.

He smirks. "I asked, will you hold these for me?" he repeats, his voice low, his clean, minty smell enveloping me as he keeps leaning over me, one hand on his legs, the other handing his sunglasses to me.

"Oh! Oh. Of course," I reply like an idiot, taking his sunglasses.

Another kiss.

"Thanks, beautiful." He pulls away, regards me for a moment, and then stands up straight to grab the surfboards. The muscles in his back and shoulders flex as he pads across the sand, carrying one board under each arm.

"*Tatum.*"

"What?" Geez, is that my only response today?

"Chernell asked you a question," Lucy scolds me.

"I'm sorry. I didn't hear you. I think I'm light-headed due to hunger."

"I said, there's a remarkable likeness between Shelby and that young man of yours, isn't there?"

"There is," I agree, still ogling Jake as he walks into the water. Neptune, thy name is Jake.

"How long have you been together?" Chernell asks me.

This brings me up short, and I turn my head toward her. She sits primly in her beach chair, her knees together. I swear she is wearing pantyhose.

"We're not together," I correct her.

Chernell raises her painted-on eyebrows.

"I mean, we're having a baby," I tell her, "but we're not, like, together, together."

"Very astute," Lucy murmurs, and I shoot her a glare.

"Well, I think it's wonderful that Jake and Shelby are getting to know each other. Shelby is a sweet girl, kind and smart and sees the goodness in everyone."

"That sounds a lot like Jake," I respond automatically, checking myself when I see both Lucy and Chernell giving me a Look. "I mean, from what I know about him. We don't know each other *that* well."

Another Look.

"Anyway. What's in the cooler?"

Chapter Twenty-Nine

Jake

"THAT STORY IS *NOT TRUE*, NICK ECHEVERRIA. I'VE NEVER SHED a tear a day in my life, and you know it."

That is from Lucy, who is giving Nick Echeverria—I suppose I can just call him Nick now—a look that would make many grown men weep. He just stares at her stoically and holds up his right hand.

"Hand to God," he says in a deep voice from where he is seated directly across from me. "You may not cry now, but you definitely did when you had that six Band-Aid bicycle crash."

"I was five!" Lucy exclaims two seats down from Nick, Summer between them.

"Still happened," he responds, before taking a pull from his Corona. His other arm is wrapped securely around Summer's shoulders; she's trying hard not to laugh at Lucy's outrage, but it's a losing battle.

Is it weird that I am having dinner with my secret half-sister, her grandmother, my one-night stand who also happens to be the mother of my unborn child, and her entire family?

Or is it weirder still that I am enjoying every minute of it?

After I spent the afternoon in and out of the water with Shelby, the fog started to roll back in. Tatum invited us to go to the Brew for dinner, promising something call "the full setup." And here we are, at two long tables pushed together—Tatum, me, Shelby, Chernell, Nick, Summer, Lucy, and Tatum's mom, grandfather, and two nieces, Sarah and Violet. We've been fed by Julia and her husband, Lincoln. So far, I've had soup, beans, salsa—the three of those all mixed together, by the way—garlic fried chicken, spaghetti, and French fries.

And an entire loaf of bread.

"I'm so full," Summer says, placing her napkin over her plate.

"But we haven't even had the blue cheese," Tatum reminds her. "Actually, I don't think I'm supposed to eat that," she adds, frowning.

"If it's pasteurized, I think you are okay," I tell her confidently.

Tatum looks at me strangely, as do Lucy and Summer.

"I read it in the baby book," I add sheepishly.

"Hmph. Well, I'll ask Julia if it's pasteurized when she comes back." Tatum looks devastated at the thought of not eating blue cheese.

"Auntie Tatum, you can have more of my French fries," her niece Violet tells her from where she sits on Tatum's other side. She is seven years old and has pretty much eaten as much as I have.

"Oh, that is nice of you. French fries make everything better," Tatum tells her.

"Amen to that," Summer adds.

"Will you teach me how to surf, too?" Violet asks, rapidly changing the subject and turning toward me.

"Well, sure. If your parents say it's okay," I tell her.

"Summer taught me how to do the yoga," she explains. "So now you can teach me how to surf."

"She's quite the little fish," Tatum tells me. "Impossible to get her out of the water, no matter how cold it is."

"Do you have a wet suit?" I ask Violet.

"Yup! We practice putting it on at lifeguard camp. Whoever gets it on first gets to run into the water first," she adds.

"That sounds like...not a great prize," Lucy pontificates from across the table.

"You're not supposed to pee in your wet suit," Violet continues seriously.

"Oh my gosh, *Violet*," her older sister, Sarah, groans from beside her.

"Thank you for telling me," I say to Violet just as seriously.

"But I think it's okay if you pee in the ocean. Uncle Nick told me it's like God's bathroom."

"Uncle *Nick*," Sarah now groans. Nick's ears pinken at Violet's revelation, and he shrugs, looking innocently at Tatum before shooting Violet a wink.

"Blue cheese!" Violet is off on another subject when Julia brings several plates filled with—you guessed it—large wedges of blue cheese.

"None for you, mama," she tells Tatum. "It's not pasteurized."

"Told you," I tell Tatum with a smile, draping my arm over the back of her chair.

"Damn," she mutters. "More French fries, it is."

"Looks like your grandfather and Chernell are getting along," I tell her, looking toward the end of the table where Shelby, Elaine, Chernell, and Antone—Tatum's grandfather—are chatting.

"They're cute," Tatum muses. "Chernell is a hoot."

"Yeah? What'd you young ladies chat about while we were in the water?"

"Nothing of consequence…" Tatum's voice trails off. I glance over and see her face is pale.

"What is it?" I ask. She doesn't respond, and her eyes are directed toward the front of the restaurant.

"What is it? Are you okay?" I look down at her stomach, as if that could tell me something.

"I'm fine. I feel fine. It's nothing," she responds in a low monotone, her gaze still transfixed on the front of the restaurant. I look and see nothing out of the ordinary; the hostess is walking a small family to a booth.

I look back to Tatum and see her eyes tracking the family—a man, a woman, and a small child on the woman's hip.

"The audacity," Lucy mutters across from us, having followed Tatum's gaze.

"What?" Summer asks from beside Lucy. Her eyes dart where we are all looking and widen slightly. "Oh. *Oh,*" she says.

"What is it, Sunshine?" Nick asks her in a low voice. She responds quietly, too quietly for me to hear. Nick's face darkens, his brow furrowed as he shoots a glare at the family.

Or, more specifically, at the man.

And then I think I understand—

This man is something to Tatum.

Or *was* something.

I automatically don't like him.

Tatum

It's a truth universally acknowledged that we all will make a bad decision at some point.

Maybe many bad decisions, plural.

You live. You learn. You move on, you rise above, you do a million other clichés, and hopefully you wind up on the other side of the mountain smarter, wiser, and better equipped to avoid cheating, lying sociopaths in the future.

At least, that was *my* particular lesson.

My spectacularly bad decision is here, in my sister's restaurant, in the flesh. He *knows* it's my sister's restaurant. Not because we ever came here together; in fact, he was very careful that none of our excursions would be local. No, he knows it's my sister's restaurant because I mentioned it. I talked to him about Julia and Lincoln and my nieces. I talked to him about my mother, my grandfather. I shared with him my concerns about Nick—a pre-Summer Nick who had just left the NFL in devastating fashion after a brutal injury and sudden divorce. I cried to him about my big brother, about my concerns that he would never recover, at least not emotionally or mentally, that he would never be the brother I once knew.

I shared truths with this man that I've only shared with a few other people in my life. I did this with the false impression that he was special, that I was special, that *we* were special. I shared my body with him, sure, but my body is the least interesting thing about me. I shared my innermost thoughts and my fears about the future.

I was vulnerable.

And this man just shit all over everything.

The issue wasn't that he didn't share back and didn't allow himself to be vulnerable in the way that I was. Although, that was a red flag I was only too happy to overlook.

The issue wasn't that he didn't express any interest in meeting my friends or family. Not even my brother—and let's be honest, more than one football fanatic has feigned an interest in me romantically in a bid to meet my brother.

The issue with this man—Trevor is his name, although he lives in my head now as Dr. Douche—is that he was very much married.

Something I was totally oblivious to until he told me that his wife was pregnant.

And he was the father.

Now, Dr. Douche and Mrs. Douche—who might be a lovely woman, for all I know—are here at my sister's restaurant with what must be the fruits of their labor, a cherubic, towheaded young child held on her mother's hip.

And I am here with my twenty-three-year-old one-night stand. And I am pregnant with *his* baby.

I think I might barf.

"Auntie, you look like you might barf," Violet comments to me in a worried tone. "Do you want me to get you a bowl from the kitchen? I like to keep a bowl with me when I feel like I might barf."

"Who is that, Tatum?" Jake murmurs on my other side. His arm rests behind me along the top of the chair, his fingers clenching slightly around my shoulder.

"It's no one." *Just a bad decision.*

"I can hold your hair if you're going to throw up," Violet says from my other side.

"*Violet,*" Sarah groans next to her. "No one is throwing up." Sarah leans forward, her brow furrowed in concern. "You're not throwing up, right?"

"No one is throwing up," I echo her statement. "Although, if I keep going with the setup," I continue, referring to the full Basque meal we've spent an hour eating, "I might split the seam of these pants."

"Are they stretchy?" Lucy asks from across the table. Her voice is casual, but her expression says *I am ready to do murder if you need me to.*

Not so different from her usual expression, then.

"They are stretchy. They have this great panel in the front that stretches as I…stretch," I respond. *No murder. At least, not yet,* I tell her with my eyes.

"Neat." Lucy bites into a piece of fried chicken with gusto.

Jake's been watching Lucy and me trade comments across the table. He suspiciously eyes Dr. Douche, who is now sitting on the other side of the restaurant in a booth, before bringing his gaze back to me. "Do you want to bounce?" he asks.

"Yeah. Yeah, I think I do," I tell him, suddenly so tired. "But let's ask Julia if we can have some fresh bread to go," I add.

I'm tired and displeased at seeing Dr. Douche, but I'm no dummy.

Bread will make everything better.

The telltale pressure in my lower abdomen informs me there is no way I can make it the fifteen minutes back to St. Bishop's without a pit stop. I look across the table at Lucy and Summer.

"Gonna use the ladies' before we go. Come with me?"

"I'm just saying, Tatum," Lucy says from the sink where she's washing her hands, "we could get Julia to casually slip something in his meal."

"No way," I tell her, meeting her eyes in the mirror. "Knowing who he is, he'd get the health department to shut down the restaurant if he got so much as indigestion."

Lucy scoffs. "Well, I don't like him being here. He never once came here when you two were together," she continues, ignoring my wince—*so many red flags,* "so why the hell is he here now?"

"Doesn't he live in north county?" Summer adds.

"He does. Or at least, he did. And honestly, I don't know why. Maybe they're having a nice day on the bay. Maybe he totally forgot my family's connection to this restaurant."

Lucy snorts. "Doubtful."

"It's not like we've communicated at all since the breakup. I mean, I haven't talked to him in almost two years." I dry my hands before using the towel to mop up the excess water on the bathroom sink. "I don't think he means anything by it. And in his warped mind, there's nothing wrong with visiting the restaurant owned by your side piece's family. It's just in his DNA—nothing he does is wrong."

"Woof. Sounds like Erik," Summer shudders, referencing the man she spent nearly a decade married to before returning to Estero Bay and linking back up with Nick.

I shudder right along with her. Erik honestly makes Dr. Douche look tame.

"They are birds of a feather, for sure," I tell her.

"Please," Lucy interjects, holding up her hand. "I only have so much room in my head to hold space for underwhelming, unimpressive tools who think they are God's gift to the earth simply because they were born with penises."

"But there are *so many* of them," I tell her plaintively.

Lucy gives an uncharacteristic grin at that, her dark eyes flashing in amusement. "No doubt. But you know who *doesn't* fall into that category?" She jerks a thumb toward the door. "Your young Romeo out there."

"Who looked ready to do battle with Dr. Douche, by the way," Summer adds, crossing her arms over her chest. "Kinda hot."

"Totally hot," Lucy agrees.

"You don't have to give me a speech about how I deserve to get laid. You already did that," I tell Lucy. "In another bathroom, I might add."

"You really do your best pep talks in bathrooms, don't you?" Summer asks her.

"Whatever. Go out there to your youngster and his swinging dick," Lucy instructs me. "Tell him what he needs to know, have an orgasm or two, and forget that you ever saw hide or hair of Dr. Douche."

I pause before exiting. "You don't think—"

"Beg to differ," Lucy interrupts me.

"I was so blind with Trevor. *So blind*," I tell them, shutting my eyes briefly. I'm embarrassed at how I ignored all those red flags.

"I know to do better, for sure. But instead of doing better, I'm having a baby with a guy I barely even know. How is that…how is that *better*?" I throw my hands up in exasperation.

"Who's to say it's not?" Summer asks me pointedly. She narrows her brown eyes at me. "I seem to recall a certain someone questioning whether it was the best idea to enter into a serious relationship with Nick so soon after getting divorced."

Ugh, that was me.

"That was you," Lucy confirms with an evil grin.

"I know, I know," I mumble.

"All I'm saying is, you have these rigid ideas of what's appropriate behavior in relationships. How old we need to be when we do x, y, and z. How long of a break we need to take in between relationships. When it's appropriate to jump your best friend's older brother when the two of you are horny and lonely on a boat in the middle of Estero Bay," she adds the last sentence with a wicked smile, referring to her, Nick, and I don't even want to know what else.

"I don't need to hear about your sexytimes with my brother," I groan, placing my hands on my protruding stomach to shield the baby from this epic grossness.

"Why do you have these preconceived ideas?" Summer asks rhetorically, as if I haven't spoken. She shakes her head, her long, coppery hair flowing around her shoulders. "I don't know! And guess what, Tatum?" she asks me.

"Um, what?" I'm afraid of her answer.

Summer's sweet, but once she's on a roll, there's no hope for you.

"*You* don't know either. So you got knocked up by a younger man. So what?! He's obviously into you. Don't ignore it just because you think it doesn't align with what's 'right' or 'appropriate' when it comes to relationships."

"She's using air quotes," Lucy whispers to me theatrically. "I think that's not good."

"Okay. Okay!" I tell her hastily. "I hear you."

"Do you?" Summer asks me seriously. "Just…go with the flow."

I shake my shoulders dramatically. "Literally breaking out in hives as you say that."

Summer rolls her eyes. "Don't be so dramatic. Go be with your man. *Be* with him," she adds emphatically.

"I'm going! I'm going," I mutter, more to myself than her, as I exit the restroom and make a beeline to where Jake stands next to the table, chatting with his sister. I avoid looking anywhere in the vicinity of where Dr. Douche is sitting.

"Proud of you, butterfly," I hear Lucy tell Summer as they follow behind me. "The student has now become the master."

Chapter Thirty

I LIKE TO THINK I'M A PATIENT DUDE.

I'm not aggressive. I don't like conflict. I am pretty amiable, most of the time.

But the more I see how…*off* Tatum is as we leave the restaurant, drive back to St. Bishop's, and get to her house, the more I wish I had done things differently.

Demanded to know who that smooth-looking older man was at the Brew. Demanded to know what he did to make Tatum less of herself.

And yes, maybe punched him in the face.

I bet Nick Echeverria would have helped me. And I wouldn't fuck with that guy.

"I can take Janet out," I tell Tatum now, tossing my keys on her kitchen counter. Shelby and Chernell are staying the night at my rental. The rental that, to be honest, I've used less and less the more time I spend with Tatum.

"Actually, can we take her for a walk together?" Tatum asks me, looking up from where she's been scratching her dog behind the ears. "I want to tell you about…some stuff, and I think it'll be easier for me if we are doing something else."

"Like picking up dog shit," I offer.

Tatum smiles understandingly. A little bit of the weight lifts off my shoulders. "Like picking up dog shit."

Janet, mercifully, handles her business less than a block from Tatum's house.

She's now happy to casually walk with us through downtown. We stroll past the old barbecue joint, a few Italian restaurants, some dive bars, the art gallery. It's quiet out, although I know from experience that around eleven p.m., this place will be crawling with college students out for a night on the town.

Literally one year ago, that would've been me, pregaming at my shitty rental with my fraternity brothers, before heading out to one of the college bars, before eating my weight in grease, before passing out around three a.m.

It feels like a lifetime ago.

"So." Tatum interrupts my train of thought, and I look at her. She's focused straight ahead, not making eye contact. "You may have guessed that I saw someone I knew at the Brew. *Used* to know. Or thought I knew. Shit," Tatum mumbles this last part, blinking and shaking her head.

"Tatum." We are holding hands, and I give hers a little squeeze. "It's okay, whatever it is. I'm not going to lo—respect you any less," I tell her, catching myself before I make a declaration neither of us is ready for.

At least, Tatum's definitely not ready for.

"So, I dated this guy. Trevor."

I hate him.

"He was there, you may have seen. Light-brown hair, polo shirt?"

I nod, my jaw tight.

I hate him and his stupid polo shirt.

"You also may have seen that he was there with his wife and…their child."

Not that I want to hear about how this guy broke Tatum's heart so many years ago, but she needs to get it off her chest. "So, I am guessing a bad breakup between you two."

"Yeah. But even before then, there were… I should have seen it coming. I should have been more suspicious."

I'm not following, but I let her continue.

"He never wanted to meet my friends. He never met my friends, Jake. Can you believe that?"

I am about to respond that, no, I honestly can't believe that, because

Tatum is clearly a package deal with Lucy, Summer, and her family, and I imagine she's always been that way. But Tatum continues.

"He never wanted to go anywhere around town. No Sidecar. No Giuseppe's. He never wanted to go to Estero Bay—like, my favorite place ever. He never wanted to go hiking with me, unless it was farther from town. He never even wanted to go get taffy with me."

"Okay…" I tell her slowly, still not sure I'm following.

"Because he was hiding something," she tells me forcefully, stopping on the sidewalk near a park downtown, and turning to face me.

I look down into her hazel eyes, sadness and regret in their depths. "Hiding…"

"Hiding the fact that he was married."

My head snaps up, and I unconsciously take a step back. "Married— but you… When did you date this guy?"

Tatum's head drops, her focus on the concrete. "We broke up a little less than two years ago."

I open my mouth, shut it. Think about years and time and math, and you know what, it was never my strongest subject.

But I have a suspicion…

"How did you find out he was married?"

"He told me," Tatum begins, her voice wobbly, and she pauses before continuing. "He told me that his wife was pregnant. That they'd actually been trying for a baby for a little while. And that—" she stops again, visibly gathering her emotions "—that he was so excited to be a father, but he hoped we could still—" she sniffles and clears her throat "—hoped we could still spend time together." Tatum raises her head, jutting out her chin defiantly, her eyes threatening to spill over. "He still wanted me as his side piece." She squeezes her eyes shut, and the tears make quick paths down her cheeks.

"Hey, hey, hey," I murmur, grabbing Janet's leash from Tatum's hand. I gather Tatum close to me, as close as I can, and wrap my arms around her. She nestles her head right under mine.

Her back shakes with her sobs as she cries into my sweatshirt. This woman, the smartest, prettiest, sexiest woman I've ever met—she's reduced to tears because of some fucking asshole who, I am sure, was never worth her time in the first place, his marriage notwithstanding.

What idiot *wouldn't* want to take Tatum anywhere she wants to go?

What moron *wouldn't* want to show Tatum off?

What absolute dipshit wouldn't realize how lucky he is to have her, even for a little while?

Although I hate the guy, I can understand why he would ask to keep Tatum.

Once you've had the best, you can never go back.

"It's okay, beautiful. Tatum, it's okay," are the only things I can think of to say as I rub her back. "It's okay."

And it *is* okay.

Because while Trevor sounds like a lower life form, his loss is my gain.

Tatum is to be treasured, not hidden. And I'll do my best to ensure she never feels so low again.

Chapter Thirty-One

Tatum

AFTER UNLOADING ON JAKE—FIGURATIVELY, BY SHARING A portion of my past I would rather not discuss, and literally, by leaving a trail of snot and tears on his sweatshirt—I am exhausted.

I feel like I could sleep for a year. Which is nothing new.

We make it back to my place, my sanctuary, and I engage in my routine. I water my plants. I sweep the kitchen. I wash my face and moisturize and apply cocoa butter to my belly, which supposedly will help with the stretch marks, but we'll see.

I brush my teeth and blink once, twice, before thinking I might actually pass out here at the sink.

I hear Jake call Janet to her dog bed, and I smile. We've got quite the little thing going here—Jake's toothbrush is in the holder next to mine. His clothes are in my overflowing closet. His Rainbows are lined up on the porch. He rinses and hangs his wet suit on the porch railing as soon as he gets back from surfing.

I don't hate any of it.

I turn off the bathroom light and shuffle to my bedroom, all but falling face first onto my pillow.

"You okay?" Jake asks from where he is already under the covers, shirtless, his hands tucked behind his head, his blue eyes etched in concern.

"I'm fine," I tell him, shaking my head in contradiction to my words.

Just…how did this become my life? This hot man, the father of my child, in bed next to me like we are an old married couple?

Jake gives me a crooked smile. "Come here."

I turn away from him so we can do the spoon thing—he's always the big spoon—and yawn. "I don't know why I am so tired all the time."

Jake hums into my hair. His chest vibrates against me, pressed right up close against my back. His smell envelops me, like the ocean and mint from his toothpaste. "You're growing another person inside your body. Like…like a parasite," he offers.

I snort a laugh. "That's super disturbing. And don't call our baby a parasite," I say before I can think about it.

Our baby.

I haven't really given voice to that aspect of this whole thing. I am forever gesturing to my stomach or talking around it or using dumb euphemisms.

But it is our baby.

Our little parasite.

Jake tightens his hold around me and hums again. "*Our* baby is perfect," he murmurs, and I melt a little.

I also have a little indigestion, and something flutters in my stomach. Or is it…

"Oh!" I jerk instinctively as I feel the fluttering again.

I feel Jake lift his head up from his pillow. "What's up?"

"I think—" Another rumble. "I think the baby is kicking," I tell him quietly, concerned that if I say it out loud, the movement will stop.

"No shit?!" Jake says excitedly, and he adjusts his position behind me. "Are you sure? Are you okay? Can I get you something?"

I smile at his enthusiasm. "I am fine," I tell him, and this time, I do *not* shake my head.

"Come here," I add, taking one of his hands and draping it along the bottom part of my bump, where I had the feeling a moment ago. "Let's see…oh!" I turn my head to the left to see Jake staring down at my stomach. "Did you feel that?"

He keeps his gaze down, away from my face. He doesn't respond for a moment, and when he does, it sounds like he has pebbles in his throat. "Yeah. I felt it."

I fall asleep with Jake's arms securely around me, one hand resting like a guard on my stomach.

Part IV

The Third Trimester

Chapter Thirty-Two

Jake

AS A PREGNANT PERSON PREPARES FOR BIRTH, THEY ENTER A period called "nesting."

I admittedly have not been around very many pregnant people in my life. Not before Tatum.

Nesting is kind of what it sounds like—getting the space ready for the baby. Making sure the towels are folded, the laundry is washed and hung up, the bottles and nipples and pacifiers and diapers—*so many diapers*—are put in their proper place.

Here's the thing, though. So far as I can tell, Tatum was already a nester before she got pregnant. She's neat. She likes things orderly. She enjoys a good deep cleaning. She takes everything out of her refrigerator, cleans the entire refrigerator, and puts everything back once a month.

Once a month.

I'm sure I don't have to tell you how many times such a task was completed in the house I rented with my four buddies less than a year ago.

That would be zero.

Tatum even washes and disinfects *the trash cans.* The kind that sit on the curb, the kind that smell, the kind that opossums and raccoons and who knows what else like to get all up in.

This ultra-nesting phase has essentially turned Tatum into a heightened version of herself.

And don't get me wrong—I am a huge fan of Tatum and all her personas.

But as I sit here, watching her obsessively remove every single store tag, sticker, and piece of tissue from baby clothes, while also reviewing her many, many Google sheets listing everything to do before the baby comes—I wonder if there's something I can do.

Something to take the load off.

"Here you go," I say as I enter the nursery, placing a giant tumbler filled with ice water and cucumber slices on a coaster.

Of course, on a coaster.

I know who the mother of my child is.

"Thank you," Tatum says, her eyes rapidly scanning something on the laptop computer delicately balanced on her stomach. Janet lies on the rug next to her—a beautiful, cream-and-aqua rug we purchased to go with the other colors in the room. Turquoise, aqua, and other light blue colors fill the space. Tatum says we are going for an underwater, ocean theme, which works fine for me.

Julia said to make sure we don't get baby crap on the rug, a solid piece of advice if I ever heard one.

At eight months pregnant, Tatum has a full-fledged human being inside her, one that kicks, somersaults, and causes quite a bit of heartburn.

My kid has wicked energy.

I smile at her and give a quick perusal of the nursery. Nick Echeverria—I really just have to start calling him Nick now—and Julia's husband, Lincoln, came to help me get it ready. We built a crib, moved old furniture out, moved new furniture in, and basically performed many tasks that made me feel like a worthwhile contributor to this process of bringing a child into the world.

Aside from…you know. My initial contribution.

"Can I help you do something?" I ask Tatum, kneeling on the floor in front of her. She's seated in a padded rocking chair, one we both tested at the furniture store to make sure we liked it. And I've got to say, that lumbar support is something else.

"Noooo, no, I think I'm okay," Tatum says distractedly, eyes still glued to whatever spreadsheet or checklist she's reviewing now.

"Do you want to eat something before we go? Or just wait until we get there?"

This gets her attention. "Yes. I mean, what? What time is it?"

"It's 10:30, and we should leave here at noon for the shower," I tell her.

The shower is the baby shower, which is being held this afternoon at the Estero Bay Yacht Club. Apparently Lucy has some sort of cache there.

Honestly, not surprising.

Although she doesn't seem the most nautical person.

"Well then, food, definitely. We definitely need food. And I should probably shower." Tatum shuts the laptop and places it on the side table next to the chair. "Help me up?" she asks.

She lets out a grunt as I grip her hands in mine and help her to stand. "Jesus," she mutters, rubbing her lower back. "You'd think I ran a marathon."

"Remember the parasite," I tell her innocently.

She glares at me. "Jake. Our angel baby is…well, an angel." She pauses and waggles her eyebrows.

"Wanna watch me take a shower?"

I smirk.

Hell yeah, I do.

Sex with an eight-months-pregnant woman is not without its challenges.

Not because I am turned off by the thought of having sex with Tatum. I still think she's as fucking fantastic as ever. I don't mean to sound crass, but her breasts are absolutely enormous. I could spend hours, days, months happily playing with her tits and die a happy man.

After all, I'm just a man.

Her curves are plentiful, her lips are plump, and her skin is glowing and warm.

She's still perfect, in my eyes.

But to get hypertechnical, the logistics of placing my P in her V are difficult. We last attempted penetrative sex a couple weeks ago, and it was like the most awkward threesome ever. I could see the baby moving around in her stomach, which…was cool and wonderful and the miracle of life is amazing, et cetera, but it was also a little distracting.

That distraction magically evaporated when Tatum got on all fours and let me fuck her from behind.

The whole shower thing started as an accident—just like this pregnancy. Zing! Tatum's claw-footed bathtub requires someone with shorter limbs to really lift their foot to step into the tub. Tatum has shorter limbs, so for the last month or so, she has needed my help stepping into the tub.

Which, let's be clear, I am happy to provide.

Naked Tatum?

Sign me the fuck up.

But the last time I helped her into the tub so she could shower, I didn't leave. I just…stayed. Like a creeper.

Tatum pulled the shower curtain around the tub, and I leaned against the pink bathroom counter, hearing the normal sounds of a normal shower.

The snap of the shampoo bottle cap.

The pitter-patter of water hitting porcelain.

The sigh from Tatum's mouth as she washed her body.

Or whatever she was doing. I'm really not sure.

But in my brain, she was washing her body.

Slowly, letting the soap lovingly caress her skin, lifting her breasts to the showerhead…

You see where I am going with this.

Those innocuous sounds, combined with the sweet vanilla smell of her body wash, the steam in the air, the mirror fogging up like a car windshield does when two people are making out…

Well, it made me hard.

Like I said—

I'm just a man.

"Are you still out there?" Tatum called to me over the sound of the shower.

"Yep!" I squeaked, immediately clearing my throat. "I mean, yes. Hi. I'm here."

"What are you doing?" Tatum asked with a smile in her voice.

"Honestly, I am imagining what you are doing behind that curtain."

Tatum cackled a laugh, like she couldn't believe how goddamn funny I was. "Sexy things, man, let me tell you. You know," she continued, "everyone tells you that when you get so far along, you can't see your feet. But that's bullshit. Because if I just crane my neck forward a little bit—" at this, she flung open the shower curtain, giving me a view of Naked, Wet Tatum "—I see my feet just fine."

"Uh-huh," I replied distractedly, clenching the bathroom counter while I tried not to get a full-on erection. Are her breasts even bigger now? Her nipples are darker than they were when we first got together.

"See?" Tatum asked expectantly, and I jerked my head up to her face. Whatever she saw there had her chuckling. "Really?"

"Really, what?"

"You have a look like, you know."

"I don't know. What?"

"Like you want to bone down." Tatum thrust her hips as best she could with the extra weight attached to her stomach, making her breasts sway obscenely. I clenched my teeth to keep from groaning out loud.

"You know what I can't see, though?" Tatum continued talking, leaning back to rinse her hair under the showerhead, putting her body on full display.

"Uh-huh?" I grunted, trying my best to maintain composure.

"My pussy," Tatum replied, and I nearly choked.

"What?"

"I. Can't. See. My. Pussy," Tatum spoke slowly, like she was talking to a child. "My stomach is too big. I can't prop a leg up to see what's going on in the ol' undercarriage. No one told me that. You think Julia would have given me a heads-up, like, hey, there will come a point in time when your snatch might be a foreign land—"

I didn't give Tatum a chance to finish her speech, because I pushed off the counter, shoved down my boxer shorts, and got into that fucking shower like my ass was on fire.

"Jake!" Tatum's hazel eyes widened, but she laughed as I rinsed my head in the water. "What are you doing?"

I leaned in to give her a kiss, softly caressing her lips, moving my hands to feel her heavy breasts. I held them gently as I pulled away and met her eyes.

"I see it just fine," I told her softly, before kneeling in the bathtub. Let me tell you, that shit is not the most comfortable thing in the entire world, but I was motivated.

"What are you doing?" Tatum repeated, her smile fading as I stroked one hand up her leg to cup her center. She gasped and flung her hands up, as if looking for something to grab on to.

"I see your pussy just fine," I told her, feeling how wet and warm she was. "Want me to tell you what I see?" I asked her with a smirk, looking up to see her lips parted and her skin flushed, and not just from the steam.

"No, no, I don't want... Oh fuck, Jake, that feels good," she moaned as I let my fingers part her and play with her.

"It looks good," I replied, teasing her folds, skirting around her clit. "Let's see if it tastes as good as it looks."

There's no way Tatum could have put her foot on the ledge to allow me easy access, but she widened her feet as best she could. "Good. So good, beautiful." I leaned in to get a taste, and I didn't know if it was the shower or the pregnancy hormones, but my girl was unbelievably wet.

"You taste amazing, Tatum," I whispered, so softly she might not have been able to hear me. But as I lapped at her, as I licked her, as I stroked and flicked and sucked, I definitely heard her. And when she followed my instructions and came all over my mouth, I savored every last drop.

And she tasted fucking delicious.

Tatum

When I ask him if he wants to watch me take a shower, Jake's face lights up like a Christmas tree.

I have a healthy relationship with my body. I respect it, and I am thankful it can do the things I want it to do.

But Jake has been a little obsessed with my body as it's changed over the past several months. And I won't lie, it's good for my ego.

"Hell yeah," he mutters, ushering me quickly into the bathroom. Janet lifts her head to watch us leave and then goes right back to dreamland.

I start the shower, letting the water get just right, and undress. It's freezing; this winter has been cold and uncharacteristically wet for central California. My feet are like ice on my bathroom tile, and the sensation creeps up the back of my legs. I don't hesitate to take Jake's proffered hand and step into the shower.

"Oooohhhh," I sigh as the warm water skates over my skin.

"Kinda get jealous when you make those noises," I hear Jake say from behind me.

I give him a little shake of my hips—at least, the best I can, given this person who has taken over the entire front of my body—and shut the shower curtain.

Jake says nothing, and I say nothing as I go about washing my hair, using my favorite shampoo. I give the occasional sigh of contentment as I rinse, shave my armpits—the only place I've been shaving lately—and use my conditioner.

I peek my head out of the shower curtain, anticipating seeing Jake half hard and his eyes half-mast with arousal. But instead, he's serious. Serious for him, anyway.

He smiles casually at me as I poke my head out.

"Are we—are we not fooling around?" I ask, confused.

"Tatum, I love you," he says quietly.

Well.

That is not what I was expecting.

I open my mouth slightly, not really sure what's going to come out, but he beats me to it.

"I know you're not going to say it back. I know you don't feel the same way, at least not the way I feel about you. And that's fine." Still the smile.

Does this man ever stop smiling?

Instead, I stand there, with my giant stomach and my giant breasts, in front of this man who has carved a giant hole in my heart with his giant dick.

"That's fine," he repeats, holding up his hands to assuage me. "I just wanted you to know."

I manage to close my mouth. I think of water conservation efforts and turn around to shut off the water.

And I turn back to him, thinking that perhaps the only logical thing to tell him is the truth.

I hold out my hand to his, palm up, the same way he's done to me a million times. He grabs my towel in one hand and takes my hand in the other, before carefully helping me step out of the tub.

I keep my eyes on him the entire time so he can see I am definitely *not* freaking out and definitely *not* thinking of how exactly I am going to relay this conversation to Lucy and Summer later.

I secure my towel around myself and take his hand again.

"Thank you for telling me," I say honestly. I lean in to give him a kiss, hoping that I can express with my lips what I am not ready to say. I hold his jaw in my hands, feeling the strength there, breathing in his scent.

I suppose that in any other situation, this might be awkward. *Man declares love; recipient does not return his affection!*

But I remember what Summer told me at the Brew late last year.

Go with the flow.

Okay, that's a nonstarter for me.

But perhaps I can just accept this for what it is. Accept that Jake loves me, against all odds, and enjoy this moment.

I move away from his lips and rest my forehead against his, sighing and closing my eyes.

I can do this.

"You're welcome," Jake says gruffly.

Chapter Thirty-Three

Tatum

THE BABY SHOWER IS BEING HELD AT THE ESTERO BAY YACHT CLUB, which is Lucy's home away from home.

I can't remember how my friend, who doesn't really like to swim, doesn't own a boat, and favors Doc Martens over Sperrys, got involved with the yacht club. The median age leans toward eighty, but Lucy says if she leaves, they'll have no one to do their books, so she insists on staying.

The yacht club hasn't changed in my lifetime, and probably since before then too. It's brown. Very brown. Brown wood paneling on the walls, brown floors, brown round tables. Sawdust covers the floor, or at least it once did, as it looks pretty sparse now. Even though it's almost two months into the new year, I still see glitter and "Happy New Year" confetti mixed in with the sawdust. A few yellow and aqua balloons are on display on a table next to the cupcakes Lucy made, lemon blueberry with a lemon buttercream frosting, if she followed my instructions. There's also a very subdued sign that reads, in gold lettering, "CONGRATULATIONS. YOU MADE A BABY."

The view in this place can't be beat. The building sits on the north end of the Embarcadero, and the entire west side consists of large windows. Estero Rock looms outside, watching over the jetty, the bay, and the boats dotting the smooth water. That is, if it's not foggy. On a foggy day, you can't make out the Rock at all.

Such is today, a late February, gloomy, misty day. The jagged bottom of the Rock is visible in the distance, walkers and cyclists taking their exercise around its circumference. The water is gray glass, an otter occasionally popping up, a few fishermen resting their poles on the wooden fence along the dock. It's quiet and peaceful outside.

Inside the Estero Bay Yacht Club?

Not so much.

"More diapers!" I say gleefully as I unwrap another large package.

"There are a *lot* of diapers," Jake echoes.

"Trust me, not enough," Lincoln calls from one of the round tables. "I never appreciated the digestive system until I had a kid."

"That means I pooped a lot," Violet tells me matter-of-factly. She has offered to be in charge of writing down who gifts what, although, given her seven-year-old penmanship, we also have Summer as backup.

"Sarah too," Violet adds helpfully.

As if on cue, Sarah groans from where she sits next to her father. Such is the life of a preteen, always embarrassed by the younger sibling.

"Everybody poops," Lucy calls helpfully from another table. "Isn't that a book you already got?"

"Sure is," Jake responds, rummaging through another bag and holding up the book.

"And another book," I continue, opening more wrapping paper. "*On the Day You Were Born,*" I read aloud.

"Oh boy," Lincoln says, turning to Julia next to him and wrapping his arm around her shoulders. At the same time, Sarah groans again—of course—and Violet shrieks with glee. Julia just smiles.

"What?" I ask them.

"It's my favorite book," Julia tells me. "I read it to the girls approximately five million times. And I cried every single time. Still do."

"Still does," Lincoln confirms.

"It's like the *Velveteen Rabbit,* then!" Summer chimes in from the next table over. "You know, an automatic tearjerker at any age," she clarifies, to Nick's confused expression.

"I don't think I've read the *Velveteen Rabbit,*" he admits.

"Well, you will, and you will cry. Guarantee it," she predicts.

"That's kind of a low bar," Lucy says. "Nick's really in touch with his emotions."

"Not a lie," he concedes diplomatically.

"Will *I* cry?" Lucy asks.

Summer bites her lip and considers Lucy, clad in black from head to toe, thoughtfully. "Does your body produce tears?" she asks innocently.

"Doctors have wondered," she responds.

"All I'm saying is," Lincoln interjects, "*that* book—" he gestures toward the one in my hands "—makes Julia cry even now."

"I obviously don't read it as much as I did when they were toddlers," Julia adds, "but when I do, *whoosh*," she says, touching her temples. "It's very emotional. It might also be because it was, like, *the* book I relied on when they were little. Our go-to book."

"Can I see it?" Sarah asks, and I hand it to Jake, who hands it off to her.

"The next one is my go-to book," Lincoln tells me.

Sure enough, there is one more book in the pile, and I read the title and burst out laughing before handing it to Jake.

"Which one's that?" my mother asks from where she sits next to Nick.

"*Go the…*" Jake pauses, eyeing Violet next to me "…*Bleep to Sleep.*"

"Now, that sounds like more my style," Lucy declares.

"You said a bad word!" Violet exclaims.

"I didn't!" Jake insists.

Julia is laughing along with me. "Yeah, there were tears with that book too. For a different reason."

"Because kids don't sleep," Lincoln explains. "I mean, you already know that," he adds, gesturing to me because, yes, I was very much around and aware of how neither Sarah nor Violet had much interest in sleeping, ever.

"You *read* this to me?" Violet asks incredulously, flipping through the pages. "But Daddy, there are really bad words in here."

"Well, I just bleeped them," Lincoln responds sheepishly. "It was more of a suggestion than anything else."

"Hmm," Violet responds, her eyes growing wider as she turns each page, her mouth forming the words silently.

"To be fair," I interject, "*you* taught me all the good curse words before I finished kindergarten." I nod to my older sister. "So I don't think this book made a big difference on their…language abilities."

"Julia Echeverria Cruz," my mother says in mock outrage. "Is this true?"

"Damn right it is," Nick mutters loud enough for us all to hear. My mom playfully scolds him, nudging his shoulder.

"Well, thank you both for both of these books," I tell Julia and Lincoln. "We will have tissues at the ready."

"For both of them," Jake adds.

"This one is from Miss Chernell," Violet tells me, handing over a large yellow gift bag.

"Oh, you didn't have to get us anything," I tell Chernell, who is seated at another table with Shelby and my grandfather. My grandfather, who asked several times if Chernell was going to be here today, I might add.

Jake has spent more time with Shelby over the past several months, and he invited her and her grandmother to come today. Shelby has been quiet—I think she might be a little overwhelmed by the whole family—but she's very sweet and obviously so happy to have Jake as a big brother.

Jake also invited his mother, Kimberly, who is *not* here.

If he's upset about that, he hasn't let on. But I, for one, am a little irritated at the woman. Having a baby with me may not be what she had on her bingo card for her son, but Jake's a good son.

He deserves a good mother.

"I got you something too," Shelby offers hesitantly. "It's in the envelope in there."

"Thank you, Shelby," I tell her with a smile, and her cheeks redden as I open the envelope to find the gift card inside.

"I really don't know what the best things are for babies. I don't have much experience with babies. I mean, I don't have a baby. Um, so I just thought that you could pick out whatever it is that you need," Shelby rambles, tucking her blond hair behind one ear.

"I don't know what the best things are for babies either," Jake says with an easy smile. "So, this is perfect."

"Oh my gosh," I whisper as I pull out the most beautiful afghan. It's my favorite color—a deep forest green, with light tan and yellow decorative elements knitted throughout.

"Chernell, did you make this?" I ask her.

"I did. I hope you like it." Chernell smiles at me, not a hair out of place, wearing her signature outfit of a button-down belted dress, this one navy blue with little white flowers.

"I *love* it," I gush, wrapping the blanket around my shoulders, taking care not to let it hit the floor. Sawdust will be a bitch to get out of this thing. "It's my favorite color. Did you know that?" I ask her.

"Of course. Well, Jake knew, and he told me," Chernell tells me.

"You did?" I ask Jake in surprise.

He smiles at me, his blue eyes clear and bright. "Of course I did." He dips his chin, giving me a knowing look.

I love you, remember?

My skin warms, and I press the palm of one hand to my cheek. "That's, um, that's very nice of you."

"I'm a nice guy," he demurs, still with his easy smile.

A nice guy who loves you.

When has that ever happened?

Never, that's when.

"It's so beautiful, Tatum," Summer coos, pulling me out of my Jake-induced trance.

"It really is," I agree. I manage to pull myself up—white folding chairs were not designed with comfort in mind, and this holds doubly true for pregnant people—and waddle over to Chernell, leaning down to give her a kiss on the cheek.

"Thank you so much," I tell her.

"You're welcome, dear. You're going to be a wonderful mother," she tells me confidently.

More confident than I feel, anyway.

"Glad you think so," I tell her.

"Tatum is a caretaker," my grandfather pipes up from where he sits next to Chernell. "She was taking care of things from the moment she was born. She will be a wonderful mother."

"You say 'taking care,' but all I hear is 'bossing,'" Nick says, but there's humor in his eyes.

I heave a dramatic sigh. "Nicky, Nicky. You say 'bossy' like it's a bad word." I return to my chair and reach for Jake's hand. He helps me lower my big body down onto what really is a torture device.

"You okay?" he asks quietly.

"I'm great," I tell him, avoiding his eyes. My view is drawn toward the windows and the muted landscape beyond. Still gray, still misty, still… still. Everything is still.

"Whoa," I mutter, placing a hand on my stomach.

Because this baby? Is *not* still.

"Ohhhh, baby kicks?" Violet asks from the chair next to me.

"Baby kicks," I confirm. "You can feel if you want to."

Violet has been pretty interested in everything the baby is doing, at all times. "What is the baby eating?" "How does the baby go to the bathroom?" "Can the baby hear me?"

When I answered that last question with "probably," Violet immediately began her quest to share her life story with the baby, from birth to present and the future beyond. She also has been sharing Taylor Swift's entire catalog with the baby. This baby will be born a Swiftie if Violet has anything to say about it.

"Hello, baby," Violet says loudly.

"You don't have to yell, Violet," Sarah grumbles from her table. I look to see that she's still flipping through *On the Day You Were Born*, casually wiping under her eye occasionally.

I catch Julia's eyes and subtly nudge my head in Sarah's direction. Julia glances at her and back to me.

"See," she says out loud to me. "I told you."

Jake

"Okay, those are all the presents." Nick hands me the last of the gifts, and I load them into my Jeep. Nick has some of the larger items—including a stroller that looks like something the military would use and I am not sure I will ever be capable of setting up—in the back of his truck.

"Thanks, man," I tell him.

"No problem." He doesn't move to go back inside, just stands with his feet planted, his arms crossed over his chest. His hazel eyes—the same as Tatum's—regard me thoughtfully, and he cocks his head to the side. The weather is cold and gray, and while it's not quite raining, condensation gathers on his shoulders as we stand.

"Did—did you want something?" I ask him, suddenly a little nervous.

"That other guy was a dick," Nick spits out, and I straighten up to my full height.

Which, I am just saying, is maybe an inch taller than Nick Echeverria.

Maybe like half an inch.

"That other guy…"

"You know. The one from the restaurant a few months ago. At the Brew."

My spine goes ramrod straight when his meaning becomes clear.

"Yeah." I shift my eyes to the Rock across the bay. "Yeah, no argument from me on that point."

"He was no good for her," Nick continues.

"Again, no arguments." A large pelican swoops down, breaking the smooth pane of water, scooping something up with his beak before taking flight again.

"I don't like guys like that," Nick tells me, and I turn back to him in surprise. We've conversed casually over the last several months, about things like our favorite music—we both like 90s grunge and both agree Dave Grohl is The Man—but we certainly haven't had a Serious Conversation.

"Guys who think they are better than women, just because they are guys," Nick explains, mistaking my surprise for confusion. "Guys who use women as a prop to make themselves feel better about their own inadequacies, while bringing down women in the process."

Now, I am surprised, and I raise my eyebrows.

"I've been doing a lot of reading," Nick offers by way of explanation.

"Okay," I tell him, unsure of what else to say.

Nick clearly has something he wants to share with me, and I'm no dummy—I'll let him speak.

"You don't seem like that type of guy," he says grudgingly.

I smile, but it doesn't reach my eyes. "I'm not," is all I can tell him.

I spread my hands open, palms to the sky. "I'm not," I repeat myself. I eye him a moment and decide to go for broke.

Who knows when I'll have the chance again?

"Did you know that I told Tatum I love her?"

Now it's Nick's turn to look surprised. He still has his arms crossed over his chest, but he relaxes his posture and shifts to one side. "No shit?"

"No shit." And this time, when I smile, I can tell it reaches my eyes. It feels good.

"She love you?" Nick raises one eyebrow.

I bark a laugh. "Not even a little bit."

Nick shakes his head slowly. "Nah, it's definitely more than a little bit."

I shrug, as if to say *what can you do?*

"She's tough," Nick adds. "Real tough. Loyal. Honest. And like our Pops said, she's a caretaker."

"I can see that." I pause, looking to the Rock and then back to Nick again. "She's really easy to love."

He nods, apparently accepting what I have to say.

"That guy *was* a total dick," I add, "and frankly, I don't blame her for being a bit jaded." I look into Nick's eyes, hoping he can see the truth of my intentions.

"And I'm not going anywhere."

Chapter Thirty-Four

Tatum

AT FIFTY-THREE MONTHS PREGNANT, THIS BABY IS NO LONGER the only thing sucking the life out of me.

My job is sucking the life out of me.

Walking from my living room to the bathroom is sucking the life out of me.

Having ankles the size of softballs from doing nothing more than sitting at my desk—while keeping my feet elevated, mind you—is sucking the life out of me.

Life is sucking the life out of me.

And I'm nine months pregnant, not fifty-three, but you get the gist.

I've wrapped up all the pressing items at my work and am officially on maternity leave.

I've nested so hard that all other nesters will pale in comparison to my nesting.

All the baby clothes are washed, dried, and hung up. The nursery is ready. Our many, many diapers are carefully set out and ready for use.

There is nothing to do but…wait.

God clearly made more than twenty seasons of *Law & Order* for just this occasion.

It's me, Janet, Briscoe, and Curtis—still looking fine as hell—assisting the two separate yet equally important groups as they solve crime and put the bad guys away. I am one with my couch, one with my green afghan, and one with my tumbler full of cucumber ice water.

And I am going out of my mind.

I've never felt such giddy anticipation and impatience all at the same time. Is this what being received by the queen or having a meet-and-greet with Beyoncé feels like? They keep you waiting forever and make their entrance only when they are damn good and ready?

The baby's due date was March 9. It is now March 17, and *I am ready to meet this baby.*

I drank some pineapple juice, having read somewhere that this will jump-start the baby into joining us topside. I've been going for walks, which are necessary for my sanity—and Janet's too—but I'm also hoping that the movement will get the baby to *move* out of my uterus.

So far, no dice.

The shouts on the television pull me out of my misery where NYPD's finest are collaring the bad guys. Actually...

Those shouts are coming from outside.

It's the middle of the day, but did I mention that it's St. Patrick's Day?

And if you live in a college town, you *know.*

St. Fratty's Day, as it is known around town, is an absolute shitshow. A drunken, boisterous shitshow.

The bars on Main Street open early every St. Patrick's Day, weekday or weekend. As in, six a.m. early. And the college students are motivated, I'll give them that, because they are known to begin pregaming even earlier than that.

Wake up at four a.m., eat a big breakfast, do shots, head to the bars, and get home by noon to pass out.

I can't judge—I went to college and had many a good, drunken adventure—but Jesus Lord, if there was ever a time I felt so far removed from the college experience, this is it.

Fifty-three months pregnant, with cankles, heartburn, and a bladder that has shrunk to the size of a grain of rice.

"Ooomph," I mutter, raising myself from the couch to go to the bathroom. I head toward the hall when I hear more shouts, laughter, and a bang on my front door.

"Fuck me."

Not really, though.

Because my sex drive has gone the way of my ankles.

That is to say, it is nowhere to be found.

I consider ignoring the knocking, but Janet is already up and excited. She barks at the door, someone pounds again, and she barks some more.

I am not expecting anyone—Jake would just let himself in, and one of my family members or friends would have let me know they were coming.

I can afford to be rude.

"*Go away!*" I yell and wait a few beats.

More pounding.

Sighing, I make my way to the front door and open it a crack.

Three young women are on my porch, dressed in sparkly, emerald-green bikini tops—did I mention the high today is fifty-five degrees?—and cut-off shorts. They all wear perfect makeup, eyelashes applied properly, highlighter on their cheekbones, their hair blown out just so.

"*What?*" I bark at the girls.

They have the wherewithal to look surprised, but also have the warm glow of early-morning inebriation.

"Um…isn't this Jameson's house?" one of the girls asks.

You have got to be kidding me.

I swing open the door dramatically, and Janet rushes excitedly to the girls, sniffing and wagging her tail, having decided that three college girls in bikinis pose no threat.

"Do I look like Jameson?" I bellow, like an old sea witch. My hair is in a messy bun, and my long maternity dress is just barely holding my tits in, which threaten to spill over the top.

"You definitely do *not* look like Jameson," the girl in the middle declares, looking me up and down, her eyes catching on my stomach. She is a tall, lithe blond type.

To be fair, these girls are all tall and lithe and blond.

The blonde on the end leans down to pet and coo at Janet, who eats it up.

"Well. There's your answer. I am not Jameson, he is not me, this is not his house. Janet, come," I bark at my dog, turning to go inside, when I feel a warm trickle down the inside of my leg.

"Oh fuck," I mutter, lifting the hem of my dress to see a little puddle on the floor.

"What is that?" Blonde Number Three shrieks.

Janet immediately goes to the puddle and sniffs it.

"*No!*" All of us—the Three Blondes and I—yell. Janet lifts her head and looks at me.

"What—what's going on?"

I look up to see Jake, just returned from surfing, wearing his Rainbows, shorts, and a hoodie, his hair still damp and sticking out at odd angles.

I sense the Three Blondes' antennae move toward him like ants seeking sugar. "Do you know Jameson?" one of the girls asks innocently.

"My water broke," I tell Jake plainly.

His eyes widen, and he moves through the trio with ease.

"Really? Seriously? When? Oh." He answers his last question himself when he views the little puddle on the floor.

"Okay. This is okay. This is great." He looks up at me, his face calm. "This is *great*, Tatum," he tells me in a low voice, resting his hands on my shoulders, the smell of the ocean still on him.

"My water broke," I repeat, my voice cracking.

"I know. I know, beautiful." I hear one of the Three Blondes suck in a breath, which pulls me out of the sheer terror that enveloped me a minute ago.

I peer around Jake at the girls.

"Why are you still here?" I bellow. Yes, bellow. I am still an old sea witch. And I am ready to bring my little mermaid into the world.

Chapter Thirty-Five

Jake

I CAN'T STOP CRYING.

Not the heaving, loud sobs some people have when they are devastated or emotionally drained. No, I am content to let the tears roll quietly down my cheeks. I occasionally lift my hand to wipe them away. They are part of me now, and I accept them.

I am glad I brought another shirt to wear—not knowing how long this labor thing was going to last—since I am basically using it as a tissue.

Tatum, as expected, was a champion. With Julia and Elaine on one side of her and me on the other, Tatum pushed and pushed and had an epidural when the pain became too great for her, and then pushed some more and fought back against the nurse trying to give her Pitocin and…pushed. I saw the very, very top of the baby's head on one of her pushes, but that was it.

A lot of dark hair, and I almost lost my shit right there. That's definitely when the tears set in.

After what felt like days—but was really around six hours—the doctor came in and checked Tatum. His arm was so far up inside Tatum, I thought he was going to pull out the baby right then and there. Tatum didn't bat an eye. Those epidural drugs are no joke.

Everything was fine, the baby was fine, and Tatum was fine, but the doctor gave a little speech about the placement of Tatum's pelvis and the small area that the baby was trying to squeeze through.

"I know that it's really, really important for some mothers to give birth vaginally," the doctor said, speaking slowly and with the caution of someone who had delivered this speech a million times before, to a million different women, with a million different expectations regarding childbirth.

"I believe that you could push for another twelve hours, and the baby will still need to be delivered cesarean."

Tatum didn't hesitate. "Then let's do that," she said drowsily.

And that was that.

Everything was a blur thereafter. These doctors and nurses don't play. We were wheeled into what I assume was an OR of some kind. Julia and Elaine stayed behind. A little sheet hung right below Tatum's chest so she wouldn't have a front-row view of what was happening.

"Dad, you can take pictures if you want," one of the nurses said.

Dad.

They were talking to me.

"Do you mind?" I asked Tatum, gripping her hand.

"No, go for it. I want to see this all…later," she said with a weak smile.

I pulled out my phone, stood up to see the other side of the sheet, and held down my photo button to capture what was truly the most awesome thing I've ever seen. The doctor cut a small incision into Tatum's lower abdomen, much tinier than I thought he would need to, and inserted his hand inside the incision, and then—

He pulled out a baby.

A bloody, screaming, scrunchy-faced baby with a cone-shaped head and her legs all wrapped around herself, like she was sitting crisscross in Tatum's stomach for the past several months.

Yes, she.

I have a daughter.

She was—and is—the most beautiful thing I have ever seen.

Now I sit with Tatum and Julia in Tatum's hospital room, holding the baby skin-to-skin, meaning I'm shirtless, and she wears a tiny diaper. The baby is quiet now after screaming bloody murder for the last three hours.

Apparently, this little lady was quite happy in Tatum's stomach and was very displeased to be pulled out of her warm, confined space into a bright, loud, cold world.

Honestly, I can't say that I blame her.

"Lincoln wants to know if he can come with the girls," Julia says softly. She looks up from her phone to Tatum. "How do you feel about that? I can have them come tomorrow."

Tatum shakes her head. "Nah, they can come. I feel pretty good. But tell Lincoln if he doesn't come with a giant burrito, I will never talk to him again."

"Noted." Julia resumes texting. "I'm going to go grab a coffee. You guys want anything?"

"What time is it?" I ask her, looking back down at the baby. Her little eyes are shut; while they were blue before, one of the nurses said they might change color after the first few days.

"Almost seven." I look blankly at Julia. "At night."

I have no concept of time. If you told me I'd been in the hospital for a week, I'd believe you.

"Yeah, I could go for a coffee. Small."

Julia nods and comes over to where I sit, looking down at me and the baby with a smile.

"She's perfect," she whispers.

And I'm crying again.

I hear the quiet click of the door when Julia leaves, and I am content to simply stare down at the baby.

My baby.

Our baby.

The silence is interrupted when one of the nurses comes in, a short, young woman with dark hair. "How are we doing?" she asks with a big smile. Her name tag reads "Neera."

"We are good," I murmur, still entranced by the baby in my arms.

"Mom, how are you doing?" Neera asks Tatum, offering her some water.

"Good," she replies softly, smiling at me and the baby. "Tired."

"I bet," Neera says sympathetically. "Any thoughts on names?"

Tatum and I both look at each other.

We had agreed we would discuss names once the baby was born and we knew whether it was a boy or a girl. But now that it's time—

I honestly have no idea.

"I have some ideas," Tatum tells me.

"It's St. Patrick's Day!" Neera chirps. "One of the other families is going with Patricia—"

"Absolutely not," Tatum says immediately. Neera doesn't bat an eye.

"Well, think about it. You don't *have* to pick a name before you leave, of course," Neera says, "but it's easier to file all the necessary paperwork if you do pick one here in the hospital, rather than once you're out in the wild." She checks Tatum's vitals and leaves the room.

"No Patty for you, huh?" I ask Tatum with a rueful grin. She rolls her eyes.

"No Patty for me," she replies.

"But you do have one in mind? Because I'll be honest with you, Tatum, I have no idea. I thought that once I saw the baby—saw her—it would come to me, and I am still clueless about what she wants to be called, and—"

"What about Constance?" Tatum interrupts me.

"Constance," I repeat.

"Yeah." Tatum clears her throat, looking tired and a little embarrassed. "She is just… I just had this feeling. Right when they held her up and showed her to me." She looks down at the baby in my arms, who is still fast asleep, totally oblivious to the moment between her mother and me.

"She is *it*. She is the one. She is…she is my constant. I just knew the moment I saw her, you know?" She pauses, a sheen in her eyes. "Did…did you feel that way too?" Tatum looks up at me, seeking reassurance.

My eye sockets tingle, threatening tears once again. I'll be crying non-stop for the first year, if the past several hours have been any indication. "I did. And I do." I look down at the baby again and try it out. "Constance."

"We can call her Connie for short, if you want. If you like it."

"I love it. Constance…" My voice trails off. We haven't really talked about last names. I am not so old-school that I would demand Constance have my last name, but I am also not going to lie and pretend that I *don't* want her to have my last name.

If that makes sense.

"Jake. I see the wheels spinning." Tatum gives me a gentle smile. "How do you feel about a hyphenate?"

"Constance Echeverria-Lundquist?" I try that out too. "It's…a lot of vowels."

"Eh. There are worse things in life. And we can forgo a middle name to make it easier."

"Yeah." And here come the tears again. "Yeah, I like it. Baby Connie," I whisper to her in my arms. My tears fall on her little face, and she scrunches her eyes shut even harder.

"Give her here, Dad," Tatum demands.

I need to give her over anyway, because now the tears come in earnest.

I can't imagine it getting any better than this.

Chapter Thirty-Six

Tatum

I SEVERELY UNDERESTIMATED HOW OBSESSED I WOULD BE WITH THIS baby.

Baby Connie.

Because I am pretty sure that no parent in the history of the world has been as obsessed with their child as I am with mine.

"She's so tiny," Summer says from where she holds Connie in the hospital room, Nick leaning over her. Lucy sits in the chair next to Summer, also peering at the baby, her normal taciturn expression absent, a calm look on her face.

"She didn't feel tiny inside my stomach, that's for sure," I tell Summer in between bites of my California burrito.

Lincoln made good on his promise to bring me a burrito, and I am happily enjoying the second half of it the next day.

"But you are," Summer coos to Connie. "You are a tiny little burrito, all wrapped up."

"Pretty sure she's bigger than a burrito, Sunshine," my brother tells Summer with a twinkle in his eye.

"She's perfect," Lucy declares and looks up at me. "And you? How are you doing?"

I shrug. "Sore. Tired. I would love a shower at some point. My stomach is throbbing," I add, indicating my lower abdomen where the C-section wound is all bandaged up. "But honestly, it was a lot less dramatic than I anticipated."

"And how's Jake?" Lucy asks.

I can't help but smile. "He's…he's great, actually. He can't stop crying. It's annoying," I tell her. Lucy rolls her eyes.

It's not annoying.

"He's on the phone with his mother now, I think."

Lucy nods and looks at me thoughtfully, uncharacteristically silent.

Summer pipes in. "He loves you, Tatum."

I jerk my gaze to see her looking at me, also with a thoughtful expression on her face. I changed my mind—the two of them are annoying, assessing me.

But they aren't wrong.

"I know," I tell them quietly. "I know he is."

The truth is, Jake is just as obsessed with Connie as I am. I could see it in his eyes the moment the doctor pulled her out—which is still bizarre to think about, by the way. Jake said it was like the bloodiest magic trick he's ever seen.

While he could see what the doctor was doing, I could only see his face. His eyes were so big and blue, even more prominent in his face than normal on account of the hospital mask he wore in the OR. His eyes went from nervous and excited to awestruck in a matter of moments. He kept muttering "Oh my god, oh my god" under his breath, and I don't even think he was aware of it. And then he was quiet.

Quiet when the doctor held up Connie.

Quiet when the doctor let him cut the umbilical cord.

Quiet when the nurse wiped Connie down briefly, wrapped her up, and gave her to Jake to hold.

When he came over to me so I could see her scrunchy little face, I saw the reason behind his silence—tears streaming down his face in an endless river.

"She's so beautiful," he whispered to me.

And then I was the one muttering "Oh my god, oh my god," as I met my daughter face-to-face.

"Hi, baby," I told her. "I'm your mommy."

And for the next three hours, we all cried—Jake and I quietly, Connie at the top of her lungs.

"She's definitely a crier," I tell Lucy, Summer, and my brother now.

Lucy scoffs. "Seems pretty quiet to me," she says, gesturing to where Summer rocks Connie in her arms.

"Just wait," I promise.

"If she's anything like her mom," Nick offers with a wry smile, "she'll make herself heard."

I glare at him, but… "You're not wrong." I take the last bite of my burrito. "Now bring her to me."

Summer smiles and rises carefully so as not to jostle the baby. "Here you go, Mama," she says quietly, laying Connie down in my arms. There's a giant stuffed giraffe the length of my arm on one side, which I've been using to prop up Connie while I try to get the breastfeeding thing down. But for now, Connie appears content to sleep.

Her little eyelashes flutter against her pink skin, her lips pursed like she's thinking about something in her sleep. She wears a little pink-and-blue striped cap, and underneath, she has a full head of dark hair. Her arms and back are also dotted with fine dark hair; Julia says her girls had "baby fur" too when they were born.

What I am saying is—she's basically the most perfect thing I have ever seen.

"I can't imagine it getting better than this," I murmur to Connie.

Part V

The Fourth Trimester

Chapter Thirty-Seven

Tatum

THREE WEEKS LATER, AND IT IS DEFINITELY *NOT BETTER*.

Does breastfeeding drive most women to the point of lunacy?

Do all people who attempt nursing end up rocking back and forth on the bathroom floor, surrounded by an endless supply of nipple accessories—and not the fun kind?

Asking for a friend.

Because my breasts—and my nipples, specifically—are *wrecked*. We are chafed, we are chapped, we are blistered and bleeding.

The bathroom looks like a tornado ran through it. On the counter is a thick substance that I am supposed to put on my nipples to soothe them, something supposedly safe for the baby to digest. Also on the counter are ice packs, now floppy and warm, also for soothing my skin. There are lettuce leaves, limp and room temperature, previously frozen, previously inside my nursing bra to—you guessed it—soothe my absolutely ravaged nipples.

I have an endless supply of milk and no way to get the milk into my baby, aside from pumping.

I have tried nursing approximately eighty million times. According to the lactation consultant I met with in the hospital, my nipples are slightly inverted in their normal state, making it harder for little Connie to latch on to my breasts.

To his credit, Jake did not make a comment about how he has never had such a problem, my inverted nipples notwithstanding, though I could see the joke percolating in his mind.

The lactation consultant also gave me something called a nipple shield. It's a clear silicone piece with a nipple shape right in the center. I am supposed to place the shield—which looks like a tiny sombrero—right over my breast. A little hole is poked in the top, and the idea is that Connie will suck on the silicone nipple, think it's my real nipple, and get her milk that way.

So far, so good.

But I have to get over this threshold of pain first.

Julia told me this would come. "You will cry. You will cry harder than the baby. You will feel like a glorified cow. You will be in pain, and nothing will help."

Helpful!

But here I am, on the floor of my bathroom, crying and in pain, and nothing helps.

I hate it when older sisters are right.

"Tatum?" I hear Jake on the other side of the door. There is a tentative pause, and I bet he is weighing what to say, because the last time he asked me "Are you okay?" for the goddamn ten millionth time, I let him know that I was *not* okay and if he asked me that one more time, he also would not be okay.

I may have thrown in a threat to his testicles.

I'm not really sure.

Because I am also sleep-deprived.

"Can I come in?" Jake asks.

"Free country," I mumble.

He opens the door a couple inches and pokes his head in. He's got the same circles under his eyes I do; Connie wakes everyone up, and we're all feeling the fatigue.

Even Janet is a little less hyper about life than she usually is.

"I brought you some water," he says, opening the door a few inches more. His eyes widen when he sees me laid out on the floor surrounded by…crap.

Just a bunch of crap.

"Thank you," I tell him through my sniffles. I wipe my eyes and reach for my tumbler, filled with ice and cucumbers.

Another thing Julia warned me about—the thirst.

The never-ending thirst, like I've been binge-drinking on a hot day in Las Vegas while also running a marathon.

Basically, I'm thirsty. Producing all this milk is not for the faint-hearted.

I guzzle my water and lean my body against the wall, letting my head fall back, shutting my eyes. I hear some rustling, and then Jake is there, next to me, on the floor.

"What are you doing?" I ask him, my voice plaintive.

"I don't want you to be alone. Connie is asleep and seems like she's going to be that way for a while," Jake replies. He looks at me, and I see the exhaustion written all over his face. His hair is messy and longer than normal.

We must make quite the pair—unkempt and exhausted, sitting on the bathroom floor.

A floor that, when I look around, I notice needs to be cleaned.

I haven't cleaned once since we brought Connie home. My mother has been coming by to help with that, as has Lucy, but let's be honest—

No one cleans a house like me.

And as I see the layer of dust and hair and I don't even *want* to know what else congregated around the bottom of the toilet, I actually whimper.

"Tatum," Jake says softly, holding his hand out to mine, palm up. I take it and look down at our hands and just…

Lose my shit.

Crying with snot and hiccups, and I probably smell and I still am wearing a giant mattress in my underwear postpartum and I *just*…

Can't stop crying.

My wailing gives Connie a run for her money, because that girl has lungs like an opera singer. But I am exhausted.

"I don't think I can do this," I whisper through my tears, my head resting on Jake's shoulder.

"Then don't," he tells me easily.

I jerk my head up and look at him incredulously. He gives me a tired smile. "I mean don't breastfeed." He shrugs. "Lots of new parents don't. If you want to do it—if you want to keep at it, get over this hump, whatever—do it. But, Tatum." His smile vanishes, and he looks at me with those ocean eyes.

"You don't have to do this. And it won't make you any less of a mother."

Julia said as much to me. Apparently, Sarah was easier to nurse than Violet. With Sarah, she nursed for one year; with Violet, Julia said she could only get three months.

"And then she bit me. Right on my nipple. No teeth, you know, but those gums clamped the fuck down. And I was done."

"If you want to, you can pump and bottle-feed." Jake recites this information methodically, telling me stuff he knows I already know. "We can use formula. Formula exists for a reason."

I drop my head back down to his shoulder and sniffle.

"Whatever you want, beautiful," he whispers, rubbing my back through the thin fabric of my old UCLA t-shirt.

One week later, my nipples are somewhat healed.

I pumped nonstop for a couple days, waking up every three hours to relieve the pressure in my breasts. Connie took bottles—thank goodness, she doesn't seem to discriminate between bottle and breast—and ate like a champion.

I'm ready to give it one more try.

The old college try, if you will.

Although I don't think breastfeeding is what that refers to.

"All right, my little piggy," I tell Connie as I get settled in the rocker. My nursing pillow is in place. I have towels lining one arm of the chair in case this doesn't go as planned and I get milk everywhere. I have my giant tumbler of water on the table next to me and a goddamn positive attitude.

"Do you want to try this again?" I ask her.

Her eyes are almost comically round in her head, still a deep, fathomless blue, darker than Jake's bright blue. Her head is a mop of dark hair, and she is more alert each day, opening her eyes wide in the morning, making little fists with her hands. Her legs are still kind of bowlegged, which the pediatrician says is normal due to the several months she spent cooped up in my uterus with minimal movement. She's supposed to stretch out within a month or so.

"What do you think?" I ask again. I release one breast from my nursing bra, really a glorified sports bra with an easy cup that I can pull right down to let the girls out. Connie gurgles and snorts in response, which I suppose is a good sign.

I grab my little sombrero, put it on my breast, and offer it to her.

And…she latches right the fuck on.

Like a pro.

"Oh!" I am almost surprised at the tingle I feel in my breast, a sign that my milk is going to let down, aka flow like a roaring rapid. And Connie keeps at it, her little mouth clamped right on me. I hear her throat swallow, see her suck, and hear her little swallow again.

"Oh," I tell her, and I deflate, letting my head loll back against the rocker, pulling out the footrest, and let my little baby eat.

It might be the best feeling I've ever had.

After twenty minutes, Connie doesn't seem to be slowing down. After thirty minutes, I take her off, burp her, and let her chill out on my shoulder for a bit. She's wiggly instead of sated, though, so I do the same thing as before and offer her the other breast.

And…she latches on *again*.

"Holy shit," I whisper.

Nipple sombreros for the win.

"Hey!"

I look up to see Jake in the doorway, a smile on his handsome face as he takes in the scene before him.

"Hey," I tell him, feeling shy. "Um, look."

"I am looking. That's so fucking cool, Tatum," he says as he enters the room, leaning over to stroke Connie's head. He looks at us for a moment and then smiles again.

"You're a badass, Tatum Echeverria."

I smile and look down at Connie. "You think so?"

"I do." He stoops down to kiss Connie's little head. He raises himself up slightly to kiss me on the lips. I'm not expecting it, and I give a hum of surprise, feeling his smile against my mouth.

I'm sure I'm disgusting. I don't know when I last showered, and when I do, I mostly have to shower while holding the baby against me. So I'm not super clean, and my hair is probably going to be in a messy bun for at least the next year, if not longer.

But when Jake pulls away and looks at me, his eyes darting around my face, I feel beautiful.

"Total badass," he murmurs. He rises to his full height before I can respond.

"Let me get you some food," he says, leaving the room before I can object.

In addition to feeling thirsty all the time, I am hungry like I have never been. Even while pregnant. And that's saying something.

Jake returns a few moments later with a full plate laden with some of the enchilada casserole my mother made, a side salad, and a cookie. Lucy made the cookies; they are lactation cookies and supposedly will help me produce milk, which I don't seem to have a problem with, if constantly waking up with wet tits is any indication.

But let's be honest, I am never going to turn down a cookie.

"Thank you," I tell him gratefully.

"You're welcome, badass."

I've also taken to walking around our house topless.

My mother suggested it when she came over and saw me with the lettuce leaves in my bra. "Get them oxygen," she advised. "I mean, no one is coming over except me, Julia, Summer, and Lucy."

"And Nick," I grumbled.

Mom rolled her eyes. "He can get over it."

So I walk around the house in my stretchy yoga pants, giant underwear, even bigger maxi pad, and no top. And guess what?

Mom was right.

Oxygen does make them feel better.

And Jake doesn't mind.

Obviously, sex in any form is the furthest thing from our minds right now—at least, it's definitely the furthest thing from my mind. But I did see a little nostalgic gleam in Jake's eyes when he came home from the supermarket one day to see me bouncing Connie on one hip, while my boobs bounced right along with her.

"They need oxygen," I explained to him.

"They definitely do," he readily agreed.

Today, I've managed to take a shower, braid my hair, and wash three of the approximately forty-three bottles littering our kitchen counter. I even put on a shirt over my nursing bra.

I hear Jake rummaging in the hall closet and the sounds of things falling.

"Are you okay?" I call. Connie is strapped to my chest, in that happy place between awake and asleep after one of our marathon nursing sessions. This little girl can eat; we've gotten into enough of a routine that I know when I sit down to nurse her, I need to anticipate at least an hour of dinnertime. I am prepared, keeping a phone charger and a book at each of the spots I usually nurse, along with carrying around my giant tumbler of ice water morning, noon, and night.

And let's be real—some Carousel taffies are also at each of these places.

"I'm fine!" I hear Jake's muffled voice. He shows up a minute later with my cleaning basket in one hand and a mop in the other.

"I'm going to clean," he declares.

I am pretty sure I fall in love with him at this very moment.

"Okay…?" I say.

"You like a clean house. I could tell the very first time I, um, I came over here," he rambles, the tips of his ears pinking at the memory of that night.

A memory now alive in the form of the very human baby strapped to my chest.

"Anyway, I know it's driving you crazy not to have a clean house. And

I can do stuff like wash dishes and bring you food," Jake continues, "but I know how to clean."

"Uh-huh," I tell him with a raised eyebrow. He knows my high standards.

"For real," he insists. "I lived in a house with four other college students," he reminds me. "I had no choice but to learn how to clean, because those idiots certainly weren't going to do it."

"By all means, clean away," I tell him, gesturing toward the kitchen.

"But you have to leave," he continues as if I haven't spoken.

"I have to…what?" I ask him.

"You have to leave. Because if you stay, I know what you'll do." Jake gives me a don't-argue-with-me face. "You'll follow me around or, at the very least, *want* to follow me around—not that I blame you, I am very nice to look at—" Jake waggles his eyebrows at me, and I have to laugh "—but you will want to point out everything I am doing wrong or the way that *you* would do it, and…that's no fun for either of us. So." Jake points to the door. "You have to leave."

"Where will I go?"

"Go for a walk. Just up and down the block, if you don't want to go too far. I have the backpack all ready for you," Jake gestures to the Vera Bradley diaper backpack, forest-green, with white and gray flowers, hanging on a hook by the front door. "Diapers, wipes, change of clothes, that weird breast-feeding cover-up if you're so inclined to use it, sun block. Bring water too."

Jake speaks fast, and when he's done, he leans in to kiss me and Connie—me first, quickly on the lips, and then Connie's perfect head, where he lingers his lips a minute. "I love you, Constance," he whispers.

And I fall in love with him a little more.

"And I love you too, Tatum Badass Echeverria." He says this to me, obviously, with a gleam in his eyes.

"I…"

I have nothing to say, if my deer-in-headlights expression is any indication.

"I…"

"*You* are going on a walk. Oh, I put some taffies in there too. And almonds. You know. Balance and all that."

And with that, he winks, turns, and walks down the hallway, I assume to start on the bathroom.

I shudder, not just because the bathroom is truly disgusting, but also because…

I have fallen in love with the father of my child.

And I never even saw it coming.

Chapter Thirty-Eight

Jake

AT TWO MONTHS OLD, CONSTANCE ECHEVERRIA-LUNDQUIST IS interested in three things.

Tatum's left breast. Tatum's right breast. And sleeping.

Everything else, she can take or leave.

I meant what I said—Tatum is a total badass. I knew this before, obviously; I knew it the moment I saw her, nearly one year ago.

Nearly one year ago, but it feels like a lifetime ago.

Tatum and Connie now exist as a cohesive pair. Where there is one, there is the other. A big reason for this is because Tatum is the food source. But another reason is that Connie already instinctively knows what *I* know—

Tatum is the best.

And she wants to be around her all the time.

This means that, while Connie is happy enough to let me hold her and sing to her and take her and Janet on walks and have tummy time and all the other things, she is also just waiting until the moment when Mom comes back. Her little eyes light up, and she clenches her fists tight. If she could fist-pump, I am sure she would.

And because Tatum *is* the best, she takes it all in stride.

But I know my girl has to be fucking exhausted.

She sleeps with Connie; she wakes with Connie. She bathes with Connie. She has gone to the bathroom with Connie still attached because she refuses to be detached. She wears Connie for naps because Connie is not a fan of being put down in the crib.

So I'm trying to pick up the slack. I had the first six weeks off work—thank you, California, for paid family leave—but as of two weeks ago, I returned to the office.

It is hard to be away from my girls, but I know Tatum has help.

I hear voices from inside the house as I walk up the path, and I smile when I hear Tatum's cackle. Nick is holding Baby Connie when I walk inside, Summer looking at him with a very distinctive, moony look on her face.

"Jesus, Summer, I hear your ovaries shrieking from here," Tatum mutters with a wry grin.

"I mean, can you blame me?" Summer asks dreamily.

"I mean, that's my brother. Soooo…yes? I think?" Tatum responds. Connie does look very cute and comfortable with her uncle Nick, who is holding her with his two hands palms up, like she's a pizza.

"Hi," Tatum says to me, and I am glad to see a smile on her face. The first few months of life are no fucking joke. I never knew I could survive on so little sleep. And at least even when I do need to pull a long night, I can up my caffeine intake the next day. Tatum is still restricting herself, given that she's nursing.

"Hi, beautiful," I respond, bending over and giving her an upside-down kiss on the lips. "Good day?"

"Good day," Tatum tells me, her eyes bright.

"Good." I hold her eyes for a moment, squeezing her shoulders. She looks relaxed. Or, more relaxed than she's been lately.

"She had a good nap today," Tatum tells me quietly.

"Mm-hm," I respond distractedly, trying to massage some of the tightness out of her shoulders.

My watch vibrates, and I remove my hands from Tatum's shoulders, looking to see that my mother is calling.

Our communication has been sporadic, to say the least, over the last couple months. After her no-show at the baby shower, I needed a break. I needed to get ready for the baby, to focus my energy where it was most needed.

On Tatum. And now, on Baby Connie.

Of course, I told my mother when Connie was born. I have held off on sending her too many pictures, which is saying something, as I think I already have a couple thousand of Connie's first two months of life. I am going to have to up my cloud storage for sure if these first two months are an indication of how many pictures I'll be taking of her.

Although it might be petty, I don't think my mother deserves to see all the pictures of Connie. If she even wants to. My attitude is, if she really wants to see Connie, she can come here, to St. Bishop's, to see her.

I dismiss Mom for now and turn back to the conversation in the room.

"She's so little," Nick comments in his deep voice.

"She's so big!" Tatum exclaims. "She's put on so much weight since she was born. I don't like it."

"She's a growing girl," Summer comments as she takes the baby from Nick and holds her sideways, swaying from side to side the way Connie likes. Connie keeps clenching and releasing her fists, her signature move.

"Hi, baby," Tatum coos to Connie, who shows us her gums in response. It's either a smile or gas.

And it's goddamn adorable.

"She knows her mama," Summer says with a smile.

"It's hard not to. We're kind of joined at the hip. Well, at the breast, I guess?" Tatum muses.

"I brought some of those bacon-wrapped dates you like," Nick tells Tatum, holding up a reusable grocery bag. "And there might be some taffies in here as well."

Tatum gasps. "My favorite brother ever."

"Your only brother," Nick comments with a knowing look.

My watch vibrates again, and it's my mother.

I remember the last time she was calling nonstop.

Another event that was less than a year ago, but feels like a lifetime.

"I'll be right back," I tell Tatum, who nods at me before taking Connie from Summer.

Tatum

I watch Jake as he heads to our bedroom to take a call.

"And *then* I told Lucy that I was sorry, but I'm really happy with Nick and he's happy with me, and we're just not interested in a ménage at the moment. Maybe in the future, though?"

"Right. Wait, what?" I snap my head toward Summer.

"Aha!" She points her finger at me triumphantly, her brown eyes dancing in mischief. "You were distracted."

"I'm a new parent. I think that's part of the deal," I respond.

"You were distracted by Jake and his…Jake-ness," she responds, gesturing her hands toward the hallway where Jake has disappeared.

"Jake-ness?" Nick asks in amusement.

"You know. He's like a happy, excited, loyal companion."

"He sounds like a dog," I tell her, laughing.

"Actually, that's not wrong," Nick comments. "He's like a golden retriever."

"Whom you want to bone," Summer adds helpfully.

Nick makes a face, and I burst out laughing. "That's disgusting! You make it sound like I have a thing for dogs," I tell her through my laughter. I look over at Janet, curled up at the end of one side of the couch. "I love you, though, pretty girl," I croon. She opens one eye to look at me and promptly goes back to sleep.

"But you do, right?" Summer asks, leaning into Nick, sitting on the chair next to her.

"Do what?" I ask.

"Want to, you know." She makes an exaggerated show of putting her hands over Nick's ears. "Want to bone Jake." Nick rolls his eyes, clearly hearing her.

"Um…I haven't thought about it yet," I demur.

"Why the hell not?" Summer asks. "He's hot. You're hot. You have a baby. He loves you. You… Well, I'm not really sure what your damage is, but why not?"

"Honestly…" My voice trails off as I look down at the sleeping, perfect baby in my arms.

Why not?

I've stopped bleeding, finally, and am no longer wearing diapers in my underwear. I actually feel pretty good for someone who had a C-section two months ago. And of course, the doctor was quick to tell me that I am able to resume sexual intercourse at my appointment two weeks ago.

"But remember," he added seriously, "it is possible to get pregnant even while nursing."

Is it weird that I didn't find that warning terrifying?

The fact that I *didn't* find it terrifying…is actually kind of terrifying.

Because in my heart of hearts, I think I would have Jake's babies any day of the week.

I look back to Summer and Nick. "You know, Summer, this is something that I am just not ready to talk about with my big brother in the room."

"Oh, thank Christ," Nick mumbles.

"But if you and Lucy want to come over one of these evenings, we can talk about that and other things, such as this new trio you are entering into with Lucy," I finish with a grin.

Nick picks up a pillow and starts to throw it at me before Summer and I jointly stop him with a hushed warning of "*Watch out for the baby!*"

Jake still hasn't returned from whatever phone call he took when Summer and Nick depart a few minutes later. "Well, no time like the present. Isn't that right, my sweet baby?" I babble to Connie as I help myself to some of the lukewarm bacon-wrapped dates Nick brought over.

Connie hums in response.

"That's right. Got to keep up my calorie intake because you *are* a growing girl," I tell her.

I tie Connie to the front of my body with the baby wrap and go about cleaning the pumping equipment, when Jake comes back into the kitchen. He's running his hands through his hair, the way he does when he's stressed, looking troubled.

"What's up?" I ask him, turning away from the sink and swaying my body from side to side.

You can never stop moving with a baby in your arms.

"That was my mother," he says grimly. "Um, she wants to…she wants to come and see the baby." He stands opposite from me in the kitchen, leaning against the countertop.

"Okay," I respond. "I mean, that's not a huge deal." It *is* her grandchild, and if she wants to meet Connie, that's no problem with me. Kimberly Lundquist may not be my favorite person, but she deserves the opportunity.

"She wants to come over tomorrow," Jake clarifies. "Because she is already coming into town. To meet with a divorce lawyer."

My jaw drops, and I put down the bottle I am holding. "*What?*" My thoughts start moving a million miles an hour. "Which attorney? Not Eddie, right?" I add, referring to my law partner, Eddie Reyes.

"No, not Eddie. Some woman I haven't heard of, and honestly, I totally forgot to write it down. I was a little…distracted." Jake looks equal parts hopeful and crushed, which is sensible.

He is no fan of his father and an even lesser fan of his father's treatment of his mother. If his mom is actually, really and truly, divorcing him, that's got to make Jake happy.

But I would imagine that, for the most part, a kid is sad to hear his parents are separating.

"How…how do you feel about that?" I ask him.

"About her leaving him?" Jake asks me, and I nod. "I guess…" He heaves out a sigh and looks down to Connie's dark head, nestled right above my breasts, her little hands clutching the fabric of my wrap. Jake's eyes crinkle at the corners, tension draining from his face.

"I guess I am happy," he says slowly, his eyes fixed on Connie. "I think my dad is a jerk." He brings his eyes up to me, a hint of defiance on his face, as if he dares me to object.

I look at him openly and honestly. "You're not going to hear any argument from me. I've never met the man," I continue, "but yeah. I think he's a jerk, too."

Jake nods. "So, if she wants to leave him, then I am happy for her."

"If?" I ask him.

"I just hope… I just hope this isn't some Hail Mary play, like, she is threatening him with divorce in the hope that he'll change his ways or have a come-to-Jesus moment or whatever," Jake explains. He closes his eyes and pinches the bridge of his nose. "Shit or get off the pot."

I snort a laugh. "That started with religious imagery and ended…somewhere else."

He gives me a tired smile. "I can't think of a better metaphor. Or expression. Whatever." His eyes drop back down to Connie. "So. Are you okay with her coming? I can be here if you want."

I also look down to the baby, who is blinking her big eyes slowly, a sign of sleep to come.

Hopefully.

And I have an idea.

"I don't want you to miss work," I tell him. "And I can handle your mother."

"But?" Jake asks, picking up on my lightbulb moment.

"But I *did* tell my mom that I would bring Baby Connie out to Estero tomorrow," I point out. "I need a change of scenery. So if your mother doesn't mind driving an extra fifteen minutes to the bay, then I am all for a visit tomorrow."

A slow smile takes over Jake's face. "So she'll meet your mom."

"And Julia, probably. I swear, this kid is giving her baby fever," I add. Julia is constantly coming over to hold the baby, to smell the baby. She even offers to change the baby's diaper, which is fine by me.

"And she'll meet your sister too."

"I could see if Lucy could come as well," I add with a wicked smile. "Really give your mom the welcoming committee."

Jake throws back his head and laughs out loud, the muscles in his throat flexing. Connie wiggles a bit in my arms at the sound, and I hum a nonsense tune as I resume my swaying.

"Let's not get too carried away," he replies, his gaze warm. He pushes off from the counter and leans in to kiss me on the cheek.

"I'll let her know your plans tomorrow and see what she says."

Chapter Thirty-Nine

Tatum

"**D**OES SHE NEED TO EAT?"

"Her diaper is dry."

"How did she sleep last night?"

"Has she been colicky before?"

My mother and Julia pepper me with questions and comments concerning the screaming, red-faced, very upset baby in my arms.

Like any other baby, Connie is life-changing. I mean that in a practical sense—I never knew I could function on so little sleep, my hygiene habits have taken a serious detour, and we all know my cleaning regimen has suffered.

But that's just because she's a baby. She has no concept of day or night or my desire to shower regularly.

She has, however, been a pretty happy baby.

Until today.

At some point during our short drive to Estero Bay, Connie decided to fuck around and find out—or maybe I am the one who did that?—because she is *unhappy*.

We drove north on the 101, the mountains and hills surrounding us lush and green, a consequence of the unseasonably wet winter we had this year. It's now spring, and it still hasn't stopped raining.

"Look how pretty," I told Connie as I drove.

She cried.

"Isn't it gorgeous?" I asked her.

She cried harder.

I drove just past Estero Rock before pulling off the highway and turning into my mom's neighborhood. There's a nice park at the entrance, the same park I used to play at with Summer and Lucy when we were kids.

The houses were designed with coastal New England in mind, jute and driftwood panels on the front, with white-trimmed windows and doors. I've always thought Estero Bay is the most beautiful place in the world, and I sighed as I took in the view of the murky Pacific just beyond the beach, beach grass edging the sand.

"Isn't it gorgeous?" I asked Connie again.

She screamed louder.

She is now well-fed, if my deflated breasts have anything to say about it. She is changed and dry, as Julia noted. She slept relatively well the night before.

I can't think of anything else that would bother her…

…Other than the fact that she somehow knows we are meeting Jake's mother today and is very displeased at the thought.

"How's your mood?" Julia asks loudly, to be heard over the baby. She stands in front of us, making silly faces at Connie, which seems to piss her off even more.

"She's fine!" I say exasperatedly as I bounce Connie in my arms. "She ate, she pooped like normal, she—"

"Not the baby." Julia looks up to meet my eyes. "How's *your* mood?"

"Me?" I ask in surprise. Who cares about my mood? I have a wailing banshee to think about. "Um, fine. I could go for a brow wax, and I don't think I remember how to blow dry my hair or use eyeliner, but…" My voice trails off as I look at Julia.

"Are you nervous about meeting Jake's mom?" Julia asks me, standing up to her full height—three inches taller than my 5'4"—and crossing her tattooed arms over her chest.

"What! No! I mean, I've already *met* her, and she's the one who hasn't—" I am cut off by a screech and a hiccup from Connie. She hiccups again…and is silent.

She takes a deep breath.

So do I.

And she resumes her crying at the top of her lungs.

"What the *fuck?*" I say in a singsong voice, squinting my eyes shut and trying to teleport my baby and myself to a tropical island where there is no crying but there is an endless supply of margaritas.

Alcohol-free, of course. Or maybe with some magic alcohol that will give me a little buzz but won't harm the baby.

"Tatum!" I am ripped into reality by my mother standing in front of me with her arms out. "Give her to me," she adds, and I gladly relinquish Connie into her waiting arms. "Who's a good girl? Who's the bestest girl?" she coos to Connie, who keeps right on crying.

"I'm going to take her for a little walk," Mom says. "Just around the block. Maybe the fresh air will do her some good."

I wave her away in defeat, watching as my mother and my heart-that-lives-outside-my-body head out the front door. Connie's crying gets softer and softer as they walk away from the house.

I immediately collapse onto the couch. Julia takes the lounge chair across from me, a big coffee table separating us.

I don't say anything as I lean my head back and close my eyes. My shoulders are tight as hell, and I reach my right arm up to massage my left shoulder.

"I always thought that babies pick up on moods, you know?" Julia says casually from her chair. I squint one eye open and see her rocking back and forth in the chair. "Like, if I was nervous about something, the girls would get fussy. Especially Sarah," she adds ruefully.

"She's a little empath," I agree, closing my eyes again.

"So, if you are apprehensive, maybe she's picking up on that and acting accordingly. Plus," Julia goes on, "it's a different routine today. You're not at home, Jake's at work, you drove out here..." Julia waves her hand in indication.

"I thought it would be good for us to have a change of scenery," I huff out.

"It gets easier," Julia says meaningfully. I hear her shift, and then the couch cushion next to me deflates as she takes the seat next to me.

I open my eyes and move just my head, turning to her. "I'm so tired," I tell her, my voice bleak.

She lays her head on the couch and turns toward me, sympathy in her hazel eyes. "No shit. Babies are not for the faint of heart." Her long hair is pulled back from her face with a red handkerchief, rolled up like a headband. Her ears glitter with multiple piercings, and she has a smaller gold ring in her nose.

"You're so cool," I tell her honestly.

"I know," she says easily. "And you have the weight of the world on your shoulders, Tater Tot." She picks up my hand in both of hers. "I promise you, it really does get better."

"Like…at the six-month stage?"

She barks a laugh. "Not even close. For me…" She bites her lip thoughtfully as she continues. "Everything under the age of five is a crapshoot. It's hard. They don't sleep, you don't sleep. I've never been so fucking sick in my life until I had kids. They bring home all sorts of germs and cooties." She shudders.

"But I'm also…" I tell Julia softly. She looks at me expectantly.

"I'm so happy," I confess, my eyes filling with tears. "I've never been so happy."

Julia smiles, one that lights up her entire face. "I know. I *know*."

"I didn't know I could be this happy," I continue. Julia nods.

"Isn't it great?"

"Great," I reply. "And terrifying. I also didn't know I could be this afraid. What if something goes wrong? What if something happens to her? What if I can't do it?" Now that I have someone to confide in, the words spill out of me. "What if I fuck it up?"

Julia rolls her eyes. "If you have the self-awareness to worry about fucking it up, you are already on your way to Parent of the Year," she emphasizes. "And Tatum, it really is trial by fire. You just…do it."

I sigh and turn my head back to the ceiling, closing my eyes again.

"I think they're coming back," Julia murmurs, and sure enough, I hear

Connie's cries growing louder and louder as she and my mother come closer and closer to the door.

My body, apparently its own biological entity separate and apart from my mind, goes into high alert, the telltale tingles of my milk getting ready to let down.

Where there is crying, from anyone, there is an eager breast ready to feed.

Ask me how I know.

Also ask all the people in Target last week, who saw me leak all over my shirt when a baby—not mine—started wailing in the dressing room.

The cries reach a full crescendo as the door opens, and my mother walks in with Connie up on her shoulder.

Someone else is behind her—someone with honey-blond hair pulled back in a neat ponytail, navy tailored pants, and a silky, cream-colored blouse.

Bold clothes for meeting your two-month-old granddaughter.

"I met Kimberly on the street on our way back," my mother tells me gently, assessing me with her Mom Eyes.

I pull myself up from the couch—my C-section scar is healed, but I still have little-to-no stomach muscles—and move toward my mom, reaching to take Connie from her. Connie settles a bit in my arms, but she's still agitated.

"Hi, Kimberly," I say, trying to infuse some brightness into my tone. "This is my sister, Julia."

"Hi." Julia reaches out to shake Kimberly's hand. Kimberly's eyes flash over Julia—all rings and piercings and tattoos—but she smiles firmly and offers her hand.

"And I guess you met Connie," I say, gentling my tone, turning Connie around so she is facing out, away from my body. "I am sure my mom told you, but she is definitely not at her best today."

I don't *want* to want this woman to like my baby, to think that my baby is the greatest thing ever created. I don't *want* to want Kimberly leave this meeting thinking, *Wow, I was so wrong to be suspect of that brazen hussy who corrupted my son, because she is an amazing mother. And that baby! Just the best-behaved infant in all of Infantland. All due to her mother, I am sure.*

I don't *want* to want these things, but I do.

I want them.

"I certainly remember Jake having some not-so-good days when he was a baby," Kimberly says diplomatically.

"Please, come and sit down. I'll get us something to drink. Water? Tea?"

"Tea would be lovely," Kimberly says, sitting on the couch next to me. She sets her purse down on the end and then turns, angling her body so she can see Connie better. She crosses her feet at the ankles, the shiny gold Tory Burch logo peeking out from the top of her heeled loafers.

I send a silent plea to Connie telepathically—

Please don't throw up on this woman.

"Hi there," Kimberly says, her eyes lighting up as she looks at the baby. "Aren't you a pretty thing?" She smiles and looks at me, her face more relaxed, looking very much like Jake in this moment.

"Her eyes," she tells me with a knowing look.

I nod and smile in agreement. "They are definitely Jake's eyes. The doctor said they might change as she gets older, and they were a darker blue when she was first born, but I think they'll stay blue."

Kimberly nods, a peaceful expression on her unlined face. "Oh, having a bad day, are we?" she asks Connie. I can appreciate that she doesn't use a baby voice.

Nothing makes me crazier than people talking in a baby voice to my baby.

Connie eyes Kimberly for a moment and hiccups, before wailing once more.

Kimberly meets my eyes again, a question in them. "Do you mind if I try something?"

"Um, sure," I say, "but I am… Well, I'm worried she's going to make a mess of your nice clothes."

Kimberly scoffs and waves her hand. "They're just clothes." She holds out her hands, and I pass Connie to her, the baby wiggling and fighting the whole way.

"I know, I know," she coos to her. She takes Connie in her arms, holding her over her shoulder and patting her back. "Let's try something," she says softly.

Mom comes back into the room with the tea, setting it up neatly on the coffee table in front of us. Julia is back on the lounger, and Mom takes the seat on the other couch next to Julia, all of us watching Connie.

Kimberly takes Connie and lays her facedown on her lap, so Connie's head is slightly hanging off Kimberly's thigh, her chubby legs hanging off the other side of Kimberly's lap. Kimberly starts to bounce her legs up and down, holding on to Connie with one hand, and uses her other hand to pat, pat, pat Connie's back gently.

We all watch in silence as Connie is jostled around—not too much, and, frankly, babies like a little movement every damn hour of the day, as I have learned. But it's a bizarre thing to see this little baby being bounced and patted. And Connie ceases wailing, hiccups, and then…just hums. Not like a tune or anything, but just a little noise in her throat, as Kimberly keeps on patting her back.

"I used to call this pat-pat," Kimberly tells us wryly, meeting my eyes. "It's weird, but it was sometimes the only thing that could get Jake to calm down when he was a baby."

"Well, she seems to enjoy it," my mother comments, sipping her tea from a large, chipped mug with a photo of baby Sarah on it. I reach for my own mug, an old Cal mug from when Nick was in college, making a mental note to get my mom a mug with her newest granddaughter on it.

Absent-mindedly, I wonder if there will be any boy grandkids. Maybe Nick and Summer will have a boy, if they ever decide to have kids.

Or maybe my next baby with Jake will be a boy.

I sputter and nearly choke on my tea. Our *next* baby? I am not even prepared to say I will have another baby ever, let alone another baby with Jake.

But again…I don't hate the idea.

I clear my throat and set down my tea before I spill it all over Kimberly and her silk blouse.

"Was Jake a good baby?" Julia asks, perhaps picking up that I am not one for good conversation right now.

"Oh, he was a sweetheart. He was very, very active," Kimberly says fondly. "Kind of like how he is now, I suppose. Always moving. You know he started crawling at five months?"

She continues, not waiting for us to acknowledge her rhetorical question.

But damn if I don't break out into a cold sweat at the thought of Connie crawling in three months.

"The first five or six weeks or so, I stayed in bed." Kimberly chuckles, shaking her head in disbelief, before looking up at me. "I was so unsure of what to do. I had…all this milk and this crying little baby who couldn't so much as breathe without me." She pauses and looks down at Connie, still humming away while she pat, pat, pats the baby's back. "I had a few miscarriages before Jake."

"I'm so sorry to hear that," my mother says automatically, while Julia and I hum in sympathy.

"Thank you. It was difficult, but once Jake came along, I was just so… determined to protect him, I guess. I wanted to give him a good home. A good life. I wanted to be a good mother. So, those first few weeks, we didn't go anywhere." She clears her throat.

"My own mother brought me food to eat, but she couldn't be there all the time. So, my…Jake's father, he doesn't know how to cook. He brought me soup. Canned soup." Kimberly shudders. "So much canned soup."

"That sounds…very unappetizing," Julia offers, the cook in her sounding horrified.

"That's a nice way of putting it," Kimberly replies. She raises her eyes to mine again, hers shining with emotion.

"I just wanted to be a good mom," she confesses to me.

I think now she's not just talking about the first few weeks of Jake's life, but every week thereafter.

I think she's talking about the biological urge to do everything for this little person who needs you to live, this little human whom you love more than you knew was possible on the spectrum of human emotion.

I think she's talking about why she made the choices she made, choices that surely include staying married to Jake's dad, but also every choice be-fore and after, choices I don't even know about.

I think she's looking for something that confirms those choices were okay, that Jake turned out okay.

And I can definitely give her that.

"You are a good mom," I tell her. She raises her eyebrows in surprise, because—let's be honest—we don't know each other. At all.

But I do know something.

"I know you are a good mom, because you have a good son," I tell her. "And he loves you. And he loves Connie."

And he loves me too.

Chapter Forty

Jake

"**S**O, IT SOUNDS LIKE IT WENT WELL, ALL THINGS CONSIDERED," I tell Tatum.

We are lounging in her—our?—bedroom, Tatum having put Connie down for the night.

Or at least, for a few hours.

Tatum has taken to sleeping with Connie in the guest bedroom, but I came out of the shower to find her under the covers in our bed.

"I can't believe it," Tatum said quietly. "Like, Connie was kind of a monster today. And then she just passed out in her crib."

I shrugged. "Maybe she's having a growth spurt."

"Maybe," Tatum replied, absent-mindedly rubbing her chest.

"I was just worried she was going to poop or throw up or do god knows what on your mom's clothes," Tatum tells me now. We're both propped up on pillows, Tatum wrapped securely in my arms, her arm draped across my body.

I chuckle. "Let me guess, white shirt?"

"Off-white. Very neutral tones. Very expensive," Tatum replies.

"Her clothing palette is minimalistic, I guess," I tell her. "She's always dressed that way."

Tatum hums. "Like I said, Connie was kind of a monster today. But your mom actually got her to calm down."

"Good," I tell her, kissing the top of her head. Tatum smells like her normal self, with a side of baby thrown in. It's the best smell. "And our baby is not a monster," I add.

Tatum snuggles in closer to my body, yawning big before she replies, "Didn't you call her a parasite?"

I smile as I rub Tatum's back slowly, stroking her soft skin. "Never happened."

"It did," she insists, her voice drowsy. "I was there."

Tatum

I wake up to the sound of…drums?

I open one eye and quickly become aware of several things:

1. It's morning, as sunlight is streaming through the window.
2. I am still in bed with Jake, who is fast asleep next to me.
3. Connie, for all intents and purposes, slept through the night, waking once around midnight to eat, but immediately went back to sleep.
4. The drums are Janet, who sits patiently next to the bed, thumping her tail on the floor.
5. *Connie slept through the night!*

I sit up in bed, careful not to jostle Jake next to me. According to the baby monitor, Connie is still fast asleep, her arms spread wide and her little mouth puckered. I smile at her before quietly rising and taking Janet outside to see to her needs.

"Stay here, pretty girl," I tell Janet in the living room. I give her a bone, and she trots off to the couch, happy to chew on her toy and ignore me for the moment.

I creep back into my room and close the door quietly. Jake is still dead to the world. He is sleeping on his side, one arm under his pillow, the other spread out in a line over the spot I was sleeping in.

He is shirtless, his muscled back and freckled shoulders visible against my white sheets. His expression is relaxed and peaceful, his dirty-blond hair tousled and messy.

I think about how easy it is to be with him, how good he is to me and

Connie. How fiercely he loves both of us without asking for anything in return, and without pressuring me to man up—woman up?—and make a decision.

Using his words, he has *not* asked me to shit or get off the pot.

And I am pretty sure I love him.

I get back into bed, pulling the sheets and comforter back over me. One last look at the monitor to confirm Connie is still sleeping, and I make my move.

I'm not ready to tell Jake that I love him. I'm not even ready to admit it to myself.

But I think I can show Jake in other ways.

Like with a morning blow job.

Jake

"Oh. Oh my god. Oh shiiiiit…" I am half awake, half asleep, and 100% hard as a rock.

Honestly, that last part is how I wake up most mornings. Or at least, how I used to wake up most mornings, until sleep deprivation became a reality.

But right now, I am simultaneously rested, relaxed, and ready to come.

Because as I fully awaken, I am treated to the vision of Tatum with my cock between her lips.

Her hair is pulled up and off her face in a messy bun—par for the course lately—and she's in whatever old T-shirt and shorts she put on last night. And she is licking up and down my shaft like it's the best thing she's ever tasted.

Her tongue travels a circuitous path up and down, up and down, and all I can do is watch her and pant like a fucking dog.

We haven't had sex of any kind since Connie joined us. And frankly, there hasn't been a lot of opportunity.

That's okay, though; that's why God invented masturbating in the shower. Quick, efficient, easy cleanup.

So, to have this woman—the woman of my dreams—in the flesh, actually taking time during our first sexual encounter post-baby to get *my* dick wet with *her* mouth?

I almost come immediately.

Tatum hums when she sees me watching, still licking me like an ice cream cone. She never engulfs the head of my dick in her mouth, she never sucks, just keeps licking.

Getting me absolutely saturated.

Tatum pulls away briefly to whisper "Good morning" before returning to her licks.

I say something in response.

Maybe.

I really don't know.

Something that sounds like "nnnngghhyuuuuuhhhh."

Tatum smiles at me, a wicked gleam in her eyes that I recall from so many months ago, and isn't that how we got into trouble in the first place?

I do not give a dusty fuck as Tatum finally, *finally* takes me into her mouth, suctioning her cheeks like a goddamn Hoover and sucking hard.

My eyes open wide, my back bows, and I know, I just *know*, I am going to come.

Already.

"Tatum," I tell her dully through gritted teeth. "Beautiful, this is going to be over really soon—"

Then I can't say anything else, because Tatum starts using her other hand to play with my balls.

I want to talk dirty to her, I want to tell her what a good girl she is, how much I love seeing her suck on my fat dick, how nasty I want to get with her.

But the power of speech has abandoned me.

After all, I'm just a man.

And when Tatum takes that hand and trails it back behind my balls, applying just the slightest bit of pressure to a place that no one has been, I know she's doing it on purpose.

She wants to torture me.

I meet her eyes again, letting her see that I truly can't hold on.

Tatum lifts her head and holds my dick right there in her mouth on her tongue. Her eyes are glazed over, her expression one of yearning, and it's fucking hot to see that she's just as affected by this as I am.

"Gonna come in your mouth," I tell her in a gritty voice.

"I want you to," she responds, licking her lips and gripping my dick firmly. She opens her mouth again and licks the tip, teasing me.

"*Fuck*," I grunt as she uses her tongue for evil. And good.

Honestly, a little of both.

"Come in my mouth, Jake," she orders me, opening her mouth again, laying my fat head right on her tongue and jerking me with her hand.

Her other hand goes back to stroking me right behind my balls, and that's it.

My orgasm hits me with such force, I think I pull a muscle in my groin or maybe my abdomen and most definitely in my ass, which I clench through my climax so hard, my vision goes white. I can't get out words, can't tell Tatum how good it feels, can't tell her how much I fucking *love* her and everything about her. I can only moan and surrender and erupt in her mouth.

And erupt I do—not just in her mouth, but also all over her lips, cheeks, and down the front of her T-shirt.

She keeps her mouth open, humming all the way through my release, licking as much of me as she can off her lips, before my cock finally relaxes.

"Jesus, woman," I mutter, flopping my head back on my pillow. "Warn a guy before you do something like that."

Tatum lifts herself up and kneels on the bed, and I look back at her to see the front of her shirt is totally saturated. "Is that—That's all from me."

She smirks at me, a rosy flush on her cheeks. "No. Well, some of it. But, um, I let down during…while it was happening," she replies, referring to her breast milk.

"Oh," I tell her, surprised. "Is that normal?"

"I guess?" She laughs nervously. "I got up to feed Connie in the night, so I'm not, like, full to bursting, but I guess…" She waves her hand in the air, the way she does when she doesn't want to say whatever she is thinking.

"You guess…" I prompt her.

"I read that a let-down might happen during sex. And other stuff," she says, not making eye contact with me.

I raise my eyebrows, because this is all news to me.

"Really?" I ask her, fascinated by this woman and her body.

"Really," she says, and she meets my eyes again. She still looks a little embarrassed, but also—

I think my girl is horny.

And I can work with that.

I smile at her easily, leaning toward her when—

"*Waaahhhh!*"

We jerk our heads to the monitor to see Baby Connie, her little legs flailing and her tiny, dark head rising and falling on the mattress.

"Hold that thought, Romeo," Tatum tells me with a smile. She moves to the door but then looks down at her shirt, rubbing her face self-consciously.

"Can you get her while I clean up?" she asks.

"Absolutely," I reply.

Literally, it's the least I can do.

Chapter Forty-One

Jake

ONE MONTH LATER, AND MY DREAMS OF SEXYTIMES WITH TATUM have evaporated.

That's not true. My *dreams* are still ever-vibrant and ever-present.

But the reality remains the same.

Which is to say…no sex.

I'm not mad about it. Baby Connie has needs. She slept amazing that night and the next few nights thereafter, and then…

She was back to wanting to be with Tatum constantly, all the time.

Like I said, I can't say I blame her.

I want to be with Tatum all the time too.

And then it happens much like it did the first time.

Connie has a nightmare of a day, crying, screaming, only wanting to be held by Tatum, with me as a reluctant backup. She's fed, she's clothed, she's dry. It's a beautiful June day, neither hot nor cold, the kind of day that you think about when you think of California, maybe.

Connie does not care about the weather, the month, the year.

By the time Tatum gives her one last feeding before bedtime—and I use the word "bedtime" loosely, because it feels like we're regressing toward the place where Connie knows neither day nor night—Tatum is exhausted, I am exhausted, and we're both on the verge of tears.

She does, however, get Connie down in the crib, a rare occurrence.

And this has me thinking of the *last* time that happened.

I need to move quickly.

Tatum stumbles into the living room, bleary-eyed, hair everywhere. I set my phone down and lean forward. "You okay?"

She shrugs. "I'm alive. She's alive, you're alive. *You're* alive, sweet girl." She directs this last comment to Janet, who comes over to be petted.

"Are you going to crash now?" I ask her.

"I actually want to take a shower." She lifts one arm and sniffs, wrinkling her nose. "Definitely."

I perk right up at that.

"Can I—" I am suddenly shy.

I'm *never* shy.

But Tatum unnerves me.

This woman I love—and yes, I still tell her, knowing she'll tell me how she feels when she's damn good and ready—unnerves me. I've never met anyone like her, and I know I never will.

"What's up?" Tatum asks me.

"Can I watch you take a shower?" I blurt out.

I mean, it's worked before.

Tatum raises her eyebrows, her lips parting in surprise. She bursts out laughing. "Seriously?"

"Yes, seriously!" I laugh with her, relieved she didn't throw something at me or burst into tears.

Although the night is young.

"I mean…" She waves a hand, indicating her voluptuous figure that's been clad in a dark-green robe the better part of the week. And not a sexy-times robe, a functional robe.

I still like the idea of her not having anything on under that robe.

"Do you…" She eyes me cautiously. "Do you *want* to watch me take a shower?"

I leap up from the couch and am on her like white on rice, gripping her shoulders and bending my knees slightly so that we are more of an equal height.

"Tatum." I look into her eyes, letting her see my honesty. "I have spent the past…several months with a perpetual hard-on, watching you walk around topless. Watching you with Connie. Watching you feed our child. And I know—I *know*—none of that is for me or meant to be enticing or whatever. I know that."

I pause and take a breath. Tatum's expression is unreadable, but again, she's not yelling or throwing things.

"Yes, I want to watch you take a shower. I want to watch you take all the showers. I want to be in the shower with you. I want to touch you. I want to put my mouth on you. I want to be inside you, Tatum."

At this, I take her hands in mine and place them over her chest. "I want to do everything with you, all the time. That's not changing, despite how long it's been since you've washed your hair."

Tatum keeps staring at me, her lips parted, her eyes glassy. She doesn't even acknowledge my last sentence, which was meant to be a joke.

I don't really care when she last washed her hair.

"Okay," she squeaks out. I smile at her nerves.

"Okay?"

"Okay."

⋀

Tatum

You can imagine where the shower led to.

It led to my bedroom, the bed, and a lot of heavy petting and heavy breathing.

I've kept one of my cotton bras on, because I'm trying not to ruin these sheets with more breast milk. Jake has me good and ready for him, or at least, what in the past has been good and ready.

"You good?" he asks from where he's positioned on top of me, balancing on his forearms.

"So good," I tell him. "Now get inside me."

Jake smiles his gorgeous, lazy smile and leans forward to kiss me softly. He positions his cock right at my entrance, and he slowly pushes inside.

Well, a little bit inside.

"Holy shit, you're tight," he wheezes, staying his movements.

"Holy shit, you're huge," I reply, wondering if my vagina somehow shrunk post-birth. I've heard of women getting stitched up too tight after an episiotomy, but I had a C-section, for chrissakes.

"You okay?" he asks again, the muscle in his jaw ticking as he holds himself back.

"Yeah," I breathe out and try to relax my muscles. But the more he pushes inside, the harder it is. I mean, literally, he is hard, but it's too hard to get anywhere inside.

It's too dry.

"Tatum, I see your face. This can't be feeling good for you," Jake tells me, pausing after making it in another inch.

"No, no, it's just…I'm like the Sahara down there," I tell him, trying to shift my weight around in the hope that it feels better.

It doesn't.

"Lube?" Jake asks.

"Lube," I confirm, and he reaches toward my night table filled with all my favorite toys and accessories to get the lube.

But even after a liberal amount—okay, a *lot*—of lube, it's clear that Jake's going nowhere.

It feels like he's wrapped his dick in sandpaper in lieu of a condom.

I don't even know, and I feel like such a failure that I just—

I don't even know.

"Are you almost in?" I grit out. Now I'm the one speaking through clenched teeth.

Jake gives me a look that is both apologetic and proud. "I'm not even halfway, beautiful," he murmurs.

"Oh, fuck right off with that," I whine, and I freak out and clench up even more, and not in the good way. I can feel the tears forming behind my eyelids, and let me tell you, there's nothing less sexy than a postpartum, hairy, emotional lady preparing to wail right under you.

"Hey, hey, hey, Tatum. I was just kidding. It's okay." Jake pulls out—*fuck*, that hurts—and cups my face in his hands.

"You were *not* kidding," I cry, tears now rolling down my cheeks in earnest. "You *love* having a big dick."

"I love having a big dick because *you* love me having a big dick," Jake tells me gently, leaning down and kissing the tracks of my tears like the perfect man that he is.

"My vagina is broken," I wail, but at a reasonable volume.

I am not waking this baby up.

"It's not broken, Tatum. Remember? The nursing creates dryness. It'll come back." Jake says it so confidently, I want to believe him.

"But how are we going to fuck?" I ask him in disbelief. "I plan on nursing for at least a year!"

"Beautiful," Jake murmurs again, coming to lie beside me and wrapping his arm around my middle.

"I was a virgin for a very long time," he continues. "There's lots of other stuff we can do besides have sexual intercourse."

"If you're talking about putting that thing in my ass, I don't think I can do that either!" I tell him, a fresh round of tears threatening.

Jake laughs, turning my face toward his and kissing me on the mouth. "No, no ass play. Not until you're ready." He winks at me, and I roll my eyes. He moves to the side, back to the night table.

"You've got *plenty* of things in here to keep us occupied," he continues.

"No dildos," I caution him.

"No dildos. But…" He holds up a bright pink vibrator victoriously.

"Variety is the spice of life, Tatum."

I watch him carefully as he takes the small vibrator—no more than four inches long, with a curve at one end—and places it directly over my center.

"You still want to keep the nursing bra on?" he asks softly, rubbing through my folds.

"I-I think so," I tell him. "I don't want—" I gasp when he hits a particularly sensitive spot "—I don't want to accidentally nurse *you*," I tell him.

Jake's eyes darken, and he bites his bottom lip as he looks at my tits. "Honestly, I wouldn't mind," he mutters.

"I know, but I just don't—Oh!" Jake turns on the vibe to a low setting, but it might as well be an old washing machine for the way it affects me.

As in, this little vibe packs a big punch.

"Feel good?" he asks softly, leaning in to kiss the side of my mouth, my jawline, my earlobe.

"Fuck yeah, it does," I whimper, because holy hell, the painful penetration of just a few minutes ago is gone. My skin is tight and hot, my core burning with an intensity I haven't felt since before the baby.

"You are the fucking hottest thing ever, Tatum," Jake tells me, his eyes trailing over my body, from my head to my core and back up again to my tits. "Perfect fucking woman," he mutters, seemingly to himself.

"Oh, rub it that way. Yes, just like that," I tell him so breathily, I sound like Marilyn Monroe up in this bitch.

"I can't wait for you to come, Tatum, you know that?" Jake says casually, like we're talking about the weather. He leans forward and nibbles gently on my earlobe, before breathing on my neck. The tiny sensation sends shock waves all over my skin, every sense heightened as he continues talking. "Seeing you come is the best part of my day."

He clicks the vibe up a notch, and I'm floating, flying, climbing so high, I don't know where the top is. "Jake," I gasp. "I don't—I don't know if I can."

"You can, Tatum," he whispers right in my ear. "You can gush all over these sheets, and I'll still use them to beat off."

One firm press of the vibe at that setting right on my clit, and I'm coming, harder than I can remember, harder than I thought possible. My core clenches so hard I might give myself a hernia, my walls contracting and releasing around nothing as I climax, the pulsing sensations strong inside me.

I cry out and grab Jake's arm, needing something to hold on to, something to keep me anchored as I flail through my orgasm.

"The best, the absolute best, keep going," Jake whispers into my ear, and I do what the man says and keep going.

The peaks lessen, but the contractions are still strong, still shaking me each time one rattles through me, and a familiar sensation starts in my chest.

"Oh no," I moan, as the inevitable let-down happens, soaking my bra.

"Fuck *yes*," Jake growls, leaning forward and kissing my chest, licking my skin, trying to bury his head between my breasts.

And I keep coming.

Jake moves his soft lips all over my skin, as if he's scenting me, and I finally have to squeeze his forearm.

"Please, no more," I sob. "No more." I shudder through one last after-shock, and Jake pulls the vibe away from my body before throwing it somewhere in the room.

He reaches both hands to my head, cradling me and turning me toward him for a kiss. "Fucking love you," he mutters in between kisses. "Love you so much." He kisses my tears, my cheeks, my hairline, before cradling me to his chest and wrapping his arms firmly around my body, like I might escape if I had the chance.

Chapter Forty-Two

D O YOU NEED TO AVOID SOMETHING? ANYTHING?

A rattling noise in the car engine that you are not ready to deal with, financially or otherwise.

A leaky sink faucet.

Or a sexy, tanned, Adonis-like surfer type with fuck-me blue eyes and a giant dick?

Have a baby!

Are you uncomfortable discussing the future?

Do you shrivel and die a bit when someone wants to talk about feelings?

Do you break out in hives when you are faced with the prospect of a life-altering decision?

Have a baby!

This is one life-altering decision that will up your avoidance game like none other!

The baby does not care about your emotions, your feelings, your concerns, or your need to sleep, shower, or use the restroom.

The baby takes precedence over all! Put those feelings—and stinky armpits and hairy legs—aside. Any serious discussions of the future—along with all shaving needs—can wait, because the baby needs to be changed!

The baby needs to eat!

The baby needs to burp!

Oh, look at that, the baby threw up everywhere and needs to be changed *again*!

The baby needs to sleep!

Just kidding. The baby is still hungry!

Say good-bye to any potentially difficult conversations where your biggest vulnerabilities will be laid bare.

Say *hello* to… Wait, yes, the baby has pooped through her outfit! You know, the adorable blue-and-white Breton-striped dress with the hot pink bow around the middle? Yes, that one! In the trash it goes; there's no getting those shit stains out.

"Sorry, no can do" becomes an easy response when you *have a baby*!

"Wish I could, but I can't" is the auto reply when you *have a baby*!

"Ooh, maybe next time" is an acceptable answer when you *have a baby*!

So, don't worry about that handsome, chiseled, cunnilingus champion who happens to be the father of your child. Focus on *the baby*!

Your undying declaration of love can wait. *The baby* cannot.

Part VI

The Rest of Your Life

Chapter Forty-Three

Tatum

"There are Nine Sisters in our county," I tell the group of five hikers standing in front of me.

Well, six hikers, if you count Baby Connie, who is strapped to the front of my chest in an ergonomic baby carrier. She is four-and-a-half months old and, if I do say so myself, the most adorable baby in the history of the universe.

"The 'sisters' are small mountains, which are actually volcanic plugs that formed millions of years ago," I continue. "They make a fairly straight path from Estero Bay to the southern edge of St. Bishop's. Some of them, as you probably know, you can't hike. In the distance—" I gesture behind me, where Estero Rock sits on this beautiful July day, a gray sentinel in the bright-blue waters of the Pacific "—you can see Estero Rock. It's definitely *not* hikeable."

"Yeah, but don't people try anyway?" This comes from a guy who appears to be in his late forties, with a grizzled beard and a wide-brimmed hat.

"They sure do, and they get arrested." I don't mention that several of the people who try hiking Estero Rock—and I use the word "hike" loosely, because it truly is a *rock*, not a mountain or a hill—are on meth or other drugs. Their decision to climb a jagged rock with no equipment and no discernible way up or down is the least of their bad decisions.

"It's just not made for hiking. Plus, it's a sacred spot for many of the indigenous cultures here, and we want to respect that." Grizzly man nods in affirmation, and I continue.

"This hike is actually quite short and great for children."

"Even her?" a gray-haired lady asks with a smile, gesturing toward Connie.

I smile back at her. "Not quite yet." I bounce a little as I keep talking. "But it'll be a great first hike for her once she's ready."

"What a beauty," Gray Hair's friend says, another older woman with tinges of pink in her curly, short hair.

"She is, huh?" I ask. "Anyway, Black Hill is quick, three miles out and back, with an elevation of about six hundred feet. But today, as you know, we met here at the lookout, where it's less than half a mile to the peak."

I've been leading these hikes, organized by a volunteer group, for the past two months. Although I have returned to work part time, I found that I was going stir-crazy on the weekends, even more so than normal. I needed to get out of the house, do something active with the baby, and there are only so many walks I can do with a stroller.

I need to *move*. The more time I stand still, the more antsy I get.

I think it has to do with this baby being one of the most eager, active human beings I've known.

It has nothing to do with me trying to avoid Jake and his determined blue eyes every time he gets me alone.

It has nothing to do with the cold sweat I break into every time I think about the future.

Nope. Nothing at all.

Hence, these community hikes. Lucy suggested it to me, as some of her older yacht club friends rave about them. And this hill—Black Hill— is quick and easy, as we've driven our cars up to the parking lot lookout point.

"You ready?" I ask my group.

"Do you think I can hold the baby when we get to the top?" Pink Hair asks with a blindingly white smile only dentures can claim responsibility for.

"Hmm, we'll see. Let's go!"

Jake

"How's it hanging?" Lincoln asks me as I settle into a stool at the Brew's long wooden bar.

"Good. We're meeting Tatum here after her hiking thing," I respond, unclipping Janet's leash and letting her get comfortable under the bar.

"Beer?"

"Root beer," I tell him with a grin. "I've got precious cargo to drive home."

Lincoln nods respectfully. "I heard that." He turns away to get my glass of sugar water. His long hair—even longer than Tatum's, I would guess—is pulled back into a man-bun thing. Tattoos cover most of the skin I can see, from his neck to his forearms.

"Food, too? I've got fish tacos today," Lincoln says as he sets the root beer down in front of me.

"I'll wait for the girls," I respond.

"Copy that." Lincoln moves to the other end of the bar to take an order from a group of girls in bathing suit tops and shorts.

It's late July and a gorgeous day. I took Janet out to the beach for a swim while Tatum does her hiking thing, but I'm itching to get some surf time in at some point this weekend.

"Oh my gosh, *Jake*?"

I turn to my left and see one of the girls from the group approaching me. It's Annette, former girlfriend of my old roommate Brandon.

"Hey, what's up?" I say casually, rising to give her a half hug. She jumps into my arms, wrapping her arms around me like we are long-lost relatives reunited after years apart instead of former casual acquaintances.

"Oh my gosh, it's been *so long!*" Annette's blond hair spills out from under her Giants baseball cap, long tresses that tumble down her back. "What have you been up to? Are you working for your dad?" Her blue eyes regard me from head to toe, catching on the golden retriever at my feet.

"Did you…did you get a dog?" she asks me, confusion etched across her face.

I sit back down and angle my body toward Annette. She leans against the bar, turning so that I—and everyone else—can see her fluorescent pink bikini top and black cut-off shorts.

"Kind of. This is Janet. She's my girlfriend's dog."

Annette's eyes widen at that. "Oh my gosh" —*is that how she begins every sentence?*—"you have a *girlfriend!* So much to catch up on!"

Not really, I groan internally, but halfheartedly wave to the barstool next to me.

"Did you know that Brandon and I broke up?" she continues, on to the next subject.

"Um, yeah." *Not really*, I think again, but I kind of figured that when Brandon moved away, that would be the case, as Annette had one more year to finish. Speaking of…

"So, you're done, right? Did you graduate last month?"

"I did! Oh my gosh, you are so sweet to remember," Annette gushes.

Yes, my grasp of undergraduate graduation timelines is pretty impressive.

Three other girls meander over with bottles of Blue Moon, orange slices wedged on the rims. "Here you go, babe," one girl says to Annette.

"Thanks. Hey, ladies, this is Jake! He was Brandon's roommate last year," Annette says, placing her beer on the bar.

"Hi, Jake," the girls chorus.

"That's Ashley, Becky, and Kaylin," Annette tells me, gesturing quickly to her friends. I nod and offer a smile.

"Did you graduate too?" One of the girls—Kaylin? Although I should just call them by their bikini colors, so this one is Red Bikini—asks me.

"Um, last year, not last month. Been working pretty much since then."

Among other things.

"That's so great, Jake," Annette coos, placing her hand on my arm, which…why is she doing this?

"Um, thanks," I answer and awkwardly try to move away from her touch.

"So, how is it working with the family business? His family is in commercial real estate," Annette narrates for her friends, as if they could give a fuck. "Very successful, right?" Annette asks me, her eyes twinkling as if she knows something I don't.

"Actually, I am not working for him. For the business," I tell her, looking down at Janet to see if she can help me get out of this conversation.

She keeps her eyes closed.

Smart dog.

"Oh no, really?" Annette asks, a furrow forming between her eyebrows. "Well, what are you up to, then?"

"Working for an architecture firm in St. Bishop's," I reply easily, looking for Lincoln around the bar to see if he can help me. He's at the end, though, chatting with one of the cooks.

"Oh my gosh, how cool," Annette gushes. "And your girlfriend? How long have you been with her?"

Well, if that isn't a million-dollar question.

Officially, is Tatum even my girlfriend? That word sounds way too casual to describe our relationship.

The way I feel about Tatum is far from casual.

"Almost a year," I tell her, fudging the truth a bit.

What's the appropriate way to tell a passing acquaintance that you lost your virginity to the love of your life, had a baby with her, and want to spend the rest of your life with her, but she refuses to engage in any conversation where even the possibility of a shared future might come up?

Asking for a friend.

"Hmmm, long time," Annette says, the furrow between her brows back. Her three friends are now ignoring us and taking lots of duck-face and other suggestive selfies, using their beer bottles as props.

Where is Tatum?

Tatum

I walk into the Brew with Connie in her carrier, stopping short when I see Jake at the bar.

Jake surrounded by pretty, young things in bikini tops.

There's almost a whole rainbow, I think absentmindedly, taking in Pink Bikini—who currently has her hand on Jake's arm—Red Bikini, Orange Bikini, and Lime-Green Bikini.

I quickly glance down to see that—

Yes, I'm still wearing the ratty San Diego football T-shirt I put on this morning, a leftover from my brother's playing career. I am also wearing lightweight hiking pants, which, while extremely comfortable, are the least flattering piece of clothing ever.

I'm still fat, still nursing, still sweaty.

Connie babbles from her baby carrier, bringing me out of my funk.

"Hi, baby," I tell her softly. Her eyes light up as she spouts nonsense.

You know, I carried this child in my body for *years*. At least, it felt like years. I gave birth to her and figured out the whole nursing thing and the no-sleeping thing and how to install a car seat and how to hold a baby in the shower, and you know what?

We're doing okay.

I am doing okay.

I shore myself up and walk toward the bar. Janet is dozing under Jake's feet, oblivious to the world. There's an empty table right behind where Jake is sitting, and I put my backpack on one chair and the baby carrier right in the center of the table.

Jake's back is to us, and Pink Bikini has paid me no mind. I debate what to do—insert myself right between them? Take a seat at the table with Connie until Jake notices I am there?—when I am saved from indecision by Lincoln, who appears behind the bar and catches my eye.

"Hey, Tater Tot," he calls to me, making his voice heard over the conversations going on around us and the Jackson Browne song playing on the speakers.

"Hey, Linc," I reply, and Jake turns around, his eyebrows rising and a grin breaking out over his face—a relieved grin, if I am not mistaken—when he sees me and Connie.

"Hey!" he exclaims. "I was wondering where you two were."

Connie starts kicking her chubby feet when she hears Jake's voice. She knows her daddy, that's for sure. He steps closer to us and leans over the baby carrier. "Were you a good girl? Did you have a good hike?"

"She was great, honestly," I tell him, keeping one eye on Jake and Connie, the other on Pink Bikini, who is now looking between Jake and me with a very confused expression on her face.

"You need anything?" Lincoln calls from behind the bar.

"Just water, please," I tell him.

"Come here, my little munchkin," Jake tells Connie, unstrapping the five million buckles on the baby carrier and taking her out. He holds her over his shoulder, bouncing slightly, clearly a professional dad.

I glance back at Pink Bikini, whose eyes now look like they might fall out of her head. She wears a baseball cap, her long, blond, beachy waves artfully draped over her breasts. She has a toned, flat, tanned stomach, bee-stung lips, and wedges on her feet that make her legs look a mile long.

I try really hard not to shrink into myself.

"Jake?!" she asks in exasperation. I raise my eyebrows at her apparent familiarity with Jake.

Jake, for his part, turns to her in surprise, as if he forgot she was there. "Oh, right," he mutters. "Annette, this is Tatum—" he motions to me "—and this is our daughter, Connie. Annette was dating Brandon," he says by way of an aside toward me.

"Brandon… Oh my gosh, *Brandon!*" I finally recall Jake's old roommate, because man, does that feel like a million years ago. "The axe murderer!" I add.

Annette's eyes get even bigger. "The axe… What are you talking about? Who are you? Is that your…your…" Annette directs this last question to

Connie, who is happily gurgling and chewing on a baby giraffe—a silicone toy, not a real one—as she looks around the restaurant.

"This is my daughter," Jake repeats easily, "and Tatum is my girlfriend. The one I was telling you about."

Several emotions flood me when I hear Jake refer to me as his girlfriend.

Elation, like I'm a giddy teenager with a crush.

Nervous, as is my go-to emotion any time I think about our future together.

And strangely, disappointment.

Shouldn't I be more than that?

"Your girlfriend," Annette repeats, eyeing me up and down.

I know what she sees. Messy hair, thick middle. I'm older than Jake. I'm no young college co-ed. I am not in a bikini.

But I am pretty sure I can make him happy.

"It's nice to meet you," I tell Annette, offering my hand.

"Yes. It is nice to meet you too," she says, giving me the limpest handshake in the history of the world.

Jake is still busy with Connie, walking her up and down the bar and pointing out various items, casually chatting with her as if she's an old friend.

"And there's your uncle Lincoln," he tells her, Lincoln's eyes crinkling at the corners as he wiggles his fingers at her from by the register. "That's some hair, huh? Think you're going to have long hair like that?"

Lincoln flips Jake off, and Connie laughs. "Uncle!" Jake exclaims in mock outrage. "Not in front of the baby," he adds.

"Don't bring her around Julia, then," Lincoln calls.

Jake smiles and returns to where Pink Bikini is still standing awkwardly next to me.

"Annie, you ready to go?" Lime-Green Bikini asks, not looking up from her phone.

Annette jerks her head from her friends back to Jake, before giving a wistful sigh at the sight of Baby Connie in his arms.

Or maybe that's just me.

"Probably pointless for me to suggest we should get together sometime, huh?" she asks me in a low voice. I look at her in surprise.

"Um, yeah," I respond slowly, not offended in the least.

I mean, I would want to get together with Jake, too.

"Well." She shrugs. "Can't blame a girl for trying." She pauses and turns back to me, her light-blue eyes assessing me. "He's one of the good ones, you know." Without giving me an opportunity to respond, she grabs her purse, sets her beer bottle on the bar, and turns to leave with her friends.

I watch them go, all tanned legs and shiny hair, their whole lives in front of them.

And then I turn back to Jake and Connie, my whole life in front of me.

Jake is still having a one-sided conversation with Connie. He looks up at me questioningly.

"You good?" he asks, concern in his eyes.

I smile back. A sense of calm descends over me. I am alive, my blood rushing through my veins, my heart pounding so hard, I feel it in my fingertips and toes.

"Yes," I say. "I'm good."

Chapter Forty-Four

Tatum

"**M**R. JACKSON, THE LAST TIME WE WERE HERE FOR THE FIRST session of your deposition, we were discussing your testicles."

"Objection!"

That's right. I'm back with Mark Jackson, wannabe fuckboy extraordinaire, and his attorney, Carson. After the last shitshow of a deposition, Carson and I attempted to stop the bleeding, exchanging several settlement demands and responsive offers. Unfortunately, the matter did not settle.

Frankly, my clients are unwilling to give Mark Jackson a dime, and I don't blame them.

But that means I have to put up with him and finish his deposition.

"I'll rephrase," I tell Carson placidly.

He glares at me.

Don't blame me, I tell him with my eyes. *You chose to represent this guy.*

Carson keeps on glaring.

"The last time we were here, we discussed some texts you exchanged with Ms. Manriquez, another nurse you worked with. Do you recall that?"

"Yes," Mr. Jackson says, eyeing me suspiciously.

As he well should.

"And you had texted Ms. Manriquez that you wanted to meet in the On-Call Room Deez Nuts. Do you recall that?"

"Objection. Asked and answered," Carson states in a monotone voice. "You can answer," he adds to his client.

"Yes," Mark echoes through clenched teeth.

"To clarify, there is no On-Call Room referred to in the hospital as 'Deez Nuts,' correct?"

"Correct." Mark looks anywhere but at me.

"And are you aware of whether there is even an On-Call Room D?"

"I don't think so."

"Did you intend to ask Ms. Manriquez if she could meet you in another room?"

"No," Mark answers slowly.

"Did you intend to meet with Ms. Manriquez at all?"

"I'm not sure?" Mark phrases it as a question.

"I guess what I'm getting at, Mr. Jackson, is that if you really never intended to meet with Ms. Manriquez at all, what was the purpose in sending her this text, the one where you asked to meet with her in 'On-Call Room Deez Nuts'?"

I'll work that phrase into the transcript as many times as humanly possible.

"It was a joke," Mark spits out, turning his gaze back to me.

"A joke," I repeat.

"Yeah, a fucking joke, okay?" There's no question pending, but I'll gladly hand this guy the shovel to dig his own grave. "Do you comprehend that?" Mark continues, gesturing with his hand, talking slowly like I'm stupid. "Do you know what a joke is? Probably not, you fat fucking cu—"

"Objection!" Carson says loudly, but I am really, really done with this guy.

I stand up suddenly from where I am seated across the conference room table.

"Mr. Jackson," I bellow. Yes, bellow, like the old sea hag that I am.

"I am entitled to ask you questions. You may not like them—"

"Off the record?" Carson asks nervously.

"*No.* I will not go off the record, and in fact, I want a clear record of this so that when I go to the judge and tell him or her—"

"It's a her," Carson mutters.

"—her that this man, who has filed a lawsuit *as the plaintiff,* claiming to have been wrongfully terminated, thinks it's appropriate to respond to questions not with answers, but with profanity the likes of which I have *never* been subjected to" —*I may be overdoing it here just a tad*—"the judge will have no choice but to award sanctions to my client."

I level Carson with my gaze. He doesn't look away and then gives one nod.

"Mr. Jackson," I continue, turning to Mark, "I deserve to be treated with respect. I realize the concept of treating a woman with respect might be somewhat foreign to you—"

"*Objection!*" Carson almost shouts, but I'm not done.

"—but I would insist, no, *demand* that you give it the old college try. Pretend I'm your mother, if nothing else. Would you talk to her the way you talk to me? The way you talked to Ms. Manriquez?"

"Don't talk about my mother," Mark snarls.

"Don't call me a cunt, you misogynistic son of a bitch!" I yell, slamming my hands on the table.

The room goes silent, and I hold Mark's eyes for a moment. He's still angry, but a hint of fear has entered his expression. I look to Gabe at the end of the table, who is sitting with his mouth agape, hands over the stenographer, ready to document whatever comes next.

"Off the record," I snap, suddenly exhausted.

"Yeah, but I want that last comment transcribed…" Carson begins before I level him with another look.

"Off the record," I repeat.

Five hours later, and I am utterly drained. I managed to calm myself, and Mr. Jackson, while not exactly pleasant, managed to answer my questions without resorting to profanity.

I'll worry about the fact that I called a plaintiff a son of a bitch later.

Right now, I just want to go home.

"Well," I tell Gabe after Carson and his client have left, "not one of my better days."

Gabe shrugs. "Honestly, I think you were justified. It's video-recorded, too," he thoughtfully reminds me, "which I think captures the whole picture.

I shudder. "That's…not good." Not good at all.

If Carson wanted to, he could report me to the state bar.

I don't think he will, but he could.

"I'm going to have to have a come-to-Jesus with Carson," I sigh, flopping back into the chair.

"Yeah, but at least you'll never have to deal with that Neanderthal again," Gabe quips, and I give a half smile.

"What a prick," I mutter, gathering up my things.

"Cosign," Gabe agrees.

I heave my bag over my shoulder, having already changed into my sneakers, and head out the conference room doors, waving to Gabe.

I look out the lobby doors to see something that makes my day immensely brighter.

Jake, in dark denim jeans, a button-up shirt with the sleeves rolled up, and sunglasses, waiting for me outside.

Jake's office is a couple blocks from the court reporter's offices, and I had told him I would be here today for this disaster of a deposition.

He's facing away from the building, hands in his pockets, the jeans doing wonderful things for his butt. I still haven't got nearly enough time with his butt as I'd like.

I sigh and smile, thinking of how nice it is to get home and snuggle Connie—my mother is watching her today—when there's sudden movement out of the corner of my eye.

I turn and see Mark Jackson approaching me, rage on his face.

"You fat bitch," he mutters, eyes bulging and cheeks red. Dude is going to have a coronary right here if he's not careful.

I back up as much as I can, but he's moving quickly, and before I know it, I am pinned between him and the wall next to the elevator.

"You have no right. *No right*," he spits, and I mean, really spits, as I am showered with his saliva as he rages.

And then he has the audacity to grab my arm.

"What the hell, Mark? Get your fucking hands off me!" I shriek as loud as I can, but he is blind with rage, either not hearing or not caring about what I have to say.

"You fucking feminist bitch." Later, I will think to myself, *that's not the insult you think it is.* "Can't take a fucking joke!" he continues. "Always have to be whining about something."

I am aware of the doors to the conference room opening at the same time the lobby doors open. Gabe rushes out of the conference room as Jake runs into the building.

Gabe, bless his heart, is about 5'2" and maybe 150 pounds soaking wet. But he does his best to grab Mark by the arm and yell "Knock it off, *cabrón!*"

Mark doesn't budge an inch.

"*Get your filthy fucking hands off her!*" Jake yells, gripping Mark's shoulders and pulling him away from me with such force that Mark stumbles backward across the other side of the lobby.

"Where the hell is Carson?" I ask Gabe breathlessly.

"I don't know," he responds, his eyes wide as he watches Jake advance on Mark. As soon as Mark moves toward me again, Jake holds out a hand.

"I'm giving you one warning, asshole," he mutters, his body still, poised to strike. "Get the fuck out of here."

"Who the hell are *you?*" Mark spits out, trying to look over Jake's shoulder to me. I shake, my hands trembling as I try to get my phone from my tote. Gabe sees me and puts his hand on my arm. "Don't touch me!" I cry out, stepping away. Gabe holds up both his hands in surrender, his eyes sympathetic.

"If you give me your bag, I can grab your phone," he says quietly. I hand it over and lean against the wall, putting my hands on my knees, trying to take deep breaths.

"I am with her. And you need to *calm the fuck down,*" I hear Jake tell Mark, calmly but lethally.

"Man, fuck you too, all wound up over some fat bitch—"

I don't hear what the rest of Mark says as he tries to get around Jake, who grabs his arm and twists it behind Mark's back. Mark is big and beefy, but Jake has a little height on him and holds his arm tight.

"One warning," Jake says. "We're downtown. We only need to go a block or two to find a cop. Is that what you want?"

"Where the *fuck* is a security guard?" I yell to no one in particular, still feeling short of breath. This isn't a Los Angeles high-rise office tower, but there's usually a security guard walking around the building or the court-yard outside.

"Hi, this is Gabriel Velasco. We need a police officer right away, please," I hear Gabe say rapidly into his phone as he rummages through my tote. He hands me my phone, but my hands are shaking so badly I can't enter my passcode, let alone hold still long enough for it to recognize my face.

"Let go of me, prick!" Mark yelps as Jake does his best to hold him steady. Jake's face is as red as Mark's, a venomous expression that I have never seen before on his face.

"Is there a problem here?" A loud voice sounds from the far side of the lobby, and I look up to see a heavyset, Latino man, maybe about ten years older than me, wearing blue jeans, a button-down shirt, and a black tie. He's exiting another suite, and behind him are at least three other office work-ers, all watching through the glass windows with wide-eyed expressions.

Jake looks up in surprise at the man's voice, and he must loosen his hold, because Mark jerks away, pushes Jake back, and immediately heads toward me, murder in his eyes.

And you know what?

Fuck this guy, this day, this case. Whatever problems Mark has, they're definitely not my fault or Ms. Manriquez's fault or feminism's fault.

So I don't think.

I just react.

I drop my tote bag, wait until he's close enough, and reach out for Little Mark.

The family jewels.

The twig and berries.

Basically, I set every ounce of professionalism aside and grab his crotch as tight as I can, squeezing my hand shut around what is definitely his flaccid dick and tiny, tiny testicles.

I give Deez Nuts a healthy squeeze.

Mark shouts, then whimpers, immediately dropping to his knees, which—thankfully, if I'm being honest—dislodges my hand from his crotch.

But I've disabled him, and I step back, shaking my hand out. As I do, two police officers rush in, their hands resting on the service weapons attached to their hips.

One cop, an Asian female with her hair pulled back in a tight ponytail, quickly surveys the lobby. I try to picture what she's seeing—me, red-faced and breathless, in front of a pretty large dude on his knees, clutching his nutsac. Gabe, next to me, holding his phone in one hand and mine in the other. Jake, across the lobby, bent over with his hands on his knees as he catches his breath.

"Everyone stay where you are," the cop says, loudly but calmly, holding one hand up and keeping her other hand firmly on her hip. "Which one of you is Gabriel?"

"That's me," Gabe says weakly.

"All I heard was that dude—" the man in the black tie interjects, gesturing toward Mark "—yelling and cussing up a storm. He was yelling at her," he adds, gesturing to me.

"This man attacked her with no provocation whatsoever," Gabe adds.

"So she kicked him in the balls," Jake wheezes out, still looking at Mark with daggers in his eyes.

"I actually grabbed him by the balls," I murmur, looking down at my hand. "Ew."

Gabe does some more rummaging through my bag and hands me hand sanitizer.

"Thanks," I tell him, squirting a healthy amount.

"Okay, okay," the female cop says. "Officer Maldonado and I will take statements. Ma'am—" she gestures to me "—I'll start with you."

Did I just get ma'am-d?

"Gladly," I reply, collapsing on the bench in the lobby.

Chapter Forty-Five

Jake

I LIKE TO THINK I'M A PRETTY MILD-MANNERED GUY.

I love my mom. I make friends easily. I can go with the flow and am not quick to anger.

But seeing that fucking oaf put his hands on Tatum triggered some visceral reaction in me, one I didn't know I had until the switch flicked on today.

How *dare* he touch my girl?

I was furious. And while I am glad that Tatum had the wherewithal to squeeze him where it counts, I am horrified this guy still assumed he had the right to talk to her like that, to place his hands on her in the first place.

After spending what felt like an epoch talking to the cops, we are back at Tatum's house. After we filled her in on what went down, Elaine left to go back to Estero Bay, and Connie is happily nursing with Tatum on the couch.

I am spent, and I think Tatum feels the same way. She's been mostly quiet, other than talking to her mom briefly and cooing to Connie, who was excited as always to get to eat. Tatum took a phone call from Carson, the lawyer who represents the guy who lost his shit, which involved a lot of Tatum saying things like "Mm-hmm" and "I understand" and—which I really liked—"Glad you are seeing things my way."

Tatum looks down at Connie now, filing her little fingernails while she nurses. It's a trick Julia taught her, because those nails are like talons, and it's impossible to get a baby to sit still.

But when Connie is eating?

She is pretty oblivious to anything else that's going on.

"You want me to heat up the leftover Thai?" I ask Tatum from the kitchen.

"That'd be great, thank you," she replies softly, focused on Connie's fingernails.

I heat up the food silently. We eat silently, all three of us. It's not an awkward silence; I think we just need to process what has happened instead of talking about it to death.

I lean over Tatum and kiss her cheek before grabbing our plates.

"I'm going to take a shower. You want me to put on *Law & Order*?" I gesture toward the television.

Tatum finally looks at me, and to my relief, a hint of a smile crosses her face.

"That would be great. Season eight, please."

I smile back.

"You got it, beautiful."

⌃

Tatum

"I didn't like that guy putting his hands on you," Jake tells me later, after I've put Connie down for the night—or for a couple hours; it's really a crapshoot these days—and am snuggling him in bed. He's fresh from the shower, smelling so good and clean.

"I wasn't a fan either," I tell him dryly.

"I wanted to kill him," Jake tells me softly, his harsh words a contradiction to the soft drag of his fingertips up and down my arm. "I've never been so angry."

"I think this means you like me," I tell him lightly.

"I fucking love you, Tatum," Jake growls, still stroking me absent-mindedly. "You know that."

I do know that. Because Jake not only tells me, he shows me. In the way he cares for Connie, the way he cares for me. The way he has more patience with me than anyone I know, despite the fact that, yes, he's younger.

"You're a good guy, Jake Lundquist," I whisper into his chest, briefly resting my lips on his warm skin, tracing lines over his abdomen, feeling his muscles tighten and flex as I do.

I prop myself up on one elbow, meeting his blue eyes. He regards me lazily, but I can tell he's still a bit wound up from this afternoon's events.

"That's why I love you too."

Jake's expression shifts, and he moves so fast, jerking up to a sitting position and placing his hands on my shoulders, that I giggle.

He tightens his hold on my shoulders and looks at my face, his eyes darting everywhere. "Yeah?" The hope in his voice—and his apparent doubt that I could—makes me fall in love with him all over again.

"Yeah, I do," I tell him, now a little shy, dropping my eyes to the sheets.

"Fucking right you do," he mutters, lifting my chin with his fingers so I have no choice but to meet his stare. "I'd do anything for you, Tatum," he says seriously, his expression honest, raw. "I know you think this was just a one-night stand—"

"It's been a lot more than one night, Romeo," I tell him sarcastically.

"—but it's not for me. It's never been that for me." Jake cradles my jaw in his hands, his eyes imploring me to understand him. "I knew from the minute I saw you…you were it. You are, like, the apex predator of women."

I burst out laughing. "Meaning I eat other women?"

Jake smiles, dropping his hands down my neck, stroking my shoulders and arms. "No, but you've definitely given me a great mental image I will cherish forever."

I scoff a laugh and mockingly push his chest.

"I just mean…you are it, Tatum," Jake's tone turns serious again, and he drops his eyes to my mouth. "There's no one else. I don't need to have dated a hundred women. I don't need to sleep with a thousand women—"

"Damn right you don't," I grumble.

"—because you're it. You're *my* constant," Jake tells me earnestly.

I suck in a breath and feel tears gathering behind my eyes.

"Connie is the best fucking thing on this planet, and she's only here because I met you," Jake continues softly.

"You had a little part in it too," I remind him, my throat tight.

"A *big* part," Jake corrects me, waggling his eyebrows.

"True." I lean forward, letting our foreheads touch. I hold out one of my hands, palm up, and Jake puts his hand in mine.

"You are not what I expected," I tell him honestly, and Jake gives me a cautious look. "You are *better*," I continue emphatically, and he grins in response. "I thought we were just going to bump uglies one time and that would be that, but then you had to go and knock me up—"

"During my first time, too. Don't forget," Jake adds.

"And here I am," I whisper, "and everything is so much better." I look into his eyes, those perfect ocean-blue eyes, and see my forever there.

"I love you. I love Connie. And I love our future together."

Chapter Forty-Six

Jake

I T'S THE DOG DAYS OF SUMMER A MONTH LATER.

I sweat through my undershirt as I exit my office, eager to get home and head out to Estero Bay with Tatum. It's hot there too, but there's an ocean in lieu of air conditioning, and we are going to stay the weekend at Tatum's mom's house.

I put my sunglasses on and roll up my sleeves as I walk the two short blocks to the courthouse. Tatum told me to meet her here, as she is wrapping up…something that involves court.

Honestly, I wasn't really paying attention.

I walk up the steps to the old government building and do a double take when I see a tall, blond girl standing in the shade just outside the building.

It's my sister, Shelby, who smiles and waves. She wears a white dress with forest-green Hawaiian flowers on it, her long hair curling down her back.

"Hey! You look so fancy! What are you doing here?" My words rush out as I embrace Shelby. We've grown close the past year, and she loves to come and visit and hold Baby Connie.

"Thanks. I'm waiting for you," she tells me.

"Okay?" I am still confused. "But I didn't know you were coming this weekend. Did you bring your board?"

I got Shelby a surfboard for her birthday, and she's gotten pretty good. We try to make it a point to go out to the bay whenever she comes to visit.

With Chernell, of course.

"It's a surprise," Shelby says, a dimple in her cheek popping as she smiles a secret smile. "Want to go in?" she adds, jerking toward the door.

"To the courthouse? Not really."

"Trust me." She links arms with me, and we go inside, getting through security quickly. I guess not a lot of people are eager to go to court at four p.m. on a Friday.

"Um. Did Tatum tell you she was going to be here?"

"Sure did." Shelby says nothing more, her eyes sparkling with humor.

"Are you going to tell me where we're going?"

"To see Tatum. Duh." Shelby grins and leads me to a set of double doors labeled "Department 4."

"Come on." She opens the door and ushers me in before her.

The courtroom itself is unremarkable. It's old-looking, with wood paneling on the walls, fluorescent lighting, and a big seal of California on the back wall, behind where the judge sits. There's no judge up there now and, really, no one else in the courtroom, until I turn to my right and see Tatum and Lucy, the latter of whom is holding Connie.

"Hi, handsome," Tatum says casually.

"Hi, boy wonder," Lucy says, bouncing Connie in her lap, trying to avoid her tiny fists.

"Hi!" I say and pause. "So…what's up?"

Tatum stands, and I notice she's wearing a dress similar to Shelby's, only hers is forest green with white flowers.

I then notice perhaps the most unexpected thing of all—

Lucy is also wearing a dress.

It's black and short and boxy, but still. I didn't think she owned anything besides black fishnets.

"What's going on?" I ask slowly.

Tatum hops up and takes my arm, and Shelby sits down in her place. Tatum leads me toward the front of the courtroom, stopping just before two little swinging doors where the lawyers would enter, I guess.

"So." Tatum looks up at me with mischief in her eyes. Her hair is also curled, I notice, down around her shoulders. She takes my hands in hers and quickly leans up to kiss me on the lips.

"I love you," she tells me quietly.

I can't help the grin that spreads across my face. "I love you too, beautiful."

"Do you want to get married today?" Tatum continues, as casually as if she's asking what I want on my pizza.

Which is always pepperoni, but I digress.

I raise my eyebrows, and my jaw drops open. I squeeze Tatum's hands unconsciously. "*What?*" I yelp. "Right now? Right here?"

"Right here, right now. We have witnesses." Tatum gestures to the back of the courtroom. Shelby waves excitedly, and Lucy gives me a smirk.

Connie babbles and coos.

"We have our daughter," Tatum adds softly.

"And, Jake," she says as I turn back to her, "I don't think I want to go another day without being your wife. If that's okay," she adds hastily.

"Are you *kidding* me?" I tell her loudly. Okay, I might yell. "Fuck yeah, it's okay! I'd marry you today, tomorrow, and the next day if I could!"

The sound of someone clearing their throat gets my attention, and I look past the swinging doors to see a middle-aged woman with black hair in a long black robe standing up in front of the seal.

Where the judge sits, at least on the TV shows.

So this must be the judge.

"Shit, sorry," I mutter to Tatum.

She grins back at me. "No worries."

"Are you ready to proceed, Ms. Echeverria?" the judge asks.

"We are, Your Honor," Tatum says in a clear, professional voice.

I realize it's probably her lady lawyer voice, and I try not to get hard, but it's difficult.

After all, I'm just a man.

"And do you have the paperwork?"

I definitely don't have any paperwork, but Shelby pipes up from the back. "Yes, ma'am. I mean, I have the paperwork," she stammers, blushing slightly.

The judge smiles kindly at our motley group. "Wonderful." She steps down from her perch, nodding at a sheriff's deputy positioned by the door.

"Please, step into the well," the judge says as she makes her way toward us.

I follow Tatum through the little swinging doors, past the long tables where the attorneys sit, and stand with her in the "well," which is basically the empty space between where the judge sits and the attorneys sit.

"You must be Jake," the judge adds, holding out her hand for me to shake. "I'm Marla Herrera."

"It's nice to meet you, Your Honor," I say solemnly.

Well, as solemnly as I can because…I am fucking stoked.

I am getting married.

I am getting married to Tatum Echeverria.

"Bride, you stand here," Judge Herrera instructs Tatum, "and groom, you stand here. Your witnesses can stand beside you."

Lucy, still holding Connie, comes to stand next to Tatum. Tatum stands directly across from me so we are facing each other, and Shelby stands beside me. She leans in to kiss my cheek.

"This is really cool, Jake," she says softly, and I look to see her eyes are shining with tears. Happy tears.

"Thanks for being here," I tell her softly, and she smiles and wipes away some of the tears.

Lucy sets down a giant tote bag that she was holding in her other hand. She pulls from it a small bouquet of white flowers, tied with a green ribbon. It's so unexpected that I burst out laughing.

Lucy winks at me, unsmiling.

I knew I'd break her down eventually.

"And you have rings?" Judge Herrera asks us.

"Got those too, Your Honor," Lucy responds, reaching into the tote and pulling out two small black boxes.

I look and see they are flexible silicone rings—a thicker band for me, a thinner band for Tatum, both in her favorite forest-green color.

"I hope that's okay," Tatum whispers to me.

I look at Connie, who's munching on her fingers as Lucy bounces her. I look into Tatum's hazel eyes. She's so beautiful, so perfect, so smart.

And she's going to be all *mine*.

And I can't think of anything to say except, "It's perfect."

Tatum beams at me and reaches for my hands.

"Ready?" Judge Herrera asks, pulling a pair of gold reading glasses from her pocket and putting them on.

"Ready," Tatum says, and I squeeze her hands.

"I'm ready."

"Do I really need to do this?" Tatum asks her mother.

"It's your wedding day. You can do whatever you want," Elaine replies. "But yes, I insist."

"You know you have to be out there too, then," Tatum declares.

Elaine shrugs. "If you say so," she says in a singsong voice.

"This is the weirdest group of single women I have ever seen," Nick says under his breath next to me, as someone puts Beyoncé on the speaker.

We're at the Brew for what Tatum called an impromptu wedding reception. We said the vows, we kissed, we signed the paperwork, and now Tatum, I, and our families are all here, celebrating with us, with more fried chicken than I've ever seen in my life.

Even my mother is here, which is a nice surprise. I look down at the end of the table where she is sitting next to Tatum's grandfather, who is talking to her about fishing or tides or something. Mom nods politely at whatever he's saying, and I smile to myself.

"It could be *any one of them*," I reply dramatically to Nick, turning back to the crowd before us.

All the single ladies—meaning Lucy, Shelby, Elaine, and Chernell— are standing in a line, waiting for Tatum to throw her bouquet. All of them, except for Chernell, look like they would rather jump into an ice bath than participate in this ritual.

"I believe in love," Chernell had declared when she got up slowly to join the other single ladies.

I couldn't help but notice Tatum's grandfather light up at that comment. "Me too!" he exclaimed.

"All right," Tatum says. "One…two…three!"

She throws, and the bouquet lands directly in Lucy's arms.

"Oh yay!" Summer squeals from where she sits next to Nick, holding Connie. She holds Connie's hands and moves them in a clapping motion.

"Oh, please," Lucy scoffs, looking at the bouquet like it's on fire. "This isn't an accurate predictor of the future, you know," she adds, giving Summer a hard look.

"I, too, believe in love," Summer declares fiercely.

I laugh at Lucy's horrified expression, and she turns her glare toward me. "Watch it, boy wonder," she says, pointing her finger at me.

I hold up my hands in mock surrender as Violet runs up to Lucy. "Can I have the bouquet? Please? Can I?"

"With pleasure," Lucy says, offering it to her.

Violet takes a deep breath from the flowers. "So *beautiful*," she says dreamily as her eyes immediately start to water.

"So many *allergies*," Julia says, grabbing the flowers from her and putting them on the table. "Let's go wash hands."

Tatum grins at me as she comes and sits down next to me.

"Hello, Mrs. Lundquist," I say to Tatum.

"Hello, Mr. Echeverria," she replies with a raised eyebrow, and I laugh.

"That was the best day in court I have ever had," Tatum tells me, her cheeks flushed and her eyes sparkling.

"I should hope so. It's not every day you get hitched in a windowless room," I reply.

"Pretty neat how I surprised you, huh?" she asks.

"It was fucking awesome," I tell her in a low voice, grabbing her curvy body and pulling her to sit in my lap.

"Gross," Nick mutters from next to me, turning to Summer and Connie, ignoring us.

"Shut it, Nicky," Tatum laughs, adjusting her position in my lap.

"I look forward to many, many more surprises from you in the future," I tell my wife.

Tatum sighs dramatically. "Don't you think we've had enough surprises already? Secret virgin, surprise baby…"

I grin and kiss Tatum on the lips. "Nah. I think I could do with a few more surprises. As long as they are with you."

Tatum holds my jaw in her hands and kisses me back. "I'll do my best to come up with something."

I smile against her mouth. I never want to let this woman go.

She is mine and I am hers.

And our future is bright.

Acknowledgements

I LOVED writing this book and could not have done it without the following people:

My husband, who is the most supportive partner anyone could hope to have. You are a total badass.

My daughter, whose entrance earthside inspired a lot of the baby moments in this book. I never knew my heart could live outside my body until you came along.

Brent, even though I am sad you have abandoned California for (likely) greener pastures. Kentucky, you are one lucky bastard.

Kiah, you are so supportive and positive and I appreciate you! Again with Kentucky being a lucky bastard. (This actually sounds like a great band name…Kentucky and the Lucky Bastards.)

Allison, for reading this thing! I appreciate your thoughts SO much and I never want to release a book into the wild without your input.

My Mom friends for everything…I never want to do life without you.

Davida, for being the best cheerleader! Can't wait to start our true crime podcast.

Lisa, for your amazing edits. I am so glad I found you!

Sarah, for the beautiful cover, as always.

Stacey, for turning a sloppy Word doc into something beautiful.

And thanks to you, reader, for spending time with this story! You probably know this but the best way for new authors like me to succeed is to get reviews, which you can leave at www.amazon.com/author/samanthabenson. I know how busy you are, and I truly appreciate even a short review to let others know about my book.

Until next time,
Samantha

About the Author

Samantha Benson lives on California's central coast, the perfect setting for real life romance stories. Sam loves dirty-talking heroes, intelligent heroines, the ocean, Lay's potato chips, Las Vegas, and 90's music of nearly every genre. When not writing, she is reading, watching Law & Order reruns, or enjoying a bicycle ride with her family.

Visit her website at www.samanthabensonauthor.com to sign up for her newsletter and be informed about upcoming releases.

www.ingramcontent.com/pod-product-compliance
Lightning Source LLC
Chambersburg PA
CBHW022109310726

48972CB00007B/1962